SMILES WHEELED on him. "Hey, this is getting weird. I don't know what the—"

"*Shhh!*" Ben hissed with crazy eyes. He peered frantically down the hallway, where a man was walking toward them from the elevators. Ben pinned Smiles in place with his scrawny arms. He whispered urgently: "Stay quiet till this guy passes, and I swear to God I'll explain everything."

Ben peered out, pulled his head back again, and put a finger to his lips. Smiles felt like a tool for playing along, but he did. The man looked about as nefarious as a copier salesman. He walked down the hall in an off-the-rack suit and a buzz cut, passing the alcove without a look.

Ben didn't breathe until he was gone.

"That could be the NSA guy—the one I'm supposed to meet about my paper," he said.

"So what?"

"Just stay here for a sec until he's gone."

"You're scaring me, Ben. What's this all about? I thought you won a million bucks."

"No, it's bigger than that."

"Bigger than a million bucks?"

Ben nodded, but he didn't look happy about it—he looked terrified.

"Smiles, I've changed the world."

THE CIPHER

JOHN C. FORD

speak

SPEAK
An imprint of Penguin Random House LLC
375 Hudson Street
New York, New York 10014

First published in the United States of America by Viking,
an imprint of Penguin Group (USA) LLC, 2015
Published by Speak, an imprint of Penguin Random House LLC, 2016

THE LIBRARY OF CONGRESS HAS CATALOGED THE VIKING EDITION AS FOLLOWS:
Ford, John C. (John Christopher), date-
The cipher / John C. Ford.
p. cm.
Summary: "Robert 'Smiles' Smylie and his friend Ben become embroiled in a high-stakes
negotiation with a pair of suspicious Feds when Ben cracks a code with the power to unlock
all the Internet's secrets"—Provided by publisher.
ISBN 978-0-670-01542-9 (hardcover)
[1. Ciphers—Fiction. 2. Adventure and adventurers—Fiction. 3. Computer crimes–Fiction.
4. Internet—Security measures—Fiction. 5. New England—Fiction.] I. Title.
PZ7.F75315Cip 2015
[Fic]—dc23
2014019432

Speak ISBN 978-0-14-750942-0

Designed by Eileen Savage

Printed in the United States of America

1 3 5 7 9 10 8 6 4 2

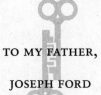

TO MY FATHER,

JOSEPH FORD

THE RIEMANN HYPOTHESIS is a real mathematics theory, first proposed in 1859, which remains unproven to this day. The things you will read in this book about its importance to modern encryption systems are true.

The rest, thankfully, is not.

"I don't believe in mathematics."

—Albert Einstein

SIXTEEN YEARS AGO

THE MAN IN the stolen car called himself Andrei Tarasov.

He drove west out of the city, fleeing Boston into a black December night. The car's heater had gone out, and an icy wind knifed in through its rusted-out frame. The man's frozen breath swirled before him; his fingers stung with cold. He ignored the pain. There was no time to think about comfort.

He had been awake for two days straight, ever since the men had come for him, and his body was long past the point of exhaustion. Fear alone kept him alert now. His eyes darted over the highway, watching for any sign that they had picked up his trail. He saw none—just the sparkling lights of Boston receding in the rearview mirror, slipping back through the snowfall that danced across the road.

The car shuddered with effort up a rise. In the rearview mirror, the city lights jostled with the vibration.

A vast skyline jittering in the night—it was just how Boston had appeared to him the first time, years ago, his face pressed to the cold plastic of an airplane window. He had been a different person then, with a different name.

An innocent kid with a gift for mathematics, brought to the United States on scholarship. He'd never been outside Russia, much less seen an American city, and its glistening towers had filled him with awe. Now, a wanted man, he watched the city vanish behind him and knew he would never see it again.

The men had appeared the day before. Rounding the corner on his walk home, he'd spotted a black sedan sitting fifty yards from his apartment. The car was far too nice to belong on his street. His neighbors were poor immigrant families who lived on top of one another in broken-down homes, the narrow gaps between them webbed with laundry lines. The man who called himself Andrei Tarasov was not wealthy, either. He knew things of tremendous value, though, and he had a good many secrets.

At the sight of the car, he'd dashed into a corner market. Nestling behind a cooler at the window, he took shallow breaths that betrayed his sudden panic. A part of him had known the day would come; the dread of it kept him up nights, drawing dark circles under his eyes. If he was right, the men in the car worked for the State Department. They would have a long file on him. They would know of his contacts with the Russian spy network.

He had been the ideal recruit: an advanced student of cryptography at Harvard, doing government-sponsored research on intelligence systems. A perfect candidate to funnel information back to Moscow.

He waited behind the cooler for long minutes, until finally a man opened the passenger door. The flash of metal on his overcoat might have been an American flag pin. The curl of plastic extending from his scarf might have been an earpiece. The man walked the length of the street and back again. If you weren't watching closely, you wouldn't have noticed the attention he paid to a particular apartment fifty yards from his car.

The man who called himself Andrei Tarasov did notice, and he knew then that his life was over. He rushed out the back exit and made it to the Jamaica Plain community bank just before closing, where he withdrew his meager savings. Within an hour he had bought the Avenger and an unregistered Walther P88 pistol from a Ukrainian man on his block known to traffic in stolen goods. Over that night and the following day, he put his affairs in order as best he could while staying clear of the men keeping watch over his apartment.

As far as he knew, they hadn't caught up with him yet. He sped forward, blowing warmth into the curled fists of his gloveless hands. The car was all but empty—he had left his possessions behind. The only two things that mattered now lay beside him on the passenger's seat: the gun and a thin brown package.

They skittered across the cold-hardened plastic as he turned off the highway. The rattle of the engine softened as he eased onto a two-lane road, taking comfort in the blanketing darkness of the suburb. The men would have a hard time taking him by surprise out here.

The snow was falling thicker now, frosting the handsome trees of the suburb. A pristine white carpet materialized on the street as he drove on—still checking for followers, still finding none. It was a fairy-tale place, this suburb. He was used to cramped spaces, littered pavement, the blare of city life. Here the lawns stretched endlessly away from the street, rolling back to majestic houses ablaze with warm lights.

He watched for street numbers on the gates outside the homes. The one he had been searching for appeared on his left, a grand brick affair with gleaming white columns lining the front. He eased to the curb and cut the engine. The quiet of the snow muffled what little sound he made exiting the car. Against the curtains in an upstairs window, the shadowed form of a woman cradled a child against her shoulder. Calming it from a bad dream, perhaps.

The woman's head was bent to the child, her full attention occupied. He had little fear she would notice as he approached the house by the front path. Crouching at the door, he eased the mail slot open. The package he balanced there appeared an ordinary thing from the outside: a regular brown package, just large enough to hold a pad of paper. At his push, it whispered to the floor.

He retreated down the steps and stationed himself under a tree. In his right hand, he held the gun.

The snow slanted down through his vision, and in that final moment he was no longer standing under a tree in Massachusetts. He was a kid in Saint Petersburg, packing a suitcase while a blizzard blew outside his window. He was standing in the roadside slush, waiting for the bus to the airport. He was kissing his mom good-bye, wiping snow from her graying hair. His eyes filled with tears, but it was only the winter wind. He was seventeen, a prodigy on his way to America, and he had never been more excited.

He had a great dream then: a dream to solve the Riemann Hypothesis. It was the goal of all great mathematicians. Whoever did it would stand with Newton and Einstein as one of history's greatest thinkers. The man who called himself Andrei Tarasov had been bold then, and when his plane lifted off from Saint Petersburg, he thought he would be the one.

But mathematics was a young man's game, and he was over thirty now.

His season for greatness had passed, and now he stood under the brittle branches of the tree, his shoulders flecked with snow, and considered the mother and child in the window. The woman's shadow waved across the curtains and rested her young one down in bed. One day that child would understand what he had left inside the package. That would be his legacy now.

He shut his eyes, raised his right arm, and hoped the shot wouldn't disturb the child's sleep.

"Mathematics is the language in which God
has written the universe."

—Galileo Galilei

THURSDAY

"A man has a hundred dollars and you leave
him with two. Boy, that's subtraction."

—Mae West, *My Little Chickadee*

2

IT WAS HIS eighteenth birthday, and what was he doing?

Was he sitting front row at some amazing concert? No.

Was he in the bleachers at Fenway, scarfing cheese dogs and nachos? No.

Hot-tubbing with Melanie at the cabin on Squam Lake? No, no, no.

It was his eighteenth birthday, at nine thirty in the morning, and the biggest thing on his agenda was a trip to Massachusetts General Hospital.

Smiles had thought a lot about his eighteenth birthday over the years. It was, after all, the day his $7 million trust fund kicked in—and if his life hadn't gone haywire in the last year, he would have been celebrating in style. But his life *had* gone haywire, and now his gut was twisting in that way it did every time he had to go to Mass General.

He had woken up five minutes ago, stirred by a harsh band of sunlight inching across his living-room couch. Smiles had crashed on it again last night. A constellation of potato-chip crumbs were stuck to his cheek; they cascaded softly to the carpet as he squinted at the bare white walls of his one-bedroom apartment.

Smiles lived at the Pemberton, an apartment building in Cambridge distinguished mostly by its crumbling brick and loud plumbing. It charged exorbitant rent on the sheer force of its pretentious name and proximity to MIT, where many of its residents attended college. If Smiles had realized the nerd-to-normal-person ratio was so out of whack at the Pemberton, he never would have set foot in the place, but it was too late for that.

He'd rented the apartment back in the fall, shortly after getting the boot from Kingsley Prep. Which, on the whole, was one of the better things that had happened to him lately. There was a certain embarrassment factor to getting kicked out of school, sure, and it didn't help any that his dad was Robert Smylie. But of all the disasters that struck in the last year, it would hardly sniff the top-ten list. There were a lot of fringe benefits to the deal, including a license to sleep as late as you wanted. Smiles, who rarely woke before ten, decided to stay put another fifteen minutes out of principle.

As he closed his eyes, he heard the scrape of a flier being shoved under his door. His landlord was at it again. The guy always had some urgent bulletin to share about the laundry room (*Please retrieve your clothes in a timely fashion, in consideration of your fellow residents*), or the parking garage (*Please respect the handicap spaces, in consideration of the disabled*), or somebody who had left the community room a mess in yet another failure to consider their fellow man.

The sun pierced his eyes and Smiles reminded himself,

for the fiftieth time, that he should really invest in some curtains. Groaning, he dislodged the stray bag of chips from the cushions and fished out the remains for breakfast. Jalapeño. Not bad.

After that, there was nothing to do but start his morning routine. It began, per usual, with a survey of the damage to his apartment from last night's festivities. (Moderate to extensive, depending on whether a spilled bottle of Jägermeister caused permanent carpet stains.) Next he hopped in the shower, then fed the thirteen exotic fish in the three giant tanks he kept in his apartment. The tanks were a major violation of his lease, but besides that, caring for his fish was the most responsible thing Smiles did on a daily basis, an accomplishment he was rather proud of. As far as commitments went, that left only the trip to Mass General. Time to rip off the bandage. Smiles laced his shoes and gathered up his keys.

On the way out the door, he bent to scoop up the flier . . . only to realize it wasn't a flier at all. It was a card, with his name written across the envelope in precise little letters. Smiles knew the handwriting—the card had come from Ben, the wacko kid who lived across the hall and went to MIT. He was only sixteen years old and a certified geek, but somehow the two of them got along.

Smiles took the card with him as he left the apartment, experiencing a tickling sensation that he was forgetting something. This was an extremely common occurrence and easy to ignore.

It was washed from his mind completely by the time he

got down to Watson Street, swept the usual complement of parking tickets off the windshield of his Infiniti G37, and got going. The Infiniti was his most prized possession, and Smiles rarely drove it under the speed limit. Only on these trips to the hospital did he drive extra slowly, extending the ride as long as possible without bringing traffic on the Longfellow Bridge to an absolute halt and/or getting rammed from behind. Even then, the trip always seemed to pass in one short, dreadful breath.

His stomach tightened as he traced a slow path over the Mass General campus. Smiles knew his way through the lifeless gray buildings and construction zones all too well by now, just like he knew the giant knot overtaking his insides: a huge, pretzel-shaped thing that would tie up his guts until he got out of this place.

He grabbed a ticket at the parking garage and found a spot on the third level. Smiles knew he should get out of the car right away, but he could never make himself do it. Instead he stayed there, frozen, while the sports-talk-radio guys babbled on about the Red Sox's struggling bullpen. His thumb rubbed across the parking ticket with a half-conscious worry reflex.

Grasping for an excuse to put things off, Smiles plucked the card off the passenger seat and opened it—some generic thing with rainbows that Ben had probably grabbed blind from the drugstore shelf. Smiles laughed at the perfect, miniature handwriting:

Happy Birthday, Smiles!
(And thanks again for the computer.)

Your friend,
Ben

P.S. Don't forget to pick me up.

Two weeks ago, he had given Ben one of the ten laptops sitting unopened in his closet. They came from his dad, who got all the latest computers for free. He had hundreds at his office—he passed them out like Tic Tacs.

Smiles closed the card with a sudden, overwhelming sadness.

All the computer companies tried to impress his dad with their latest products. You couldn't buy a computer anymore without finding the logo for his company, Alyce Systems, stuck on it somewhere: the two interlocking keys that had become the universal symbol for computer security. Over the last decade, Alyce Systems had become the biggest success story in Boston. *Time* magazine had actually called his dad "the Man Who Changed the Internet."

And then a year ago, the Man Who Changed the Internet went to see his doctor about a nagging headache and they discovered it. A brain tumor. Nobody knew how long he'd live.

The whole thing was unreal.

Smiles yanked the key from the ignition and laid his head against the seat. He shut his eyes, letting his head fill with the buzz from the parking-structure lights. Sometimes this was as far as he made it. He'd sit in the car for a while, then retreat to the apartment and play online poker, lying to himself that he'd return to the hospital later. Today was Smiles's birthday, though. His dad was expecting him. It wasn't exactly like he could call up and say, *Sorry Pops, can't make it, not feeling too well.*

With a monumental effort, he forced himself out of the car and headed for the hospital.

This was it. This was his eighteenth birthday.

3

SMILES ELBOWED OPEN the door to the neuro-oncology unit.

He was double-fisting the coffee order he picked up at the café downstairs every time he visited: a small black in his left, a large decaf with light cream and cinnamon in his right. Shanti liked the way he did the cinnamon. She was his favorite nurse, with her smooth caramel skin and sexy ropes of bronze hair. There was something graceful in her walk, and Smiles believed he had detected, beneath the shapeless cover of her hospital blues, a magnificent rack.

Smiles may not have been Brad Pitt in the looks department—he was a gangly six foot one with a washed-out complexion and hair the color of a sun-faded paper bag—but he didn't care about that. If you had half a personality, he had found, you did just fine with the ladies. Not that he'd cheat on Melanie or anything. It wasn't even an issue, anyway, since Melanie had told him she needed a "break." Just another thing that had gone wrong in the last year.

The door sighed closed behind him, leaving Smiles alone

in the sterile fluorescence of the waiting area. The long curve of the reception desk was vacant, the air heavy with carpet cleaner and the general sense of doom that clung to Smiles here. He put Shanti's coffee on the ledge and checked his phone for procrastination material. It offered only a text from Darby Fisher ("*IPO baby!!! Is it a buy at $35 or what?*") and two calls he'd slept through from a 510 number he didn't recognize. Silence on the Melanie front.

The coffee wasn't helping the knot in his stomach. Smiles tossed it and lurched down the hallway to the whiteboard that said *Ro er Sm l e*.

They wrote the patients' names outside the rooms. His dad had been admitted two months ago, and bits of purple ink had come off in the meantime, leaving his name like a half-completed crossword answer. Everyone knew who he was, of course. They probably wanted to install a plaque: DISTINGUISHED PATIENT ROBERT SMYLIE: FOUNDER OF ALYCE SYSTEMS, HARVARD PROFESSOR OF MATHEMATICS, PHILANTHROPIST, TWO-TIME *PEOPLE* MAGAZINE TOP-100 SEXIEST MAN ALIVE.

True, all of it. They probably wanted to feed him grapes by hand. He had asked for no special treatment, though, so he just got the whiteboard. He hadn't been able to stop them from putting him in a private room that happened to be the biggest on the floor.

Smiles hesitated at the entrance, stopped by a cascade of familiar thoughts.

Robert Smylie: It was his own name, too. But to think of himself accomplishing what his father had . . .

To think of himself being worthy of such respect . . .

Being half the man who lay inside, dying . . .

"Robert?"

His dad had seen him.

Smiles steeled himself. He forced some energy into his voice as he entered the room. "Hey, Dad."

"Ahhh, he appears at last. Happy birthday, son." The hospital bed hummed as he raised it to a sitting position. He still had the runner's body, the lean face, the crystal-blue eyes. That was the freaky part—when you couldn't even tell.

"Yeah, thanks," Smiles said as his dad beckoned him for a hug. Smiles dipped in, forgetting for a moment that the last seizure had left him paralyzed on one side. Now Smiles had pinned his dad's good arm awkwardly beneath him. He pulled away quickly, embarrassed.

They had found a second tumor after his last seizure, one they couldn't remove without touching parts of the brain that control, like, breathing and other stuff you don't want to be screwing with. Then the paralysis set in. The doctors had given Smiles plenty of updates, their coats as white and blank as his shock-numbed mind. He couldn't keep up with all the technicalities, didn't really want to, but he got the basic vibe: This train's a-rollin', and it ain't stoppin'.

His dad motioned to a speaker on his nightstand, which as usual was playing some obscure classical number. "Turn that down, will you?"

The iPod docking gizmo was the only luxury his dad had allowed himself. He didn't even keep the gifts that arrived—he had them distributed to other patients. (When the diagnosis first became public, Smiles had seen flower arrangements from the Kennedys, the mayor, and Bill Gates. Bono had probably paid off Equatorial Guinea's national debt in his name or something.) Even after two months in the place, the room was still a spare white space—all blank walls and utilitarian furniture. It fit him all the same. Smiles could hear his dad's mantras in his head: *Live simply, stay humble, take no shortcuts,* etc. etc. When Smiles had brought the Infiniti back from the lot, his dad had eyeballed it coolly. "Flashy," was all he'd said, but the bite in the single word could have broken skin.

The only hint of personality in the entire room came from the framed picture of his mom on the nightstand. There was something new today, though. A green screen had been erected at the front of the room, blocking out the window to the hallway. Beneath the screen, black boxes with metal closures lay on the floor, all marked with the logo of a video production company. Maybe his dad was spending his off-hours starring in an action movie.

Smiles turned the iPod thing down, but not too much. His dad loved his classical music.

"That's better," his dad said as Smiles dragged a chair to the side of the bed. He always sat in the same spot, near the picture of his mom. As if she could still break the tension between Smiles and his dad.

Smiles nodded to the screen. "Filming something?"

"Oh, that. For the IPO." His dad rolled his eyes. "They tell me I should make an address to the troops on Tuesday."

Alyce Systems was going public that day. If you had a pulse and lived in Boston, you'd heard about it in a thousand breathless news reports, with countdown clocks in the corner and interviews with working stiffs ready to bank their life savings on Alyce. All the stories were the same. Each one contrasted his wise and mature dad with all the Internet phenoms from Silicon Valley who'd reached too far, too fast, or whatever. The IPO seemed to consume everyone these days, even his old Kingsley friends like Darby Fisher, who were all suddenly talking like CNBC anchors. Smiles tried to ignore it as much as he could.

"So what's this I hear about you and Melanie?"

Oh, that. Smiles hadn't said anything about it. But of course his dad had found out anyway. Perfect.

"Oh, you know, she's just got a lot going on right now. It'll be fine."

It was hardly fine. Melanie had told him she needed "some space," that she wanted to "take a break," and several other code phrases for the fact that she'd be dumping Smiles for good any minute now. When he thought about it, he felt like his heart was being sledgehammered by one of those guys in the made-for-cable strong-man competitions he sometimes flipped past in the middle of the day. He didn't see the point of talking about Melanie, though—it hardly seemed like a big deal next to a case of brain cancer.

Up close, Smiles could see now that his dad was looking weak. His eyes fell shut while the piano tinkled on, driving Smiles slightly mad. Why couldn't he ever think of anything interesting to say? Why couldn't he keep his dad entertained, for just five minutes a day?

His dad smiled lethargically. "Is that GED prep boring you to death?"

The GED stuff. This is what hurt.

"It's not so bad," Smiles said, although he had spent much of the last few months coming up with excuses to cancel his tutoring sessions for the test. He had barely opened the prep manual. Actually, he didn't even know where it was anymore. The cover was green, he knew that much. Meanwhile, his old friends, perched safely in the high thin air of Kingsley Prep, were going to Yale and Harvard and Brown—maybe Duke if they were dumb.

"It can't be much of a challenge."

"No, it's not," Smiles said sharply.

He couldn't keep his voice smooth, couldn't keep the raw edge of his anger tucked away. Talking about the GED with his dad. His dad, the genius. The math professor who, fifteen years ago, had revolutionized computer technology and turned Alyce Systems into a Fortune 500 company.

"Well, what subjects are you—"

"It's for idiots, Dad. It's stupid stuff."

His dad's face settled into a familiar cast of tested patience. "Just push through it, then."

"That's what I'm doing." Although, of course, it wasn't.

He was being sucked into the black hole of shame that gobbled him up whenever he entered this room. His dad had toiled for years coming up with his breakthrough on computer encryption. What had Smiles ever pushed himself at? Getting Melanie to go out with him the first time, that chain email scam that backfired, and, briefly, *Call of Duty*. That was about it.

And now, as his dad patted his arm, Smiles felt Phase

Two of the black-hole syndrome. It was a reflex by now: a sudden urge to be serious. To be diligent. To get passionate and work hard at a subject he found interesting. It would be a subject that was mildly cool and could lead to a fortune like his dad had made if he applied himself for a while. But . . . what?

Smiles never knew, and after a while the feeling would pass.

He was staring at the floor tiles, losing himself in a vision of Shanti's rack, when he felt his dad grasp his arm.

"Robert, we need to talk about something."

The trust fund, Smiles thought immediately. This was going to be about the money. A responsibility talk about what it meant to have $7 million. It was only a fraction of his dad's fortune, but he'd always been big on Smiles "finding his own way." *Be honest, take no shortcuts, find your own way.*

Then a cloud passed over his dad's face and he said, "We have to be realistic about this."

Oh. This wasn't about money at all.

"Yeah, Dad," Smiles said in a soft scratch of a voice.

His dad held his gaze. "Things aren't getting any better."

He never talked like that, and Smiles knew right then that he'd be dead within a month. It should have floored him. It should have hit him like a car going seventy. But all Smiles felt was a vaguely embarrassed feeling.

"You . . . you're a fighter, Dad."

You're a fighter? Did I really just say that? Smiles wished someone would punch him in the face.

"Yes, I am. But listen. There's something else, and it's

important." His voice had gone thin and pained. "You've been through too much for a young person, Robert. Far too much."

His dad's eyes slipped over to the picture of his mom. Smiles swallowed hard, feeling ambushed, wishing he could be somewhere else.

The picture had been taken at their wedding—an artsy black-and-white shot with flower girls dancing at her feet, her head tossed back in laughter. She was his stepmom, if you wanted to get biological about it. Smiles didn't think of her like that. His "real" mother had abandoned him when he was two. Fine. He'd gotten something better in the deal. Her name was Rose Carlisle, and she was his favorite person in the world. She had lazy blonde curls and big green eyes like life on fire. She looked like fun, and she was. And Smiles could seriously relate to her. And now she was gone.

She had died almost a year ago. In the crazy year of things going wrong, nothing else could compare; it sat at the very top of his top-ten list of bad things, and it would sit there forever. The accident just happened—a freak thing with her car. No warning, no good reason for it, no good-byes. She just . . . died. Tough luck. Sorry, Smiles.

"Your mother," his dad said, "she wanted you to have something when you turned eighteen."

Smiles had gone dizzy with the memory of his mom, but he didn't want to miss this. "She what?"

"She left you a letter. And . . ."

His dad's hand fidgeted with the sheet—his good hand, on his left side. Watching it tremble turned Smiles cold. The whole time he'd been sick, Smiles had never seen him crack.

Now this. This was what it had been like when she died, when his dad had wept for a week.

"And what?" Smiles prodded gently. He needed to know what his mom had left for him.

His dad shut his eyes, his brow furrowing with some kind of memory. Finally, just when Smiles began to wonder if he'd nodded off, he spoke.

"There's a package."

"A package? Like . . . a gift?"

"You could say that. But not a regular gift. It's a notebook."

His dad pressed the button for the nurse then. Smiles wondered if he was getting a migraine from the swelling and needed morphine.

He was reeling with questions—*What was in this notebook? Why did she leave it for me? And what's with the letter?*—but his dad raised his good hand, fending him off.

"That's all I want to say about it, I'm afraid. Ask Marshall for the letter, okay? He has it."

Marshall Hunt, his dad's lawyer and business partner since forever. He was Melanie's father, and also the trustee of Smiles's trust. Smiles remembered now that they had a meeting about the trust today—it was the thing he'd forgotten that morning.

"Yeah, Dad. I'll ask him."

"Okay," his dad said firmly. "We're done with that now."

Shanti appeared at the door then. She raised her coffee in thanks to Smiles, but then turned quickly to his dad, giving him an aren't-we-clever look.

"Ready anytime," his dad said with a wink, and Shanti

disappeared happily back into the hallway. There was something going on that Smiles wasn't grasping, but he wasn't sure he cared.

"Just give her a minute," his dad said.

Smiles nodded as a delicate silence fogged the room, his mind still spiraling with questions about his mom's letter. Staring at the green screen, he flashed on a memory of his once-firm plan to become a movie director. He'd gotten the idea after seeing this cool Italian suspense flick at Darby Fisher's one night, and he knew instantly that it would be *his own way*. But by the time the camera he ordered arrived in the mail, he was pretty much over it.

There'd been a time, before the phrase had been pounded into his head, when Smiles thought finding *his own way* would mean running Alyce Systems itself. Bouncing down the executive floor at Alyce as a kid, he'd taken it for granted that one of the silver nameplates would eventually say ROBERT SMYLIE JR. It was a stupid thought even before he got kicked out of high school. But sitting here with his cancer-stricken dad, their uncertain futures clouding the air, Smiles found himself strangely warm to the topic of Alyce.

"So Tuesday's the big day," he said. "Is there, like, a time I need to be here?"

He was going to ask if he had to wear a tie or anything when his dad chuckled. "Oh, God no. No reason to drag you over here for that."

Smiles nodded calmly, all the while feeling a fresh tide of shame wash over him. He'd thought he should support his dad on his big day, but of course there was no reason for him to come. He had nothing to do with his dad's company. He was going to be lucky to get a GED. He was an embarrassment. He was a fool.

"Yeah, okay, thanks. I'm late to Mr. Hunt's though, so . . ."

Smiles patted his dad's shoulder—the numb one, he realized too late again—and shoved the chair back into the corner. It banged against the wall, legs clattering on the linoleum floor.

"Robert, wait for—"

"I'll see you tomorrow," he said over his dad's protest, and escaped into the hall.

He took a single breath of relief before seeing Shanti headed his way, pushing a cart with a huge birthday cake on it. Half the floor staff trailed behind her. They were just starting up with the first bars of the Happy Birthday song.

Smiles avoided their eyes. "Sorry, gotta go," he said, slicing sideways through the nurses. The song petered out in confusion as he rushed forward and out to the parking structure. He drove away from it all as fast as he could.

SHE HAD BEEN scrutinizing the list so intently she didn't notice Jenna over her shoulder.

The list said this:

* * SMILES * *

Pro	Con
1. Fun	1. Never on time
2. Good heart	2. Doesn't make plans
3. Tells me I'm hot (affection)	3. Tells me I'm hot (objectification)
4. ???	4. ISSUES w/ his dad
	5. Bad communicator
	6. Drinks too often
	7. Aquariums—weird??
	8. ((school situation))

Melanie had forced herself to stop at number eight. She'd been disturbed to find herself racking up cons with ease and unable to think of any more pros. Better to just stop there, at the bottom of the page.

This project had been a total, total bust.

It was the seventh such list she had made during trigonometry, and the seventh commitment in her life in which the negatives won out. The tally for "Volleyball Team" was five to six, but none of the others was even close. (Her upcoming visit to Smith College had scored exactly zero positives.)

None of this should have surprised Melanie. She knew she was a pleaser. She had agreed to join that nightmare community garden project last summer just to avoid a mild flicker of disappointment in her dad's eyes after he suggested it. She'd done a lot of stuff like that. It was insane. She knew it.

Was the Smiles situation really any different?

Melanie circled *ISSUES w/ his dad.*

She could hardly blame Smiles for having a complex about his dad—he was Robert Smylie, after all. That was bad enough, but Melanie knew it was his mom who'd really broken him. Not Rose. No, his biological mom, who left when he was only two years old, with no explanation.

It was arrogant to pity him, but she couldn't help it. They had known each other forever, and she had always felt the need to be delicate with Smiles—like he was a cracked dish, and Melanie had to preserve the pieces of him until he could be glued together, magically restored.

Ms. Phillips droned on at the chalkboard as Melanie's pocket vibrated with a text.

Smiles: *"My life is bizarre. Call me."* He kept forgetting she didn't have a study hall this semester and couldn't talk in the afternoons. He kept forgetting they were on a break.

The list was supposed to help her decide what to do, but now it sickened her. There was something gross about evaluating a person like this. Based on this page, it looked like Melanie thought she was too good for him . . . and maybe she did. Number eight said it all: She was ashamed to have a boyfriend who had been kicked out of high school. Melanie could hardly even bring herself to say the word *expelled*. On the list she had written *((school situation))*, the two layers of parentheses like makeup over a wart.

But Smiles would never be ashamed of her, if their places were reversed. He didn't make judgments like that. Smiles, actually, had a much better heart than she did. The thought made Melanie feel both happy and sad.

The bell rang at last, but Melanie sat rooted there, studying the stupid list while the room emptied in a shuffle of bodies and books. Her fellow Kingsley students, starched and clean in purple-and-gold uniforms, clotted at the door to the brick-lined, waxed-floor hallways. They felt measurably quieter these days, without Smiles's too-loud voice ringing through them. She crumpled the page tightly, thinking she was alone until she felt the presence at her back.

Jenna Brooke was standing behind her left shoulder, waiting.

God, she had probably read the whole "Smiles" list, too.

"So we're going to Alyce tomorrow, yeah?" Jenna said brightly.

"Yeah, Jenna." They went every Friday. It wasn't news.

Jenna hugged a book at her chest. Her buggy eyes always freaked Melanie out. "Walk to physics together?"

"I'm going to my locker."

Melanie gave a smile that she hoped wasn't too encouraging, then darted.

She didn't throw the list away on the way out. For all she knew, Jenna would root through the trash for it.

"SMIIIIIIILES! HAPPY BIRTHDAY!"

Mr. Hunt grabbed the edge of his desk, heaved himself up, and greeted Smiles at the entrance of his massive office.

"Thanks, Mr. Hunt."

He was taller than Smiles and pushing three hundred pounds, and whenever he did anything remotely physical he broke out in a sweat. For such a porker, the guy looked amazingly good, Smiles thought. He dressed in creamy business shirts and ties done up in fat, perfect knots—today's tie was powder blue over a nuclear-white shirt. Mr. Hunt looked fresh and new, wrapped up like a Christmas turkey.

He checked his Rolex and gave Smiles a joking punch on the shoulder. "Came early, did ya?"

Smiles, two hours late by then, laughed. "Just for you, Mr. Hunt."

On the ride over to the Alyce Systems headquarters—a mirrored behemoth on Water Street—Smiles had managed to convince himself he shouldn't take his dad's talk of dying seriously. Maybe he'd last a long time. Maybe there'd be a miracle. But he couldn't shake the other bomb he'd dropped: the mystery letter from his mom. A message from the grave, it sounded like. And a "package" to go with it—a notebook of some kind. Smiles was beginning to think that the universe just liked screwing with his head.

As much as he wanted to read anything his mom had written him, he was getting a bad vibe about it. She had talked to him about everything—her irresponsible days in the Tri-Delt house at Boston University, the cheesy guy at the gym who always hit on her, whatever. One summer she'd kept going on rants about her athlete's foot. What *couldn't* she tell him?

It wasn't going to be good, Smiles had figured on the way over, the news of her letter turning sour in his stomach. But being in the presence of Mr. Hunt made things seem more manageable. The guy was like comfort food on legs.

"Big day, kid. Very big day."

A brisk smell of shaving lotion and mesquite-spiced cologne assaulted Smiles's nostrils as Mr. Hunt wrapped him in a bear hug. It lingered while Mr. Hunt clapped him on the back and slid into his desk chair of buttery leather. On the bookshelves behind him sat a basketball in a glass case, signed by all the Celtics on one of the old championship teams—Larry Bird and Kevin McHale and the rest of them. Beside it sat a fleet of model cars: a Bentley, a Maybach, and an Aston Martin. You could find the real versions in his garage. Mr. Hunt took pride in maintaining them himself.

"Go on, sit down." He motioned Smiles to the far windows while he gathered files. "Sit, sit."

It was a corner office, and like everything else about Mr. Hunt it was ludicrously big. You could play a game of racquetball in one half and host a dinner party in the other. Smiles crossed the plush white carpet to a seating area by the windows. Up here on the top floor of the skyscraper, they had twenty-foot ceilings. The floor-to-ceiling windows gave an IMAX view of the Atlantic Ocean, the harbor, and the streets below.

The coffee table had a spread of glossy magazines. *Wired, Forbes,* something called *The Robb Report*—thick wedges of a sumptuous kind of life. Smiles inhaled the pleasant, empty smell of vacuumed carpet. Looking down at the plaza in front of the office building, he could see its signature element: the fifty-feet-high bronze sculpture of the Alyce Systems logo. One old-fashioned key standing upright, another pointing downward, their teeth meshing in the middle. The tiny people below streamed around the huge sculpture as they went about their ant-colony business. From up above, it was hard not to feel superior.

"Over there, darling," Mr. Hunt was saying to an office worker. She left a tray with bottled water and enormous cookies as Mr. Hunt trekked over with the papers.

"All right then," he huffed. "Ready to get rich?"

They plopped into the deep chairs by the windows. Mr. Hunt pushed over a fountain pen and a document that said RECEIPT AND RELEASE at the top. Three sticky tabs protruded from the edges, telling him where to sign.

Smiles uncapped the pen, a heavy silver job that felt right for the occasion. "Can I get a drum roll here?"

Mr. Hunt liked that one. He chuckled as Smiles signed on the three lines, which were actually dotted. "You won't have to sign like this for every check," Mr. Hunt said. "Just the initial payment."

Smiles wasn't getting the whole $7 million today. The trust paid out in little installments at first. They would increase in amount until he turned twenty-five, when he would get the balance in one big chunk. Those were the terms his dad had set when he established the trust, and from what Mr. Hunt had said it was all standard stuff. Whatever—Smiles wasn't complaining.

His first payment, the check he was getting today, was for something close to $50,000. Not too shabby.

"You should realize," Mr. Hunt said, "that this will be your full inheritance. You know that your father has been . . . well, preparing, shall we say. Virtually all his holdings are going to his wildlife foundation, his educational charities, and the symphony."

Smiles knew that already—his dad was already famous for giving away basically his entire fortune. Mr. Hunt was acting like this was all extremely sensitive stuff, but Smiles had never been bothered by it. It was one of the reasons he admired his dad, even if it made him that much harder to live up to. "If I need more than seven million to get by, I'm in pretty serious trouble."

Mr. Hunt let out a roar of laughter. "Great attitude there. Okay, I just want you to be clear on that. You know that your father always wanted you to—"

"Find my own thing. I got it, Mr. Hunt, but thanks."

Smiles slid the document back across the table.

Mr. Hunt checked the pages and set them aside. For such a giant person, he could be very delicate.

"Okay, now, start a file at home. You'll get receipts in the mail after each payment. Save them for your records." Smiles nodded, fully intending to do this but also knowing he'd get lazy and blow it off.

Mr. Hunt then launched into a spiel about K-1 forms and tax stuff that Smiles nodded at but didn't listen to. He was seized with a new anxiety about his mom's message. He felt like he might suffocate if he didn't hear her words soon.

"I have to ask you . . ." Smiles blurted as Mr. Hunt bit into a hubcap-sized sugar cookie from the tray. "It's something about my mom."

Mr. Hunt paused mid-chew, then gulped down a mouthful of cookie. "Sure, what is it?"

"My dad said you have a message from her. A letter or something, for when I turned eighteen."

Mr. Hunt nodded, but his face had suddenly turned haggard. He brushed a microscopic crumb from his lapel and sighed. "I was afraid that this would happen."

"What?"

"That he would forget."

"Forget what?" Smiles wasn't getting this.

Mr. Hunt held his palms out in a calming way. "There was a letter from your mom, yes. And she wrote it for you to read it when you turned eighteen. But Smiles . . . when your father was in the hospital after his first seizure, he asked me to destroy it. I shredded that letter months ago."

"But she wrote that for me." Smiles was trying not to blow his stack. He needed to hear his mom's last words to him. Her *last words*. "What did it say?"

Mr. Hunt just shook his head. "I didn't read it. I assumed it was personal, obviously."

"But he told me about the letter today."

"Well, that's what I was afraid of. You know how it can be."

Yes, Smiles knew how it could be. His dad could have hour-long conversations and not remember them the next day. The lost spots in his memory, they happened more and more. He had forgotten about telling Mr. Hunt to destroy the letter.

"The letter was from my *mom*. Did he even have the right to do that?"

"It's not really a question of having the right," Mr. Hunt said. "There aren't laws about this kind of thing."

Gone, just like that. Destroy the letter—who cares about Smiles? His head spun as he focused on a drop of water sliding down one of the water bottles. His mom's wild laugh echoed in his mind; his chest seized with a physical ache.

"What about a package? There was a package with the letter . . . or, well, the letter was going to tell me about a package. A notebook, actually." Even as the mixed-up words came out of Smiles's mouth, he knew they sounded strange.

Mr. Hunt listened, his expression blank. "I don't know anything about packages or notebooks. I'm sorry."

So that was it then. Smiles fell back into his chair.

"You're upset about this," Mr. Hunt said carefully.

"Yeah, I am." His voice came out cold. Mr. Hunt wasn't to blame, but Smiles couldn't help it.

"You feel cheated; I can understand that." Mr. Hunt cracked open a bottle of water, measuring his words. "Your mom could be impulsive, Smiles, I think you know that. And let me tell you something else: Your dad has the best judgment of any single person I know. You have to trust him on this one—trust that you didn't want to read whatever was in that letter."

Mr. Hunt put his hands together, finished with his speech. The office rang with silence and suddenly Smiles had risen to his feet.

"Good-bye, Mr. Hunt." The words dribbled from his mouth, and then his legs were carrying him out of the office so he could get out of there and sit in the Infiniti and process this on his own.

"Smiles, wait."

He was almost to the door. When he turned around, Mr. Hunt was holding an envelope.

"Don't you want your check?"

"MY LIFE IS bizarre. Call me."

Smiles needed a good vent, and he was pretty sure Mel had a free period in the afternoon. He shot her the text as he flew over the Longfellow Bridge on his way back from Mr. Hunt's office, completely forgetting that it was Thursday and Ben would be waiting for a ride back from MIT. Smiles picked him up every week—or almost every week. To be perfectly honest, it wasn't the first time it had slipped his mind.

Luckily he saw him from the Infiniti: the tiny frame, the semi-hunched back, the determined little steps down Massachusetts Avenue. Smiles had to laugh. His next-door neighbor was a bizarre dude, no doubt, but it was a relief to see him. Much better to hang out with Ben for a few hours than to sit around alone, stewing about the letter.

Smiles couldn't resist. He floored it, angled to the curb, and jammed on the brakes. The screech sent Ben about twenty feet in the air. On the way down, his army backpack disengaged from his shoulder and landed in a spray of pens.

He really made it too easy. Smiles tried not to overdo it, but in fairness, Ben was like a walking solicitation for practical jokes. He was wearing a typical outfit today: tattered blue jeans and a yellow dress shirt that fit him like a tent, his freakishly thin body imperceptible beneath it. He looked out at the world through timid brown eyes that were the stuff of bullies' dreams.

Smiles tapped the horn as Ben gathered up his backpack. He jerked upright, his shirt billowing around him, pirate-style.

Smiles rolled down the window. "Hey, bud!"

Ben cracked the door and sat down heavily in the car. It took all of his arm strength to heft the backpack onto his lap. It looked like there were bricks in the thing. "So, like, that never gets old to you?"

It may not have been the first time Smiles had ambushed him on the sidewalk.

"Not if your vertical leap keeps improving like that."

"Well, thanks for the ride, anyway," Ben said. "Thought you might blow me off today."

"You kidding? Not a chance."

Smiles turned off Mass Ave and cut through a rat maze of back streets to the Pemberton, which was even closer to MIT than it was to Mass General. (Especially if you ignored a couple of one-way signs.) He had discovered the Pemberton entirely by chance, after getting thoroughly lost on the way back from the hospital during his dad's first extended stay there. He'd pulled over in frustration and seen a FOR RENT sign in the office window. His presence was no longer requested at Kingsley by then, so Smiles had followed his impulse and signed a month-to-month lease for the one-bedroom—theoretically, a temporary base from which he could visit his dad every day. But when his dad had returned to their home in Weston that first time, Smiles had stayed on in the city. It had been almost six months since he'd moved in, and Smiles had spent every night of it at the Pemberton.

"You're gonna be ready early tomorrow, right?" Ben said as he huffed up the stairwell to the second floor.

They were going to Fox Creek for the weekend. It was a huge casino just two hours away in Connecticut, and Ben had some nerd-fest math conference there. In the last year, Smiles had lost $22,000 playing online poker, but the last $10,000 or so was just unlucky breaks—-he was actually getting pretty crafty at it. He'd been secretly thrilled when Ben asked for a ride. A nice little winning streak at Fox Creek could make for a decent birthday celebration, after all.

"Yeah, definitely," Smiles said.

Ben was scurrying down the hall, all eager to get back to his formulas, but Smiles wasn't ready to go back to his empty apartment. He semi-forced his way into Ben's place and plunked down in the inflatable Budweiser Super Bowl chair.

"So you gotta do some gambling with me tomorrow," Smiles said. "I mean, as long as you're at Fox Creek, you should have some fun."

Ben made a beeline for his desk (shocker) and started

dumping books out of his bag. "I'm going for the confer-ence, not to goof around," he said.

Smiles slumped in the plastic chair, reminding himself that he wasn't dealing with a normal person here.

The apartment looked exactly as it had that first day, six months ago. Halfway through a game of *Call of Duty*, Smiles had heard a clunking sound outside his door and found a scrawny-ass dude trying to lug a desk up the stairs by himself. Smiles's first instinct was to whip out his phone and get it on video; it would have gone viral in a second. Instead, he had introduced himself and helped out.

This had turned out to be a brilliant move. Smiles was just doing a good deed, but then Ben had let it slip that he was only sixteen and going to MIT. Which meant: mad genius. A brain like that could pay off big someday, Smiles figured, and he'd decided right then and there to chum up to the crazy little guy.

The only furniture Ben had was the desk, a bed, a fold-ing chair, and a card table to eat his meals on. The one addi-tion since he moved in was the inflatable chair, which Smiles had picked up at the liquor store so he'd have somewhere decent to sit when he came over.

Ben had his nose buried in his notebook already. The guy was a monk. Always working away, staying focused, making himself better. Smiles watched him and wondered, as he often did, why he couldn't be more like that.

He had his doubts by now that Ben would ever become the next Robert Smylie Sr.—the questionable hygiene alone would be an impediment to that kind of success—but Smiles had to admit he enjoyed the kid's company. Hanging out for hours at a time in Ben's place helped fill his days, yes, but he also liked the feeling it gave him to steer Ben away from his more disastrous life choices (e.g., Dockers) and instruct him on the finer things in life (e.g., RRL Low Straight Carolina Wash jeans in gray, single cuff). The one time he saw Ben in the Rag & Bone Yokohama shirt he'd given him for Christmas, his downy cheeks shaved for once, Smiles realized his grooming advice to Ben was probably the most productive contribution he'd made to society in his entire life. The strange friendship had even given him his last great idea for *his own thing*: to start a comprehensive life-skills school for the socially awkward. Hopefully with students more receptive than Ben, who despite that one shining moment seemed to ignore the copious copies of *GQ* and *Men's Health* that Smiles "accidentally" left in Ben's apartment in hopes they might stir some interest in his own betterment.

Smiles had given up on the nerd-school idea after drawing up one lesson plan ("Acne: Know Your Enemy"), but he was still holding out hope for his ultimate project: getting Ben a girlfriend. Smiles mulled over strategy as he wandered to the card table. On the wall above, Ben had taped an official-looking letter from some big-shot journal called *The Annals of Mathematics*, which had accepted one of Ben's math papers for publication. Smiles desperately wanted to make a joke about how it sounded dirty, but he figured Ben wouldn't appreciate it.

"So, you nervous about meeting with those spies?" he said.

Ben had told Smiles that he had to get some kind of

government agents to clear his article before it could even get published. All top-secret and everything. That's why Ben was going to the conference—to meet with the agents about his article.

"They're not spies," Ben said. "They're just some guys from the NSA."

"The NSA," Smiles repeated, not wanting to ask.

"The National Security Agency. They do cryptography."

"Umm-hm. Cryptography."

"Code-breaking," Ben said, his voice bored now. He hadn't even looked up from his books.

"So what do you have in that paper, anyway—state secrets?"

"It's nothing special. All high-level work in cryptography has to be screened before it gets published."

Ben was playing it off, but Smiles knew the truth: The kid was a mad genius.

Melanie's reply buzzed through his cell: *"In trig. Hang in there—see you tonight."*

Tonight. Why she had agreed to come over tonight, Smiles wasn't exactly sure. Probably to give him the ax— or, knowing Melanie, maybe she was just being nice. Either way he had to make the most of it. Smiles figured he should probably clean up his place, or at least make a dent in his mountain of laundry. Just the thought of tackling it made him tired.

"Seriously, man, how do you live without a stereo?" he said, flipping through some of Ben's mail and other papers.

Ben just grunted.

"You need some music in your life. It's healthy." Smiles was just talking to himself, like he did regularly here. It was nice to have someone there to hear you, though. Ben was like having a cat, Smiles thought as he read a crinkled flier from a place called the Clay Mathematics Institute.

MILLENNIUM PRIZE PROBLEM CHALLENGE it said at the top, and underneath—

Holy shit. They had seven math problems there, and they were giving away $1 million if you figured any of them out.

"Dude," he barked so that Ben wouldn't ignore him this time. "Are you trying to solve these?" Smiles waved the flier at him.

Ben turned around. "Maybe."

"What do you mean, *maybe*?"

"I don't know. They're hard."

"I hope so, for a million bucks." Smiles read some more. Ben had circled one of the problems in pen. It was called the Riemann Hypothesis, and it appeared to be the granddaddy of them all. Something to do with prime numbers. Smiles was pretty sure his dad's system—his special encryption technique—was based on prime numbers, too.

"So come on—are you doing this or not?" Smiles said.

"Put it away, Smiles. Just leave it."

"God, that'd be pretty sweet to make a million dollars off a math problem."

"*Just leave it.*"

No, he wasn't always the friendliest dude. He got moody like this, and sometimes he'd just kick Smiles right out of his apartment. Ben had mentioned once that he was

a borderline Asperger's case—which as far as Smiles understood meant you were, like, actually medically diagnosed
as a nerd—and he chalked up most of his strange behavior
to the mental disease thing. Smiles knew that Ben didn't
mean to be harsh; he was just too wrapped up in his brainy
projects. Feisty and wise: He wasn't a cat, he was like a
modern-day Yoda.

"Don't get all pissy." Smiles carried the flier over to
the desk and swiveled the notebook toward him. "Are you
working on it now?"

Ben tugged the notebook back. He sighed again, much
heavier this time, staring at a blank spot on the desk while
he spoke. "If I promise to gamble with you," he said, "will
you let me work?"

Smiles threw up his hands. "Say no more. Work away.
Tomorrow we ride!"

Smiles went across to his apartment, happy as he'd been
all day.

AT EIGHT O'CLOCK on the nose, Melanie appeared at his door holding a huge plastic container filled with water. Something dark was coiled at the bottom. Smiles recognized it immediately.

"Oh my God, Mel."

It was the best birthday gift he had ever gotten.

Five minutes later, the dragon eel slipped into Smiles's 120-gallon tank, which had been sitting vacant since Virgil the barracuda bit it two weeks ago. The dragon eel had these fearsome little horns, and black and orange stripes across its body that a tattoo artist couldn't have drawn any better. The thing was a genuine beast, more than a foot long. It squirmed and settled around some fake coral.

"He'll be shy for a while," Smiles said, "until he gets used to it."

Melanie watched, her green eyes transfixed. Smiles understood—sometimes he just stared at his fish for hours before he realized a whole afternoon had passed. But now, he couldn't help staring at Melanie.

She didn't have freckles anymore, but you could still see the tomboy. In a month she would have a tan from cross-country practice. Her face was all elegant lines—sharp cheekbones, defined lips, the long curve of her eyebrows. Melanie was smokin' and she didn't even know it.

"Oh, look," she whispered. The eel stirred along the bottom, churning the fluorescent pebbles like flakes in a snow globe.

Smiles watched her watching the eel, and his chest caved a little. They were leaning in so close he could smell her. Clean sheets and spring mornings. Maybe it was just her shampoo. Who cared—the familiar scent lit up his brain receptors like the Fourth of July.

They made eye contact, and all of a sudden he was just doing it: dipping his head and drawing toward her. Kissing her. Tender but intense, soft but electric.

After a while, Melanie broke it off. "Umm, wow . . . Look . . . I don't know—"

"Oh . . . no, I'm sorry . . . I just . . ."

Melanie had made it clear that they weren't together at the moment, and it looked like she was hitting about 9.5 on the freak-o-meter right now.

"Well, guess I did all right with the present," Melanie said perkily, trying to laugh it away.

Then, "Don't worry about it, it's okay."

And then, after a long minute of staring at the eel together, "What was that text about anyway?"

His text. About the letter.

Smiles wasn't sure he wanted to talk about it anymore.

Maybe Mr. Hunt was right—the letter was toast, and it might be best to give up on it.

"Oh, I don't know." It was already inching its way out of his mind, carting itself off to the trash heap of failed ventures he'd tossed away over the years (making varsity lacrosse at Kingsley; fronting an alt-metal band; seducing Ms. Callan, his ninth-grade math teacher).

"Tell me," Melanie said. She slipped the palm of her hand into his, patting it on top.

Smiles decided he should probably talk about something before he went on another mad kissing spree. "Well, get this. I went to see your dad this morning."

He told her about the message from his mom, and the "package," and how her dad had destroyed the letter at his dad's direction. They sat on the couch, with Lake Jägermeister on the carpet between them. Smiles hadn't been able to get it all out yet.

The more he talked, the more Smiles missed his mom. This letter thing was stirring up the pain, like the rocks in his tank. There was comfort in the hurt, though. He wanted that bed of memories; he wanted those bits of her.

"Smiles . . ." Melanie hesitated.

"Yeah? What do you think?"

She gave him a quizzical look. "It's just that . . ."

Smiles waited for her to continue, but she just sat there, doing a kind of tilted-head thing. It reminded him of his frustrating conversation with Mr. Hunt earlier in the day. Was this something genetic? Were the Hunts programmed to turn gooey and useless at critical moments in Smiles's life?

"C'mon, Mel, just say it."

"Well, don't you think . . . don't you think that it . . ."

"*What?*"

"Don't you think the message could be from your birth mother?"

WAS IT POSSIBLE?

Could he really not see it?

Could he really not see the blazingly obvious truth?

"Oh," Smiles said. "I don't know. I hadn't even thought."

Of course it was from his birth mother.

His stepmom, Rose, had had no reason to leave Smiles some kind of weird letter/time bomb, set to explode on his eighteenth birthday. You'd only arrange that kind of thing if you knew you weren't going to be around. Rose didn't know that—she hadn't known she was going to die in that accident.

She wasn't a coward who couldn't face up to something she'd done. The letter was probably an apology his birth mother was too scared to make in person.

Smiles stared absently at the aquarium. In all their years together, he had brought up his birth mother only once. They were still small, ten or eleven, and Smiles had told her he'd tracked down her address. Her name was Alice. She was a mathematician like his father, and Smiles had discovered she was working at a think tank on the West Coast. They were up in Smiles's room when he showed her an envelope containing a letter he'd written to her. Melanie still had a sharp memory of her young self in Smiles's room, sitting cross-legged on his Patriots comforter, wondering how awkward it would be to write a letter to a mother who had discarded you.

Through the envelope, she could see the messy scrawl of his handwriting. The square dark blot in the middle was a school picture he'd included for her. He'd sent the letter more than a week earlier. It had already been postmarked, sent to California, and come back. A handwritten note near the stamp said *Return to Sender.*

Melanie hadn't understood at first. "She's not there anymore?"

Smiles had shaken his head. "It's her handwriting," he said. "I've seen it before."

He'd never brought up Alice again.

"Do you have a number for her?" Melanie asked now. She grabbed his phone from a pile of Xbox games just in case.

Smiles only shrugged. "I never looked for her again, after she returned that letter. I didn't even try to find her when my dad got sick." He seemed disappointed with himself, and Melanie felt another surge of anger at the woman who had made him feel this way.

"C'mon," she said, "we'll hop on your computer. Maybe she's still at the same place. And California is three hours behind, so—"

Melanie stopped. She had triggered something in Smiles. "What is it?"

"Probably nothing," he said, "but . . . where is area code 510?"

He brought out his cell phone and showed her a record of two missed calls from a 510 number. "They came in this morning."

Melanie had no clue where 510 was, but it couldn't hurt to try. "Call it."

She pinched her lip between her teeth as he contemplated the screen. And then he pressed the "call back" button. The tinny sound of a ringing line came through as Smiles drifted to his bedroom, the cell to his ear. Melanie followed on light feet to the doorway.

Smiles sunk to his bed, just a box spring and mattress lying on the floor. The sheets lay across it in a great swirl, a radar image of a hurricane. Even from the doorway, Melanie could hear the voice answering the call. She couldn't make out words, but there was something sharp in the delivery. It sounded female enough.

Smiles paused a moment. Melanie thought he might lose his nerve and hang up. She gripped the doorjamb with an unconscious intensity.

"Hello?" Smiles said. "Is this Alice Smylie?"

Silence for a moment, and then a muted reply. Smiles continued: "This is Rob Smylie. Your son, I think."

I think. It was heartbreaking. Melanie realized she'd cracked a nail and forced her hand away from the door frame.

Smiles nodded and then started again. "I, uh, well, you

know Mr. Hunt? I was talking to him today and he told me there was a letter that you'd left for me. And a notebook of some kind. I'm not sure I really understood, but anyway I was wondering—"

A longer burst of sound, but now the voice had a note of finality in it.

"Well, okay, but I mean the whole thing was just a little confusing. You did write the letter, then?"

Silence, and then another clipped sentence from the other end.

"Maybe you could just tell me about it then? 'Cause it turns out Mr. Hunt actually threw away the letter. It's sort of a long story, but my dad's kinda sick and—"

A louder, longer response. Smiles's head made a slow bow of defeat to the carpet. Melanie wanted to throttle this woman. She couldn't take it anymore, and worse, she felt like she was invading Smiles's privacy. If she could pick up the line and demand some answers, she would. But she couldn't, so she did the only decent thing she could think of and retreated to the living room.

Melanie waited for five minutes there, looking beyond the gurgling fish tanks to the low clouds turning to Creamsicles in the sunset. The murmured pleadings she heard in Smiles's voice pained her ears.

Since she had last been to his place, a number of golf ball–sized pocks had appeared in the living room drywall. Her shoes rested on a gigantic purple stain in the carpet with dried chunks of paper towel all over the place. Smiles had parties during the week, attended, she imagined, by people he met out at the bars who liked the idea of hanging out with Robert Smylie's son for a night. It worried her. She wondered what happened here at night during the week but never asked. Chalk up another thing she wanted to change about herself.

She was sitting on the battered blue sofa that Smiles had found in the trash area on the day he got his keys. On the wall facing her was the seventy-two-inch plasma.

The obscene hunk of black plastic was shrieking everything she didn't like about Smiles. She wasn't comfortable here. And still she knew why she had come tonight. She knew why she had confused him with her birthday gift, and why she'd kissed him back by the aquarium. If she had the list right now, she would have written: *Pro: I glow for him. Ridiculous, but I do.*

The bedroom door opened. Smiles pocketed his cell on the way out, looking haunted.

"Smiles . . . what did she say?"

"Do you want to eat?"

He was avoiding it, of course, but she hated seeing him like this.

"Kabobs?" she said. Smiles loved the smelly kabob joint across the street.

He took her hand on the way out. He almost never did it, and she could have cried at the tender offering.

⅄

The kabob place was the size of a matchbox. It had two tiny booths, and the air was thick with a smell of lamb that stuck to your clothes for days afterward. The grease had yellowed the walls and penetrated a picture frame above them, warping a poster of Cyprus. They ate in silence, scrunched side by side in the booth. Melanie was thankful when Smiles prepared to speak.

"It was her, you were right." He was a fast eater and had finished already. He wiped his hands on tissue-thin napkins.

"Yeah?"

"Yeah. She said it was for the best that I didn't read the letter."

Melanie groaned.

"What?" Smiles said.

His harsh tone took her aback. He hardly ever spoke like that.

"I just . . . I think you deserve to know what it said."

Smiles shrugged. "What could she say that's important now? Whatever—it's over."

Melanie chewed, savoring the extra time to think of how to advance this conversation. It suddenly felt like a minefield. "But after what she did to you—"

"I don't care what she did to me. I had the best mom I could want."

"I know. It's just, like, *accountability* or something."

"I'm not gonna play judge. I'm not gonna force anybody to deal with me if they don't want to." After a while he added, "Anyway, she said my mom knew about the letter."

"Rose?"

"Yeah, Rose. You know—my *mom*." He was angry now, like Melanie had been insulting the memory of the woman who raised him.

"Right, sorry." Melanie felt like she couldn't win here.

What was she supposed to do, call them Mom One and Mom Two? "But I mean, what does it matter that Rose knew about it?"

Smiles stared at her like she was dumb. "If she knew and didn't say anything, then she probably thought it was best for me not to know about the letter, too."

"Or she was just being respectful. Waiting till you turned eighteen, according to the directions for the message. Did she even read it?"

"Yeah." The harsh voice again. "I guess. They emailed about it and everything, apparently."

"Smiles . . ."

He turned to her, gearing to attack.

Why was he getting like this?

"If it were me," Melanie said, "the emailing thing would make me *more* curious."

"We're different people, then. Or maybe I'm just weird."

Melanie could feel herself getting hot but couldn't help it. She could practically see his self-esteem shrinking before her eyes, and it wasn't right. "She *gave birth* to you, Smiles. Did she even apologize for leaving you and your dad?"

Smiles balled up his soggy napkins and paper plate.

"I'm done, let's go."

"*I'm* not." She had half a kabob on her plate.

"You aren't eating that."

She wasn't, but now he was pissing her off. "You're telling me what I'm going to eat? I don't know why you're acting like this is all my fault somehow."

His stare hardened, his eyes gone bitter and dull. "I'm done with this."

And then he left.

⨯

Melanie finished her kabob out of spite. She sat on the sticky red plastic, in the hot greasy air, and she chewed slow bites that piled uncomfortably in her stomach.

She walked to the apartment building on a storm cloud of hurt. Melanie knew she shouldn't act when she wasn't thinking right, but she couldn't stop herself. She rapped loudly on Smiles's door, welcoming the pain that broke across her knuckles.

Smiles pulled the door open and retreated back inside, but Melanie didn't follow.

"It's *over*," was all she said before slamming the door shut and walking away, bloated and sick.

DID I JUST do that?

Yes, I just did that.

The Camry's tires throbbed over the cobblestone drive. Melanie got out and wafted toward the house, feeling like someone had filled her with helium.

She lived with her parents in an embarrassingly nice Tudor home, which hardly stood out in the candy-land opulence of Weston, the town motto of which should have been "Jealous?"

This was all wrong. Melanie had always imagined breaking up with a guy as a triumphant, girl-power moment. The way it sounded in pop anthems. Even if it wasn't like that— even if she didn't get over it right away—she would have three girlfriends close at her side, and they would heal their troubles together through the power of, like, sweet-potato pies, or the wisdom of Jane Austen, or maybe a magical bra. The fat and/or slutty one would keep them in stitches the whole time, and everything would be right.

Apparently not.

Melanie was happy to see the lights off and no sign of her dad's car. They must have had a thing tonight. Her parents always had a thing—an opera, a benefit, a gallery opening.

A stone path led to their front door with its black iron hinges and tendrils of ivy. Melanie trudged up the stairs and sunk onto her bed without turning on a single light. She had logged a lot of hours like this in the last couple of years: facedown on her floppy white comforter, lights off, doubting herself. But this was worse than fretting over a volleyball game or chemistry test; this was Smiles. They had known each other forever. Their fathers were best friends. Their lives were wrapped around each other like the roots of an elm.

Melanie couldn't fight it off anymore—a nauseating feeling that she had pushed things too far. She didn't know what it was like to have a mother who left you. She had basically forced Smiles to make that call. And he had done it, which must have been scary as hell, and when it was over he had held her hand softly. Like the kiss he had given her by the fish tank. Melanie couldn't replay their argument too clearly—it was still a thick brew of feelings—but now she was getting the impression that she had riddled him with questions.

Why hadn't she given him a little space? All this stuff about Alice—it must have felt like a threat to Rose, who had been such a good mom to him before dying in that terrible accident.

Melanie had loved Rose, too, and she loved even more the stories that Smiles would tell about her. How she taught him to make daiquiris (virgin for him, double rum for her) in the summer when he was little. How, when he was even smaller, she would let him work the ATM like a video game. Her password was RSJR (i.e., Robbie Smylie Junior), and Melanie went heartbroken all over at the thought of Smiles's stubby infant fingers pressing the code, his hands clapping when the money came out. Rose had programmed that same password into their home security system, and—

Melanie bolted upright.

No.

I couldn't do that.

Would it even work after a person died?

Rose had sent Alice an email about her mystery letter . . .

If Melanie could access Rose's email account, she could see it. And then Melanie would know what all of this was about.

Without thinking, Melanie turned on her bedroom light and fired up her Mac.

She was hoping that Rose's email account would still be active (she'd been dead for almost a year now, but how would an email service know that?), and she couldn't be positive she'd used the RSJR password for it.

Melanie searched her Gmail account for messages from Rose. She quickly found two messages from roseyrose65@ yahoo.com about a surprise party for Smiles they'd planned together. Melanie had never had the heart to delete them.

Now that she had Rose's email address, she went to Yahoo—the screen distressingly joyful and tidy, advertising a movie called *Pants on Fire*—and plugged "roseyrose65" into the Yahoo ID box. For the password, Melanie typed in "rsjr" and pursed her lips.

A red message: *Invalid ID or password.*

Maybe the password had to be at least six characters long. She tried "robbiejr."

Same error message.

She tried "robertjunior," "robbiesmiles," "robertsmyliejr," and "littlerob," but none of them worked, either, and Melanie started wondering if Yahoo was tracking all her failed attempts to break in to the account. She was probably raising suspicion deep within Yahoo's security programs in Silicon Valley, or Bangladesh, or wherever. Yeah, Melanie probably shouldn't have been doing this from her own computer, but it was too late now.

She had signed up for things on the Internet that required you to use both letters and numbers in your password. Melanie looked at her cell phone and found the numbers corresponding to *JR.*

And then she typed "robbie57."

And then it worked.

~

The email page freaked her out.

Good Evening, Rose! it said, as if she had just stepped out of the grave to update her pals on how the afterlife was going. Melanie shuddered away the feeling that she was doing something blasphemous.

Just find the email Rose sent.

Smiles's birth mother's first name was Alice, that much Melanie knew. His dad had started his company back when they were still together, and he'd named it after her in a cutesy kind of way. Alyce Systems.

Melanie brought up the "Sent Mail" folder and clicked on the "To" bar, which put the recipients in alphabetical order.

Amongst the *A*'s, Melanie found it. A single message, sent to Alice:

Rose Carlisle
To: Alice T <msalice@hotmail.com>
Thursday, April 3 11:53:04 AM
Subject: Alyce

I have your info on Andrei. We need to talk. Please respond—I'm not into head games here.

Rose

Melanie smiled wide. It sounded so much like her.

Rose was so much fun, but there was something wild about her, too, something half-unhinged, and she had a ballbuster at her core.

Her immediate thought about the message was a guilty one: Maybe Rose and this "Andrei" had been having an affair. It might explain the "head games" comment and the antagonistic tone. Maybe Alice had found out Rose was cheating on Mr. Smylie and was trying to exploit her knowledge somehow. But why? And what did it have to do with Smiles? Melanie had no clue, and she shouldn't be speculating like this anyway.

She was ready to close the account when she re-sorted

the emails by date and saw that Rose had sent a second email immediately after the one she'd sent to Alice—to Melanie's own father. A worried hum escaped Melanie's lips. The email read: *Marshall, I know you're in Saint-Tropez for the week, but if you get this give me a jingle. If you can drag yourself from the topless beaches, that is* ☺.

Was it just a coincidence? The email was friendly enough, but she obviously wanted to talk to him right away—she wouldn't have bothered him in Saint-Tropez otherwise. Could there be a connection between her dad, Alice, and whoever this Andrei person was? How could her own father possibly be mixed up in all this? Certainly he couldn't have anything to do with an affair. Just the thought of him on a topless beach was enough to turn Melanie's stomach. It was silly to even venture a guess—

Headlights flashed on the street below. The car swept past—it wasn't her parents—but it broke Melanie out of her runaway thoughts.

This was pretty ghoulish, what she was doing.

She printed out the email to Alice, shut off her computer, and hopped under her comforter. It was pointless to even pretend she could give this thing up—not now, not with her dad mixed up in it, too. But she resolved not to think of the affair angle, or make any other premature judgments, until she got some better information. If she was lucky, Andrei worked at Alyce Systems. It seemed possible, anyway, given the subject line. Melanie did her for-credit internship every Friday at the Alyce headquarters (with Bug Eyes, Jenna Brooke). They worked in the HR department, so tomorrow Melanie could search for employees named Andrei.

Melanie stared up at the ceiling with a crazy energy racing in her head.

There was something significant in that letter, she was sure. Something important to Smiles, to her dad, and maybe even to herself. The trauma of the night was fading already, replaced with a determination to discover what the letter was all about.

It was like a test, and Melanie was excellent at tests.

"If I were to awaken after having slept for a thousand years, my first question would be: Has the Riemann Hypothesis been proven?"

—David Hilbert, 1900

FRIDAY

"As humans we must dream, and when we dream, we dream of money."

—David Mamet, *The Spanish Prisoner*

IT WAS SIX fifteen a.m. and someone was pounding on
Smiles's door.

Not cool.

He hugged his comforter tight and buried his head in
his pillow. Usually someone knocking at his door with this
kind of brute force meant yet another noise complaint from
the semi-hot chicks in the apartment below, who had turned
out to be disappointingly anal about such things. But he
hadn't left the stereo on last night or anything, so he spent
the next ten minutes hoping they'd just go away.

They didn't, and at 6:25 in the morning—*6:25 in the
morning*—Sir Knock-a-Lot was still going at it. Smiles
wrapped the sheet around himself and stumbled to the door.

Ben.

"What the hell, dude?"

"C'mon, we need to beat rush hour," Ben panted.

He was wearing a polo the color of leftover salmon.
With pleated khakis and gray docksiders. Did nerds actually *try* to wear the lamest possible clothes? Was it some

kind of elaborate in-joke they had been playing on society for decades?

"I told you we needed to leave early," Ben said.

"Early means before noon," Smiles said, but Ben obviously had no concern for such norms of etiquette. "Give me five minutes," he groaned, since he was up anyway. "And no kidding, dude. For your own good? Change those pants."

~

When they got past Framingham, Smiles let it loose.

The Infiniti hit eighty, then eighty-five, then ninety. Cruising speed.

After rousting Smiles with the big scene back at the apartment, Ben was sound asleep in the passenger seat. Smiles had nothing to do but sit there and think about the phone call with Alice, his birth mother.

It's better left alone.

It's better left alone, she kept saying.

It's better left alone. I'm getting on a plane. I'll have to end this call now. Click.

He cranked the stereo to get the call out of his head, tapping out a Green Day song on the steering wheel and watching with some relief when Ben finally shifted upright.

"So, what do you want to play at the casino?" Smiles said before Ben could nod off again. He needed some convo to get him through this drive.

"I can't gamble," Ben mumbled, half-asleep. "I'd get too nervous."

Smiles shook his head. "There's nothing to be nervous

about. It's all about numbers, and you're a wiz with numbers. You could tear it up at blackjack. *Rain Man* style."

"What?"

"Forget it," Smiles said. Ben was already going for some book in his army backpack. He was so paranoid that he'd rigged the closure on it with an actual combination lock. His high school locker had probably looked like Fort Knox.

"So what's that million-dollar problem you're trying to figure out, anyway?"

Ben stared at him. "You really want to know?"

"Why, you don't think I'm smart enough to get it?" Actually, Smiles knew he wouldn't be. "Just dumb it down a little. Gimme the highlights."

Ben inhaled. "It's called the Riemann Hypothesis."

Smiles flew by an SUV, focusing tight on Ben's words so he wouldn't get lost.

"Probably the biggest mystery in math," Ben said, "is the pattern behind prime numbers. No one can figure it out. You know what prime numbers are, right?"

"You better break it down for me, Einstein." Smiles might have been more embarrassed about his lack of knowledge if Ben hadn't woken him up before sunrise.

Ben flicked off the stereo. "Okay, well, most numbers are the product of at least two other numbers. Like 21. You multiply 3 times 7 and get 21, right?"

"Right." Smiles was all over that one.

"But the number 7, that's a prime number. 'Cause you can't multiply two other numbers to get 7. Except 7 and 1, and 1 doesn't count."

"Okay." Smiles was totally getting this.

"Some prime numbers are huge, with, like, a hundred and fifty digits in them, but they occur more rarely the higher you go. And they don't occur in any pattern. Or, at least, any pattern that anyone's figured out in the whole history of math. Which is weird, because *everything* in math has a pattern."

"That's the problem, figuring out the pattern? They'll give you a million dollars for that?"

"More or less." Ben sounded offended. "It's only the holy grail of math problems. Some of the best mathematicians have spent their whole lives trying to figure it out, and no one's gotten it."

"Why do they call it the Rainman whatever?"

"The Riemann Hypothesis. It's named after this guy, Bernhard Riemann, who actually did a lot of the work behind Einstein's general theory of relativity." Ben waited a beat, like he expected Smiles to break out into applause for the great Mr. Riemann. "Anyway, he had this hypothesis about how it works . . ."

Ben was getting excited talking about this. His voice was rising and he was rocking back and forth in his seat. Smiles had seen him do the rocking thing in his apartment—one of those little tip-offs, like the pants, that things were a bit off with the kid.

"No one's been able to prove or disprove Riemann's hypothesis, though," Ben went on. "It has to do with zeta functions, which are a little complica—"

"Yeah, better skip the zeta functions."

Now that he'd gotten Ben all wound up, Smiles had a sudden urge to shut down the conversation. They were treading close to the topic of Alyce Systems. All this talk about prime numbers was jogging his memory, and he was sure now that his dad's discovery—the one that had revolutionized computer encryption—was based on prime numbers, too. Ben probably knew all about it.

Smiles didn't want to ask him, though, because if the conversation went in that direction Smiles was headed straight for the black hole. He was out for a good time at Fox Creek, not a reminder of his ailing father and how he'd never measure up. He tugged the steering wheel to the right, barely making the off-ramp. A horn blared behind them.

Ben white-knuckled the armrest. "What was that?"

"I need some Taco Bell," Smiles grumbled.

⨍

The rest of the drive felt like work. Traffic snarled as the morning wore on, and Ben wasn't providing much in the way of company, unless spraying the passenger's seat with churro crumbs and scribbling in his notebook counted for anything. The only voice that spoke came from the deadened female vocals of the navigation system.

That and the one in Smiles's head: *It's better left alone. I'm getting on a plane. I'll have to end this call now.*

Smiles's mood didn't improve until they saw Fox Creek rising out of the flat green landscape. If you put a McMansion on horse steroids and placed it in the middle of a farm, that's sort of what Fox Creek looked like. Smiles loved it.

He ignored the self-parking sign and drove straight to the glass-canopied casino entrance.

"Don't even think about leaving that wrapper in the car," he said to Ben, and grabbed his duffel bag from the backseat. The valet handed him a ticket, and Smiles led the way through revolving doors to a marbled lobby area. Beyond it, the casino rang to the tune of a thousand slot machines. He dumped his bag on the floor, basking in it all for a second, before spotting the hotel reception to their left.

"This way," he said, and got a few steps before realizing Ben wasn't at his side. He was still standing under the chandelier at the entrance—just frozen there, notebook still in hand (naturally), eyes pointed thoughtfully skyward. What a piece of work. Smiles marched back and waved in Ben's line of vision.

"Stargazing?"

Ben stared at Smiles like he was coming back from a dream. "Sorry, I just . . . never mind."

"Give the brain a rest, dude. It's time to gamble."

Ben scurried to Smiles's side, checking his watch as they approached the reception desk. "I need to hurry, actually," he said. "The opening session starts soon."

The receptionist guy was wearing a sherbet-blue jacket with dangly gold trim at the shoulders, like somebody had asked Walt Disney to design some military uniforms and they'd gotten shipped to a casino in Connecticut by mistake.

"Can I help you gentlemen?"

"I'm here with the CRYPTCON . . . conference," Ben said.

"Oh my," Sergeant Sherbet said. "Some young code breakers, eh? So exciting. Okay, name on your reservation, please?"

Ben pulled a sheet of paper from his backpack. "Ben Eltsin," he said, and rattled off a confirmation number. Sergeant Sherbet sprung to action at his computer, but Smiles got distracted from the rest of the exchange.

A girl was headed their way. Cutoff jean shorts. Toned legs. Sun-bleached hair. A strand of it cascaded silk-like across a pixie face with honey-colored eyes. Smiles prayed to a merciful God she would stop at the desk to check in. She did. And she gave him a grin, too.

She had a scar high on her cheek, barely the size of a fingertip, shaped like a starfish. It crinkled when she smiled. Maybe Smiles's radar was off after three hours in the car with Ben, but he thought there was something happening here. Smiles returned her grin—going for *Yeah, I'm feeling it, too.*

"Hey," he said, because you had to start somewhere.

"Hey." Her voice was like a warm bath.

"I'm Smiles." He didn't extend his arm, on the theory that they were beyond handshakes already.

"Smiles?"

"A nickname." He shrugged, meeting her eyes, thinking, *This is totally working.*

She nodded and pointed a thumb at herself. "Erin."

He was getting a better read on her now. Her face was soft—her features cute and rounded—but there was something devilish there. Those honey-colored eyes, they were heat seekers. If there was any justice in the world, Smiles would be getting some action tonight.

"Here for the weekend?" she said.

"Yeah, for this conference thing," Smiles said. "You?"

Erin gave him a teasing smile, and the starfish scar drew in on itself coyly. "Guess you need to go."

He followed her eyes over his shoulder. Ben was standing at the side of the reception desk, flapping a card key envelope at his side with a pointed look of impatience. Sometime soon, they were going to have a long talk about the wingman concept.

"Ermm . . . yeah . . ." But before Smiles could salvage the situation, Erin had stepped to Sergeant Sherbet and Ben was pulling him down a hallway with signs that said CRYPT-CON AHEAD. It looked like Walt Disney had designed the carpet in here, too.

"Was that really necessary?" Smiles said.

"Yeah, sorry. I know you were flirting with that girl."

"Flirting? She was practically giving me a *lap dance*." He sighed—Ben would never appreciate the astronomical chances of meeting a pixie sun goddess who was doing her best to throw herself at you inside of five minutes.

"C'mon," Ben said, checking the little envelope with the card keys. "Cedar Tower, room 537."

"What's the big rush?"

"They said there was going to be a special guest at this opening session. I don't want to miss it."

"Oh, I'm sure it'll be epic," Smiles said as they followed a sign to the Cedar Tower through the conference-center part of the hotel. Turning a corner, they saw a registration table with a CRYPTCON sign and a line of people straight from Dork Central worming out behind it. Smiles cringed at the collection of short-sleeve business shirts, wrinkled dress pants, and old-man walking shoes—in some cases, all on one person. Would it kill these people to hit a J.Crew?

Ben's tiny bird shoulders slumped at the sight of the line. "Mind dumping this in the room for me?" he said, holding out the gym bag that doubled as his luggage. "I really need to get in that line."

Smiles grabbed the bag, happy to be loosed on his own. "Just call me Jeeves."

Ben handed him one of the room keys. "Thanks. So where can I find you later?"

"The poker room," Smiles said. "I'll be the one with all the chips."

"I'm sixteen. You know I can't get in there."

"You don't have a fake ID?" Ben was worse off than Smiles had thought. "You promised you'd do some gambling."

"I just said that to get you out of my room," Ben said, as if they'd been over it ten times already.

"Yeah, well . . ." Smiles paused. The pixie sun goddess had just passed by, engrossed in a text as she turned the corner. The surprising part was that now she seemed to be headed straight for the CRYPTCON registration tables. Then a wonderful thing happened. She swiveled and walked backward a few strides. As she did, her eyes turned up from her phone, lit on him, and seemed to say, *You coming or what?*

"Actually," Smiles said, "tell me about this opening session again."

JENNA BROOKE WOULD not shut up.

". . . It's like, oh sure, Stace, they're totally natural—no way are those inner tubes that suddenly appeared inside your mom's lips collagen injections or anything . . ."

She absolutely would not shut up.

They rode to Boston every Friday for their "Career Explorer" internship. Melanie's dad had volunteered to host two Kingsley students in the Alyce Systems HR department, so Melanie had signed up (obviously she had, because her dad had half suggested it). It wasn't a bad deal, except for the ride from Weston—on the commuter line, then switching to the T at North Station—which Jenna inevitably filled with analysis of people's body parts and, if the subject of discussion was a girl, Jenna's inevitable suspicions about her promiscuous ways.

". . . not saying he isn't halfway cute. Have you ever seen him in his baseball uniform? I'm not gonna lie, when I saw him out there in that game against Country Day . . ."

Melanie wished that she could just drive in with her dad, but he left early and stayed late. He'd been walking out this morning, carrying a heavy briefcase and eating a bagel (both of which, like everything else her father did, made her fear an imminent heart attack), when Melanie had impulsively asked him if he knew anyone at Alyce Systems named Andrei.

Her father stopped at the door. "Tarasov?"

Melanie went with it. "Yeah, Andrei Tarasov."

"Why?"

Instantly, Melanie realized what a bad idea this was. No way could she tell him about snooping in Rose's email account. Now she had to make something up on the spot, right there at seven o'clock in the morning, and she was a horrid liar to begin with.

"Uh, yeah, I guess. I think he's a programmer?" Melanie spat out the line just to say something; a lot of Alyce's employees had something to do with programming, one way or another. "I saw his name on something last week and didn't recognize it."

That last part was actually a pretty smooth recovery. Melanie's first project in HR had been some make-work assignment entering the programmers' and analysts' information (hire date, etc.) on a spreadsheet. Melanie probably *would* have remembered the name from that whole day of tweaking the spreadsheet just so.

Her dad chewed down his bagel, while Melanie mourned every last carb he was ingesting. "What did you see his name on?"

"Umm . . . something from Framingham, I think. From payroll." A lot of programmers worked in the Framingham complex, where they also had a payroll office. Whatever.

This was disaster territory now. Melanie, who had never been inside a church in her life, had rarely felt so sinful. "I was just wondering . . ." she said, trailing off lamely.

"I doubt it would have come from payroll. He left a long time ago. Don't remember him that well."

"Oh, okay, thanks, Dad," Melanie said, relieved when he kissed her cheek and stepped out the door. He waved good-bye to her from the path, his bagel swinging high in the morning air.

The train rattled to a stop at Park Street.

"This is us," Jenna said, perky as ever, oblivious to the fact that Melanie had spent the entire subway ride zoned out on thoughts of some guy named Andrei. They climbed the dusty, traffic-worn stairs of the T and ducked into an Au Bon Pain so Jenna could get her latte fix—". . . since when would I want to be a cheerleader? It's like, yeah, having Greg Simmons palm my ass ten feet in the air for a whole football game isn't exactly my idea of . . ."—and made the thankfully short walk to the Alyce Systems headquarters.

Melanie didn't have much actual work to do, and most days she savored the light pulse of energy from the business-people gathering at the elevators, milling around the coffee station, settling into life on the thirty-fourth floor. A hush blanketed everything. Even the copy machines, which would spend the next eight hours hammering out documents, hummed a calming white noise throughout the floor.

Best of all was the window by her cubicle. You could look down and sense the order to life: the rhythm of the traffic, the march of the waves.

Melanie didn't stop long at the window today. She logged in and went to Google right away. "Andrei Tarasov," she entered, remembering the last name her dad had mentioned. Just four hits came up, three of them irrelevant. The other one, the first on the list, was a fifteen-year-old article from the *Boston Globe*'s Metro section.

The headline ran: SOFTWARE TECH FOUND DEAD AT WESTON RESIDENCE.

It took Melanie all of twenty seconds to read the article that took her breath away:

WESTON—Police discovered the body of a software analyst on the front lawn of his employer in yesterday's predawn hours.

The man, identified as Andrei Tarasov, 36, was declared dead on the scene in this genteel enclave. According to a police spokesman, he was the victim of a gunshot wound to the head. A semiautomatic pistol was found in his hand at the scene, suggesting a potential suicide. A coroner's ruling is expected within the week.

Mr. Tarasov had been working at a start-up software firm, Alyce Systems, for less than a year. The founder, Robert Smylie, is the owner of the property on which Mr. Tarasov's death occurred. Police say Mr. Smylie has been in Silicon Valley on business for the last week and is not suspected of having any role in the death.

Mr. Smylie released a statement praising Mr.

Tarasov's work and expressing regret over the
loss to Mr. Tarasov's colleagues and friends.

The deceased left no survivors.

A man kills himself on Mr. Smylie's front lawn . . . and
her dad doesn't remember him?

This didn't make sense.

This did not make sense at all.

JUST HIS LUCK.

Smiles had raced up to the room, tossed their luggage inside, and gotten back to the CRYPTCON registration in world-record time, but Erin had made it through the line already. He planted his hands on his thighs, catching his breath while Ben emerged from the hive of nerds at the registration tables.

Ben fit an orange lanyard over his head as he walked over. His eyes narrowed as he got closer. "Are you, like, sweating?"

Smiles ignored him, fruitlessly scanning the crowd for Erin. He could only hope she was as jazzed about this opening session as Ben. "So where do we go?"

"You really want to come?" Ben said, in a voice that did not qualify as enthusiastic.

Smiles saw a teachable moment here. He squared Ben's shoulders. "Lesson one, okay? When it comes to meeting girls, you've got to seize every little opportunity you get. Especially you, no offense. A girl smiles at you on the subway? Chat her up. Asks you for directions? Chat her up. You accidentally spill your beer on her? Chat her up. You never know where it'll lead. Seize the day, man. They put that crap on T-shirts for a reason."

"So that's a 'yes'?"

"Now you're gettin' it," Smiles said. "I don't need, like, top-secret clearance to get into this thing, do I?"

"No, the conference is public. You just need to be registered."

"Don't worry about that. Just lead the way," Smiles said, and followed Ben down the hall to a set of double doors. The room inside was surprisingly large—twice the size of a movie theater—with wide rows of seats descending to an empty stage. A trickle of conferencegoers flowed down the aisles at the sides of the room, picking seats at leisure.

Smiles stuck close behind a larger man as they entered. The woman handing out programs at the door missed him— and his lack of a registration badge—entirely. He picked his way forward to Ben, who was already a quarter of the way down to the stage. "I'm more of a back-of-the-class kinda guy," Smiles said, but Ben didn't hear and/or care. Smiles sighed and trailed him to his chosen spot all the way down in the second row, precisely in the middle.

"You sure you don't want to just sit up on the stage?" Smiles said, craning his neck for a glimpse of Erin.

Ben opened his notebook and readied a pen. "I know you want to find that girl, but just do me a favor, okay? Don't make a scene in here."

Smiles turned forward, annoyed with himself as much

as Ben. He should have just gotten her number at the registration desk. This had been one of his more half-baked ideas, and now it was too late to leave—the trickle of people coming down the aisles had become a stream. They had nearly filled the unbroken row of seats stretching across the width of the auditorium; it would have been a real production just to make it to the aisle.

His dark mood from the car ride returned, and again Smiles found himself trying not to think about that phone call.

It's better left alone.

Trying not to think about how he'd been so stupid, sticking his neck out.

Smiles knew, of course, why he'd made the call: trying to prove some kind of point to Melanie about his maturity. He should have known it'd all go wrong.

People couldn't find seats anymore; they stood two deep along the walls. The auditorium was packed and tingling with energy waiting to be focused. Then the air in the room stiffened, and Smiles looked up to see a mustached man in a beige suit setting himself at the podium. The microphone gave a lively squawk when he tapped it. Satisfied, he raised his arms to his sides and said, "Welcome to CRYPTCON!"

A lusty round of applause filled the theater until the man motioned them silent. "This is going to be our greatest year yet," he said. "And our special guest speaker at this plenary session is one of the reasons why. You're all wondering who it is, am I right?"

The crowd played its part happily. Cries of "Yes!" "You

bet!" and "Tell us!" rose up from the seats. A lady in the front row said, "Matt Damon, please!" and everyone roared with laughter.

The speaker took the microphone off the stand so he could walk across the stage. Really hamming it up, this guy. "We'll reveal our speaker in just a moment, I promise. But first, for the students and journalists joining us today, let me spend a moment introducing the topic of this session: public-key cryptography."

It had been months since Smiles had sat through a lecture. Too bad Ben wasn't the type for a good game of hangman. He scanned for Erin again, but couldn't find her in the sea of rapt faces.

"Without public-key cryptography, it would be very hard to imagine living in our modern world. Quite simply, it is the tool that keeps our electronic secrets secure: encrypted emails, credit card transactions, all kinds of network data. I could go on and on. It has its origins in the World War II era, when governments were looking for a better method to send coded messages to spies. One problem: If you use the same code with all of your spies, then a single breach of the code threatens all of your secret messages. Some very smart people came up with a solution, known as asymmetrical encryption." The auditorium hummed with approval.

"The brilliance of asymmetrical encryption is that it allows one to share secret messages with anyone he likes, without ever sharing a secret code." The speaker had returned to the podium. He pressed a button on a laptop, and the screen behind him, which had read WELCOME TO

CRYPTCON, became a picture of a giant mansion behind a gated driveway.

"Just to be clear," he said, "that's not my house." They loved it.

"I use this with my students to illustrate public-key cryptography, which is a type of asymmetrical encryption. The most important type, in fact. And here's how it works: If I want to receive secret messages, I use two keys." The guy actually produced two golden keys from his pockets. Smiles would have found it impossibly corny except that it reminded him of the two interlocking keys in the Alyce Systems logo. This man was about to explain the foundation of his dad's company.

"One key," he said, wagging the key in his right hand, "is my public key. I will give this to anyone. It's the key to my front gate, and if anyone wants to send me a secret message, they simply use it to open the gate, walk to my front door, and drop their message in my mail slot."

He tapped the laptop again, and the picture changed to a fancy front door with a brass mail slot.

"The other key I keep safe. It's my private key, and I give it to no one." He slipped the key into his pocket. "It's the key to my front door, and whenever I want to get my secret messages, I open my door and collect them.

"Now, I know what you're all thinking: What is he talking about? Mail slots have been around forever!" Even Ben chuckled at that one. "Of course, the mail slot is just an analogy for the way public-key encryption works. And with the arrival of the Internet, it became infinitely more important. Amazon wouldn't have gotten quite so far if it had to share a secret code with each of its customers before accepting credit card information from them, would it? Today, public-key cryptography protects not only billions of credit card transactions a day, but untold stores of private data.

"And with that background, let me introduce someone far more knowledgeable on the subject: our special guest." Some premature claps sounded from the back. "Our speaker is a brave one, and let me tell you why. At this session today, you're going to hear about some new research. But as we know, sharing research publically in our field can be a dangerous thing. Some people tell you to Never Say Anything."

Peals of laughter ripped across the room, but Smiles didn't get it. He nudged Ben.

"The NSA," Ben whispered. "They say it stands for Never Say Anything, 'cause they don't want anyone spreading information about encryption. They have, like, laws against it."

The man had reached one end of the stage. He turned on his heels and started back. "Who are these people? It's hard to know. Some say there's No Such Agency."

Smiles had lost his curiosity, but Ben whispered anyway: "They used to deny they even existed." More laughs were rippling across the seats. This guy was really slaying them.

"In all seriousness," the man said as the crowd fell obediently silent, "the consequences of speaking publicly about innovations in our field are severe. Not many scientists face jail time for merely talking about their work, but we do—

those smart enough to advance the art of cryptography and brave enough to share. The speaker I'm introducing is a professor at one of our most respected universities. One of the professor's students has done some interesting work. And the professor has courageously volunteered to present that research today—despite the risk of arrest—in order to protect that student. Ladies and gentlemen, Professor Taft of the University of California at Berkeley."

The crowd leapt to its feet before the professor even appeared, washing the auditorium in applause. Smiles didn't bother. The forest of bodies made him feel small, and he was left alone again with his thoughts. Smiles heard the microphone crackle and the speaker mutter a thank-you. The speaker's voice was female, and the scrape of the microphone reminded him of static on his cell. The crowd remained standing around him, but Smiles was somewhere else entirely—back again on that phone call with his mother, her voice so smooth and firm and far away. Polite but distant. It had a high polish, a pretty piece of wood under an inch of lacquer.

While he had talked with her on the phone, a huge gaping hunger had cracked open inside him. But her voice had said, *It's better left alone.*

She was talking about the letter, which Smiles hardly even cared about by that point. He wanted bigger answers, but there was no way to ask the questions. So he kept pressing about the letter. *It's better left alone*, she repeated. Then her voice went flat: *I'm getting on a plane. I'll have to end this call now.*

And then it was over.

The applause kept on, the crowd still on its feet. And then Ben dropped to Smiles's side, landing heavily in his seat. He gave Smiles a strange look—thoughtful or troubled or maybe just Ben being his strange self. The clapping subsided and an air of anticipation filled the room. In front of Smiles, the wall of bodies came down in pieces.

"Thank you," the female voice said into the microphone, and Smiles gasped.

That voice . . .

He could hear it more clearly now. The man in front of Smiles sat, and that's when he knew for sure. He had only seen a few pictures of her, but it didn't matter. It was in the wide set of her face, the flatness of her lips, the eyes that gazed out at the crowd. She looked like *him.*

Standing at the podium—he was certain of it—was his mother.

"**THANK YOU VERY** much for that," she said to the final notes of applause. It was definitely her—the voice from the phone, the one he'd been unable to shake all morning.

The screen lit up with a formula and she began her speech, but Smiles couldn't absorb what she was saying. He could only hear the tone of her voice, the same as on the phone but now slightly more feminine, more relaxed. Smiles almost laughed. She was more comfortable risking her freedom than she'd been during a call with her son. He watched her in a trance, feeling nothing except the blood rushing to his head.

Smiles had told Melanie he didn't think about his mother, but of course that was a lie. He wondered about her all the time. When she'd sent the letter back unopened, it had cut him deeply. He hadn't been eager to relive the experience, and he'd never sought her out again. He always imagined she was out of reach somehow, that she'd joined a cult, moved to a commune in Australia, taken off on a Peace

Corps stint in Paraguay. Even the phone call could've been made from anywhere. But now she was standing in the flesh before him.

She was playing casual to the crowd, but you could sense something rigid about her. A plain navy dress shielded her petite figure. Chunky scarlet beads circled her neck. There was something controlled about her haircut, a bob with razor-edged bangs.

She had wrinkles at her eyes—markers of the years she'd spent away from him for no reason at all. She adjusted her dark-frame glasses and looked to the screen, pointing out some intricacy in the numbers that appeared there. Smiles watched her and felt a hot spark of anger.

"As you see, it's a rather elegant approach to the issue," she was saying.

Smiles found himself shrinking down in his seat, half expecting that everyone in the auditorium would have noticed the resemblance between them. But at his side, Ben hadn't moved. He wasn't even watching the stage—he still wore that troubled look, only now his eyes were roaming over the ceiling in a searching kind of fashion. Smiles was about to nudge him back to reality when Ben placed his finger flat along his nose, his concentration reaching new levels of intensity.

And then Ben said out loud, in far more than a whisper, "It couldn't . . ."

People turned, curious at the interruption. On the stage Alice broke off at the small commotion. Smiles touched Ben's arm, hoping to neutralize whatever kind of Asperger's thing was going on, but it didn't work at all. Ben's eyes popped alive.

"No way!" This time it was nearly a shout. Smiles could feel the excitement boiling from Ben's body.

The crowd rumbled in annoyance and the mustached man leapt onto the stage, trying to locate the source of the problem. Ben was too worked up to care. He shot straight up out of his seat. Snatching his backpack, he stormed toward the aisle as fast as he could, hurtling past laps and tripping over knees in the narrow row of seats. From their position in the center, it took an excruciatingly long time.

Smiles wanted to scream: Hey, *whatever happened to "don't make a scene"?*

The presentation had stopped entirely now. The audience began turning on Ben, muttering at him as he twisted his way to the aisle. Some guy at the end of the row grabbed at him, citizen's-arrest style, but Ben spun loose and flew up the stairs. His backpack flapped wildly against his side as he took the steps two at a time, banged hard into the door, and fled out into the hall.

The air had left the room entirely.

Smiles needed to find out what was going on before the session started up again. He cringed and ventured awkwardly down the row himself, apologizing as he made his way. "Sorry, medical emergency," he said over and over. His go-to excuse had never failed him, but this was really pushing it.

The crowd was still recovering from Ben's dramatic exit. Now a grumble of confusion began spreading through the auditorium as Smiles stumbled his way sidelong to the aisle.

"Everybody, please," the mustached man was saying. Smiles heard his voice through the speakers as he wedged past the final few seats, a tight smile pressed to his face. "We apologize for the interruption," the man continued from the stage. "Hold it down, please, and we can continue in just a moment."

Before he started up the stairs, Smiles turned to the podium. His mother was staring back at him, drawn stiffer than ever.

↣

Smiles pushed into the hallway, not sure he had the capacity to handle Ben's drama, whatever it was. The door swung closed behind him with a satisfying metal *clack*, and Smiles wondered if he would be able to shut out the memory of what he'd just seen as easily as that.

The woman with the programs was stationed in a chair by the door, tearing through a sudoku and a bag of Cheetos. Smiles was about to ask her if she'd seen a crazed kid running from the auditorium when he spied Ben across the hall. He was sitting on the floor a short distance away, writing furiously in his notebook. Directly above him was a brass light fixture—the proverbial lightbulb over his head.

Smiles approached gingerly. Ben suddenly seemed like some kind of wild animal that could be stirred at the slightest provocation.

"What's going on there, bud?" he said.

Ben jabbed an index finger in the air, his attention fixed on the page.

The whole episode had been pretty disturbing, but as he watched Ben writing with such concentration, Smiles had an inkling of a thought.

"You figure something out in there?"

Finally, Ben finished writing. His arms puddled to his sides in exhaustion. "Yeah, I did."

Smiles knew of only one thing that Ben was trying to figure out—one thing worthy of making such a scene. A grin creased Smiles's face. This might not be scary at all. This might be a jackpot.

Smiles leaned into him and said, "So tell me, how does it feel to win a million bucks?"

He was sure Ben had solved the Riemann thing—the million-dollar question. But Ben just closed his notebook firmly. "I . . . I really shouldn't talk about it."

"Talk about what?" Smiles said, but Ben didn't fall for it.

"*I can't talk about it.*" It was the bladed voice he used sometimes, mostly when he was trying to kick Smiles out of his apartment. "Actually, I need to go home."

"Home?" No way.

Smiles looked up and down the hall, as if anyone else could help him reason with this guy. The space was nearly empty of conferencegoers, silent except for muffled sounds from the auditorium and the rhythmic crunch of Cheetos.

"Look, man," Smiles said, "I can see you're a little freaked out by your brainstorm here. But there's a rule, and it goes like this: When you get Smiles out of bed at six o'clock in the morning to go to Fox Creek, you go to Fox Creek. You don't turn right around and go home."

Something hard set in Ben's jaw. "You don't understand. I'm not safe here."

"You're not safe?"

So yeah, Ben had gone full-on nutcase. Next he was going to say somebody had put a chip in his brain, and Smiles wasn't equipped for this. He just wanted to play a little poker. Maybe the casino had an on-call shrink for problem gamblers who Smiles could get on the case. In the meantime, he figured he should stash Ben away.

"Okay, look, let's get you to the room."

He pulled Ben up from the floor and led the way to the elevators, amazed at how far awry the casino trip had gone in the span of an hour. He didn't think it could get any stranger, but then out of nowhere Ben yanked Smiles's shirt, dragging him into an alcove.

Smiles wheeled on him. "Hey, this is getting weird. I don't know what the—"

"*Shhh!*" Ben hissed with crazed eyes. He peered frantically down the hallway, where a man was walking toward them from the elevators. Ben pinned Smiles in place with his scrawny arms. He whispered urgently: "Stay quiet till this guy passes, and I swear to God I'll explain everything."

Ben peered out, pulled his head back again, and put a finger to his lips. Smiles felt like a tool for playing along, but he did. The man looked about as nefarious as a copier salesman. He walked down the hall in an off-the-rack suit and a buzz cut, passing the alcove without a look.

Ben didn't breathe until he was gone.

"That could be the NSA guy—the one I'm supposed to meet about my paper," he said.

"So what?"

"Just stay here for a sec until he's gone."

"You're scaring me, Ben. What's this all about? I thought you won a million bucks."

"No, it's bigger than that."

"Bigger than a million bucks?"

Ben nodded, but he didn't look happy about it—he looked terrified.

"Smiles, I've changed the world."

MELANIE WAS GOING to have to start bringing her own lunch.

Every Friday, she tried to evade lunch with Jenna Brooke, and every Friday she failed. So now Melanie was sitting there in the deli, listening to yet another stream-of-consciousness rant from Jenna. This one seemed to be a cultural history of lesbianism in which their soccer coach, Ms. Fields, was playing a major role.

It wouldn't have grated on Melanie so much, except that she had managed to pull the old HR file on Andrei Tarasov that morning. She'd slipped into the file room during a midmorning lull and found it quickly among the old records that she had organized and boxed for shipment to the warehouse.

She had stashed it in her new leather bag right when she got back to her cube, planning to sneak out for an early lunch and read it then. But just before Melanie could make it to the elevator for her absurdly early lunch—it was barely past eleven at the time—Jenna tracked her down and, of course, volunteered to join her. ("I'm totally craving corned beef. Let's do it.")

Now Melanie could only steal longing glances at the file in her leather bag, all the while hoping that Jenna would stop talking long enough to eat her sandwich so this lunch could be over. Melanie finished her vegetable soup and cleaned up her place as conspicuously as possible.

". . . Chicks who get nipple piercings? They're the new Stepford wives. Give them whatever they want, you know? Not to get like post-post-feminist about it, but—oh my God, wait, is that a new bag, Mel? It's—so—freaking—cute . . ."

Melanie didn't notice the interruption in Jenna's thoughts until it was too late. Jenna was holding Melanie's bag over the table now (dangerously close to the dressing oozing from her Reuben sandwich), spinning it around in admiration. As Jenna fondled the leather with a ferocious envy in her eyes—to be fair, it *was* a great bag—Melanie could only pray that Jenna wouldn't open it and see the Andrei Tarasov file inside.

Which of course she promptly did.

Melanie reached to stop her, but it was too late. Jenna was already pulling the manila folder out for inspection.

"Heyyyyyy," Jenna said, in a mock-naughty tone that Melanie had heard her use on numerous members of the football team. "You aren't supposed to be taking these outside the office."

She was right. The point had been drilled into them on their first day.

"Yeah. I was just going to—"

"Oh my God! It's that Russian dude." Jenna had opened the file on the table now, reading intently. "Melanie, what are you doing with this?"

"You know something about him?"

"Know something? This is the guy they were talking about. The Russian spy!"

The clatter of dishes, the steam from the dishwasher, the electronic pinging of the cash registers—all the stimuli Melanie had been aware of only a second ago faded away.

Did Jenna just tell me that Andrei Tarasov was a Russian spy?

And now, for the first time ever, Melanie was completely interested in what Jenna Brooke had to say.

"Russian spy?"

"Okay, so I'm not supposed to know anything, but I heard Chrissy and Pam talking about this guy a few weeks ago," Jenna said.

She was always trying to make friends with Chrissy and Pam, two employees in the HR department. They were just out of college, and they always did everything too cheerfully for Melanie's comfort, like their happiness was a chocolate coating over a hollow inside. Melanie had given them a name in her head: the Easter bunnies.

"Yeah?" Melanie said, and her prompting tone was all Jenna needed.

"So this is what they said, swear to God. This guy, Tarasov"—Jenna jabbed at the folder—"he was a Russian, okay? He came here for school, 'cause he was really smart or whatever. Harvard, I think they said. Wherever Mr. Smylie was teaching."

"He was one of Mr. Smylie's *students*?" Melanie couldn't keep the surprise out of her voice.

"Yeah, yeah—it's so freaky, right? Wait till I tell you. So this guy was in grad school at Harvard, working with these big math professors. I guess some of the math can be kind of sensitive, like top secret. 'Cause they use that advanced math for, like, nuclear weapons and codes and whatever. That's what Chrissy was saying. Anyway, after school he got a job at Alyce. But then they found out that Tarasov had been stealing research and handing it over to the Russian government."

Melanie's cell rang; she sent it to voicemail without checking the ID.

"It's crazy, right?" Jenna said.

Melanie leaned forward, trying to keep Jenna's voice down. "Was he stealing research from grad school or from Alyce?"

"I don't know. I couldn't hear that well."

Melanie was puzzled. "You couldn't hear?"

"Oh, well, I was sort of eavesdropping. Chrissy was explaining it to Pam in her cubicle, and I was just kind of around. In the background. Until they noticed me."

"Oh."

"I mean, how could I not listen in? I had to."

Melanie pulled the folder back across the table, thinking that Jenna had a point. It was such a wild story, so different from her speculation about an affair. Melanie was tempted to write it off, but neither the Easter bunnies nor Jenna exactly had any motive, much less the imagination, to make something like this up.

Melanie wondered if Jenna knew about Andrei Tarasov committing suicide. "So what happened to him?" she said.

Jenna shook her head. "I'm not sure. Chrissy shut up really fast when she saw me there. I think I heard something about him being deported." She swiped the folder from Melanie again and turned to the back. "Let's see why he left," she said, running her finger down the page. "Oh my God. *Reason for departure: death.*" Jenna gave Melanie a wide-eyed look. "Karma's a bitch, eh? No, I totally shouldn't say that. That's terrible."

Lunchtime customers were filling the deli now, jostling for space in the tight quarters. Melanie didn't pay them any mind other than checking to make sure none of them was from Alyce.

A passport-sized picture of Andrei Tarasov stared up at them from the upper right-hand corner of the page. Milky skin, undernourished, but not altogether bad-looking. He had a child-man quality about him; his wispy black beard looked like an effort to play grown-up that didn't work.

A part of Melanie felt guilty for not telling Jenna about the suicide, but she couldn't do that. Her dad had been hiding something this morning—Melanie was sure of that now. Telling her about a Russian spy in the company, who, by the way, had shot himself on Mr. Smylie's front lawn, might not have been ideal morning chatter, but her dad had pretended that he barely knew about Tarasov.

There was something bigger here that her dad didn't want to talk about, Melanie thought as she and Jenna gathered their things. Melanie didn't even know what the possible secrets were, but now they seemed much larger and scarier than they had just a few hours earlier.

She couldn't afford to give away any information about Andrei Tarasov. Not until she found out everything. Not until she found out that her dad wasn't mixed up in this in any way. And not until she discovered why Smiles's birth mother, Alice, had an interest in Tarasov. Alice's letter to Smiles had something to do with him, something that Rose had discovered and didn't like. But what?

Melanie felt a pang at the thought of Smiles. She had an urge to hug him.

They walked back to Alyce under a bright blue sky that mocked Melanie's dark thoughts. The April sun was weak, but Jenna beamed into it contentedly as she slipped on her jacket, savoring the promise of warmth.

"Sooo . . . what were you doing with that guy's file, anyway?" she said.

Oh God. "Oh, yeah, well, I was boxing all these files up the other day and this one just ended up in my bag somehow."

It was her worst lie on a day of many lies. Whatever—Jenna always tried to stay in Melanie's good graces; hopefully she wouldn't start an investigation or anything. When Melanie's cell rang again, she grabbed for it like a life preserver.

Caller ID: *Katie Andrews.* Her friend from the class ahead of her at Kingsley. The one who had gone to Smith College, and who Melanie was going to visit tomorrow.

"Sorry, Jenna, have to take this," she said.

"No prob," Jenna said easily.

Melanie smiled back at Jenna, feeling a strange new affection for her.

"It'll just be a sec," Melanie said, bringing the phone to her ear and knowing she'd be stringing out the conversation with Katie all the way back to Alyce.

"SPILL IT," SMILES said.

He snatched up his duffel bag and commandeered the far bed. The morning's drama had worn his nerves thin, and part of him wanted to slump over for a nap. But first, he really needed to hear this.

Ben trailed him inside, pulling a chair out from one of those completely useless tables they put in the corner of hotel rooms. "Okay, okay. But . . . well . . . you're not going to like this."

Smiles couldn't imagine how Ben's formulas—whatever they amounted to—could possibly affect him. "Try me."

Ben heaved a sigh. "I figured out something about prime numbers this morning."

"Umm, yeah, I got that much."

Ben extracted his notebook from the backpack like he was defusing a bomb. He gripped it tight to his chest. "The thing I figured out—it's more dangerous, in a way, than a nuclear weapon. It could cause all kinds of trouble."

"No joke, dude, you've got to stop talking in riddles."

"Just listen. I told you about the Riemann Hypothesis, right?"

"But that's not what you figured out?"

"No," Ben said.

Even hearing this a second time, it was still a buzzkill.

Smiles was still stuck on the idea of a million-dollar score—probably because it was exactly the kind of thing he wanted for himself someday. When he dared to, he imagined what it would be like to tell his dad that he'd started his own company, that he'd made his first sale, that he was succeeding at something. He just had to find the something, and it had to be relatively easy. Maybe he should go back to that idea he'd had to make a beer pong app for smartphones for when you were drinking but didn't have a Ping-Pong table around. It was pretty brilliant. You could make one for Quarters, too. Spin the Bottle. All kinds of stuff. There had to be tons of cash in those things, and Ben could probably do the programming with his eyes closed.

"Anyway," Ben said, "I was working on the Riemann Hypothesis, and I got to thinking about the shape of elliptical curves in space and how they—"

Smiles made a rapid rolling movement with his index finger.

"Yeah, fine. I figured out *how to fast-factor the product of two primes*." Ben said this as if he had just made the Statue of Liberty disappear.

Smiles let the silence hang for a second. He didn't have the first clue what it meant to factor the whatever of blah blah blah. Ben must have seen his confusion, because he grabbed a pad of hotel stationery and a pen. "It's like this," he said, writing:

$3 \times 7 = 21$

"Three and seven are both prime numbers. You multiply them and get 21, right?"

"Yepper."

"Okay, well, going this way is easy . . ." He wrote it with an arrow:

$3 \times 7 \rightarrow 21$

"Simple. But there's no good way to go backward, to start with 21 and get the 3 and the 7." He wrote:

$21 \rightarrow 3 \times 7$

"Or, there wasn't until today. Now I have an algorithm that can do it in a snap."

Smiles considered the page. "I take it this means something important," he said, "besides the fact that you're a math geek?"

Ben wilted with frustration. "Smiles . . . it's, like, revolutionary."

Something about Ben's disappointed reaction stabbed at him the way it would coming from his dad. "Just kidding you, man." He straightened up. "Congrats, seriously. But why'd you freak out down there? Saying you weren't safe and everything."

Ben leaned forward, elbows on his knees. "You should know, Smiles."

Was he joking? "Well, I don't."

"All computer encryption—like, your dad's whole company—is built on the premise that you can't factor the product of two prime numbers. But I can do that now."

Smiles squinted at him. "What are you saying?"

The air-conditioning was blasting into the room's heavy curtains. The air pushed ripples across the fabric, as if ghosts were gathering for a mixer back there. Smiles felt the tingle of goose bumps on his arms.

"I'm saying that if you gave me a halfway decent computer hacker, in about a half hour I could decode any message that Alyce encrypts."

"Hold up. Really?"

"Any of them," Ben said. "Anything encrypted by Alyce, or any other company that uses public-key cryptography, I could get."

Alyce encrypted messages for all kinds of businesses. Smiles didn't really know what they were, but he knew they were big ones. His blood was pumping now in a way that was different from his excitement over the beer pong app.

"So, you could get all the credit card numbers from Amazon?"

Ben let out a hard-edged laugh. "It's like the guy said this morning. Encryption doesn't just protect credit card numbers. It's how they keep *everything* on computer networks secure. People buying stocks. Wire transfers. It's how they control water systems. Airplanes and missiles. Nuclear power plants, for all I know."

Water systems.

Nuclear power plants.

The stock market.

Smiles was getting a bigger picture now, and as he did, something heavy settled over his body.

"You could see all those things?" Smiles said. "How?"

"'Cause I can generate private keys."

Smiles closed his eyes, trying to catch up.

"The gate and the door, remember that? That's how public-key cryptography works, but it's just an analogy. Your dad's the one who actually made it work electronically. Without his system, you couldn't exchange secret messages over the Internet with people you didn't trust completely. It was a total revolution, and it's all based on primes."

Smiles nodded, more to calm Ben down than anything. "So instead of keys, they use prime numbers somehow," he ventured.

"*Yes, exactly!*"

"Chill. Just break it down."

Ben pointed to what he'd written before:

$3 \times 7 = 21$

"Three and seven are primes. Because they're primes, they're the *only* two numbers that you can multiply together to get 21."

"Okay."

"So 21 is my public key—it opens my gate. And 3 and 7 are my private keys. They open my door."

"Okay," Smiles said, feeling a foreign twinge of pride within himself for keeping up.

"So say you want to send me your credit card number. You type it in the computer, and then the encryption program scrambles it up using a formula based on my public key, 21. The way the encryption is written, the only way to undo it is to know the two numbers that when multiplied together equal 21. Which only I know, 'cause they're my private keys."

"And even though people know that your public key is 21, it's hard to figure out that your private keys are 3 and 7?"

"Right! But that's what I figured out today, how to do this . . ." He underlined:

$$21 \rightarrow 3 \times 7$$

"It's always been impossible to do in a short time with really huge numbers. It's called factoring. The only way that people can do it is to basically try random combinations to see if you get the public key when you multiply them together. With the big numbers they use, it takes forever to try all the possible combinations."

"Forever? Even with computers?"

Ben nodded. "The sun would burn out before you would get the private keys to a really long public key. Literally. It'll be faster when quantum computing gets here, but for now it takes forever. When your dad started Alyce, he did this thing to prove how good his system was. He put a number out there, the product of two prime numbers. He challenged anyone to find the two prime factors within ten years. Somebody actually figured it out, but it took them twelve years. Now, with my algorithm, I can do it in under a second."

"Which means you can unscramble the messages."

"Yeah." Ben sat back in his chair, spent. "With my algorithm, I can figure out all the private keys in the world."

Smiles really needed to stretch his legs, but he was glued to the bed. "If somebody got your formula, they could, like, wreck the stock market, couldn't they?"

"They could do anything," Ben said. "Smiles, this algorithm—the government would consider it an instrument of war. They would actually consider it illegal to possess. Didn't you hear that guy talking about the NSA?"

Smiles nodded.

"They don't even want people talking about little research discoveries. But this is on a different level. This is *everything*. Do you see how badly people would want this algorithm? You see what terrorists could do with this? People would die for—"

"Slow down, slow down. I get it."

Ben was reentering meltdown mode, but Smiles couldn't blame him. He wasn't kidding about having a nuclear bomb in that backpack.

The whole thing reminded him of when he'd gotten kicked out of Kingsley, just because he'd agreed to keep Darby Fisher's weed in his closet and they happened to find it there. The problem was so huge, there was nothing to do about it.

Ben was looking at Smiles with a deep sadness in his eyes. "Honestly, I was just trying to think of a solution to the Riemann Hypothesis. I was never trying to do this." He crushed the page from the stationery and flung it to the dresser. "I'm sorry."

"Sorry?" Smiles didn't understand the apology until it hit him. "Because your algorithm could make my dad's whole company irrelevant."

"You're not mad at me?"

"No," he said quickly, though he saw the problem clearly enough. He lifted off the bed with a syrupy weight in his legs and shut off the air-conditioning. After that, he didn't know what to do. Ben took his place on the bed, staring up at the ceiling in a semicatatonic way, and the weighty silence of the room was making Smiles edgy. He felt an urgent desire to play some *Call of Duty*, to shoot some pool, to watch his fish. He could spend hours staring at them, envying their bubbled lives. No intrusions, no pressures, no expectations to meet. Eat your food, play in the rocks, waggle your tail— as far as lifestyles went, it was hard to beat.

Smiles opened the curtains just to do something. Their fifth-floor room looked out on an impossibly big parking lot, and the sun glanced back at Smiles from a thousand windshields. He would have let some fresh air into the room, but he knew they always rigged the windows shut in casino hotels so gamblers couldn't commit suicide after a bad night at the tables.

"I had a pretty strange experience myself this morning," he said suddenly, surprising himself. "You know that big-shot professor? The special guest? That was my mother. She left when I was two." He spoke slowly, talking to the view. Ben didn't answer, but it was better that way. He just needed to speak it out loud to someone, and in the silence left by Ben he could imagine Melanie listening to his words. "It was so weird seeing her up there. I thought I'd never see her again in my life. Maybe this morning was the last time, I don't know."

Smiles heard shifting behind him, and when he turned Ben was up on his elbows. "Are you serious? That was your *mom*? My God, Smiles . . ."

Ben stopped, unsure of what to say, and just as suddenly as he'd started talking about his mother, Smiles wished he'd kept his mouth shut. He couldn't expect Ben to make it better for him.

"Are you—"

"Yeah, fine," Smiles said. He needed to move. He walked to the door and turned back. "Look, you gonna be okay here for a while?"

"Where are you going?"

"For a walk, I guess," he said. And then Smiles wobbled aimlessly into the hall, wishing he were the kind of person who could deal with big problems.

"BLACKJACK."

The dealer pushed three more purple chips in front of Smiles.

The poker room had been too crowded to deal with, so Smiles was playing blackjack at a hundred-dollar minimum table. It was just him, the dealer, and a crotchety Asian woman in a tennis visor at a "high-stakes" table sectioned off from the main casino. A few people hung at the bronze railing, looking on with hungry eyes. Like they were peering into a limousine, wondering if a star was inside.

His stacks of chips teetered on the velvet. He must have been up over $5,000 with the ridiculous string of black-jacks he'd had. Any other day, it would have been cause for major celebration. The only thing he could think about now, though, was Ben's discovery.

"Blackjack *again*," the dealer said, and shoved more chips across. He tossed a black hundred-dollar chip back to her for a tip. She was definitely more excited about all this than he was.

Of course, she didn't know that a genius kid had just discovered a way to destabilize her whole way of life. To see all her banking records. To steal money from her casino. To find out any electronic secret that she'd ever had. Not that anyone would care about her little secrets, when they could cause floods and wars and who knew what else.

There'd be panic if people knew. Those people collected at the rail, they'd be rushing home, stocking up on powdered milk and canned goods and duct tape. Or whatever you were supposed to buy in, like, a code-red situation.

Smiles couldn't blame Ben for being scared. His algorithm might have been an amazing discovery, but he'd have to keep it under wraps forever—never getting any credit, never getting any reward. It was too dangerous to share with anyone. Even telling the NSA guys would be taking a huge chance. It made Smiles think of those sci-fi movies where a friendly alien comes to Earth and all the government wants to do is hold it captive and stick it with needles. Smiles wondered how long Ben could take the strain of holding on to such explosive knowledge.

The kicker, of course, was that it could take down Alyce Systems, too.

"Dealer busts." More chips for Smiles.

"Lucky boy," said a voice behind him.

It was Erin, the pixie from the registration desk. Showered and fresh, in a white sundress that showed off her tan. The tension in Smiles's neck melted away at the sight of her.

He shrugged at his tower of chips. "Guess so."

The Asian woman harrumphed at the interruption.

Smiles rolled his eyes for Erin's benefit. He liked the way hers twinkled back at him while the dealer patted the felt, asking for his bet.

"I'm sorry," the dealer said to Erin, "if you're not playing, you can't be in this area."

She plunked down a wad of hundreds. "Will that do?"

"Oh, yes, of course, ma'am," the dealer said, recovering quickly. She slid the crisp bills through her hands and onto the velvet. "Changing two thousand!" she yelled.

"Well well well," Smiles said.

Erin smiled at her chips as they came her way. "Blowing my savings," she said. "I just got this for finding a number on GIMPS."

"You what?"

Erin looked at him funny. "You're here for CRYPTCON and you don't know what GIMPS is?"

"My friend's the one at the conference. I'm just along for the ride."

"Well, you were quite the entertainment this morning."

So she was there after all. Smiles pushed away the thought of his mother, right there on the stage in front of him. "Yeah, well, my friend's a little eccentric," he said.

They played out a hand—Smiles busted, Erin won— and then the dealer got busy shuffling a tower of cards. The Asian woman didn't have the patience for it; she stowed her winnings in her purse, bound for another table.

"So what's a gimp, anyway?" Smiles said.

Erin smiled. "GIMPS. It's an acronym—the Great Internet Mersenne Prime Search. Lots of the people at the conference do it. It's just this software you put on your computer to make it search for a special kind of prime number with its spare capacity. They have rewards if your computer finds one big enough. Mine was 445 bits long."

"Bits?"

"Digits. Digits, bits, same thing."

"Hold on. They paid you for that?"

"Yeah." She said it like it was totally obvious that you would get paid lots of money for finding some useless number. "The government pays big bucks for the *really* big ones. I just got a little prize from a math foundation."

The dealer clapped her hands and showed them her palms, a magician about to do a trick. She dealt a hand and Smiles took a hit, wondering how Erin had gotten into the casino. She couldn't be twenty-one. He had used the license he got from some BU guys with an underground business making fake IDs. He'd met them out at a bar, and they gave him the license free because they'd all had such a good time that night. It happened back when Smiles was set on becoming a stand-up comedian, but the license was all he'd ever gotten from that endeavor. The name on it was Harold Bottomsworth IV.

He and Erin played out a few more hands, sitting comfortably in each other's personal space.

"So you're a huge nerd then?" Smiles said after a while. She slapped him, but her fingertips feathered against his arm as they pulled away.

"I have a complex about being into math. Half the time I'm embarrassed about it, the other half I'm pissed that people don't realize what a genius I am. Mostly the latter. I have a bit of an ego problem."

Her voice was velvety, a half notch deeper than you'd expect from a gymnast-sized girl. The sound of it soothed him like a drug.

The casino lights played against her butterscotch hair as she turned to him. "I'm not half as smart as the other people here, really. I mean, that was just luck, obviously, my computer finding that prime. But yeah, the government will pay for the big ones because they can be valuable in all kinds of applications."

Smiles didn't want to think about math anymore. He didn't want to think about Ben's problem, or terrorists screwing with the stock market, or Alyce Systems being rendered obsolete. He wanted to think about Erin.

"So how about you hang out with me tonight?" he heard himself saying.

The direct approach had worked pretty well so far, and she wasn't looking too put off by it now. "You'll have to work harder than that," she said, but there was a smile on her face.

"Bet on it?" Smiles plunked a stack of black chips inside the circle. "I win, we go to dinner."

Erin liked it. "I don't come that cheap," she said, nodding to the rest of his stack. "All of 'em, and we'll talk."

Smiles could see the heat seeker coming out. He'd known it since that morning: She loved being wild. He called her bluff, pushing all of his chips to the betting circle. They swallowed it up, spilling across the felt.

The dealer leveled Smiles's chips, counting the stacks

off efficiently. "Betting $7,300!" she called behind her. The crowd at the rail stirred with voyeuristic pleasure. A guy in a muscle shirt edged up the stairs, looking on.

"Holy crap, you're doing it," Erin said. When he felt her hands clench his arm, Smiles put it in the bank: However this turned out, he was getting some action tonight.

"Good luck," the dealer said, fist-bumping the cloth for good measure.

The dealer's lightning hands shot his cards across the table. Erin hadn't put out a bet, so it was just Smiles against the house. He drew an eight and a seven, for a total of fifteen. A terrible hand, except that the dealer showed fourteen. Every idiot in the casino knew what you were supposed to do in this situation: stand on fifteen and watch the dealer bust. Smiles reached to wave the dealer off, but Erin dug her nails into his arm.

"Take a hit," she whispered. Her breath was hot on his ear.

"I have fifteen," he said. With all the tens in the deck—the actual tens plus all the face cards—there was a huge chance of busting if you hit fifteen. This went beyond thrill-seeking; it was suicide. But Erin just leveled her gaze.

"Take the hit."

Smiles swallowed a potent mix of confusion and masculinity and tapped the felt.

"Hitting on fifteen, sir?" The dealer's voice was dubious. Erin nodded.

"Uh, yeah."

Smiles normally enjoyed the deliciously nervous moment before the dealer added a card to his hand. Now he was cringing with certain doom as she swept his next card from the shoe. She flipped up a five. Smiles had twenty.

He breathed. It was like landing in a net you didn't know was there.

"Stand," he said, before Erin could press his luck any further.

The dealer smiled and drew her own next card. Another five.

"Nineteen. Player wins."

"Holy . . ." Smiles was numb with delight. It felt like he'd gotten away with something, all thanks to Erin. As the dealer doubled his chips, she cupped his ear and whispered more softly than before. "I'm an excellent card counter, among other things."

Her words tingled as she pulled back and gave him a wink. *Time to firm up dinner plans*, Smiles thought as the guy in the muscle shirt appeared at the table.

"What's this?" said the dude, now right at Erin's side. He was looking back and forth between Smiles and Erin like they were giving him a hernia.

"Oh, you're here," Erin said, suddenly off-balance. Smiles saw her eyes go timid for a half second before she collected herself. He didn't like that look on her, nor the fact that she was putting her hand on the guy's shoulder.

"This is Smiles," she said with a head bob in his direction. "Smiles, Zach. My boyfriend."

The way his life was going lately, Smiles almost wasn't surprised.

Zach had stringy arms poking out the sides of his gray

muscle shirt. You could see, around his neck, the silver line of a ball chain that probably held dog tags. He stood an inch shorter than Erin, his most prominent feature being a tiny upturned nose. He looked like a toy poodle that's always trying to pick a fight with the Doberman down the street. How dudes like this got cool girlfriends, Smiles would never know. He watched Zach's hand curl around Erin's side and wanted to clock him.

Zach's eyes fixed on the little sign with the betting limits. "A hundred bucks a hand!?" he said to Erin. "Why are you playing *here*?"

Because it's where I am, Smiles thought.

He didn't say it, though—he didn't want to deal with this scene. He scooped up his chips, his senses still reeling with the feel of her hand, her breath, the lively spark of their conversation even through meaningless talk about the GIMPS thing and how the government would pay you for prime numbers.

Suddenly, his hand clenched tight around his chips. Smiles knew exactly what Ben needed to do. And it was genius.

Smiles grabbed a mound of black chips and dumped them in Erin's hands. "Fun playing with you," he said. "Now I need to ask a huge favor."

MELANIE SCANNED HER closet for something to go with her cardigan.

Her skinny jeans would be good, or the gray pencil skirt she liked so much. Would that be too dressy for the college scene, though? Her corduroy mini would be casual enough for sure. So the jeans or her mini . . . or maybe those cute capris?

She had been packing for a half hour now, and it was the first time since lunch that she hadn't been thinking about Andrei Tarasov. She'd spent the afternoon cabined in her cubicle at Alyce Systems, running Jenna's crazy news about Tarasov over and over in her mind: *Could he really have been a Russian spy? Could Alice's letter to Smiles have had something to do with that? And why would her dad be afraid to tell her about him?*

The last question was the most troubling of all, and the idea of concentrating on her work—some research project on the Alyce Systems health insurance plan the Easter bunnies had given her—was laughable. With all the nervous questions boiling inside her, it was all she could do not to break her New Year's resolution to stop chewing her fingernails.

Now back at the house, with evening falling on the hushed street outside her windows, she'd found a soothing respite in the chore of packing. She made the umpteenth trip from her closet to her bed and laid her capris and yet another sweater in the suitcase.

She forced herself to stop—this was getting ridiculous. You didn't need a full bag of clothes for an overnight visit to Smith College. Melanie zipped the suitcase and settled on her comforter, cracking the window for a bit of cooling air.

Katie's so much fun, Melanie thought, trying to trick herself into getting excited for the trip.

She and Katie had planned the visit back in the fall, when Melanie was still considering going to Smith. She had pretty much settled on Vassar by now, though, and with the Andrei Tarasov stuff unresolved, the idea of leaving for the weekend gave her a low-level panic attack. It felt like going out to a movie on the night before a test.

Alone in her room, Melanie felt the mammoth void of Smiles's absence. He hadn't called all day. Of course he hadn't—she'd slammed a door in his face not twenty-four hours ago. She checked her phone for missed calls, just to be sure. Nothing.

You can't be angry with him for not reaching out to you, she told herself. And for the most part, she listened.

The breeze whispered into her room. It carried the early-spring smell of thawing earth, inviting her outside. Without hesitating she slipped her feet into the nearest pair of tennis shoes, picked up the Andrei Tarasov folder, and dashed off a vague-enough note to her parents. She didn't want to stop long enough to talk herself out of it. Instead she pulled the Camry out of the garage and headed straight for Boston. Newton Street would take her to the Mass Pike and from there she'd only be a half hour away.

It would be easy enough to find it. She didn't know where exactly Andrei Tarasov had lived, but the address was right there in the file beside her.

SMILES WAS SO jacked up, he could hardly stand it. He pounded on the door to the room, forgetting for a second that he had his card key in his back pocket.

Ben arrived at the other side before he could fish it out. The poor guy looked the same as when Smiles had left hours ago, only with bed head and darker circles under his eyes. His army bag was slung over his shoulder, padlocked for safety, of course. The copious books inside made sharp angles against the green fabric. Ben looked like one of those ants that can miraculously carry fifty times their own body weight.

"Dude, problem solved," Smiles said.

"What are you talking about?"

"Where are you going? You're not leaving or anything."

"No," Ben said, a little testily. "You won't let me. I was just going down to Starbucks."

"Excellent. So listen, I've got a plan. I'll tell you on the way."

This crazy energy had been racing through him from

the instant it hit him at the blackjack table. He'd been going full tilt ever since—it was the most productive day he'd had in years.

Smiles walked in step with Ben down the hall, considering for the first time how to broach this. His idea was genius, no doubt about that. But Ben was a prickly one, and Smiles didn't want him rejecting it just because he was in a bad mood.

At the elevators, Smiles punched the down button furiously. "You're gonna love this. I swear to God, I feel as smart as you right now." And he did. He really did.

Ben looked around. "Fine, but you can't talk about . . . you know . . . out in the open like this."

Smiles nodded. It was a fair point, and he didn't want the little guy getting his hackles up. Another guest approached as the elevator opened; they rode down to the casino level with no sound between them except the murmur of the elevator pulleys.

The doors parted to reveal a huge group of CRYPTCON nerds wearing their orange lanyards and deciding where to go for dinner. Some bald guy was yelling about a craving for Chinese. He could barely compete with the earsplitting jangle coming from the casino behind them. It sounded like the slot machines were hyperventilating.

The Starbucks was in sight, away from the casino, but it teemed with over-caffeinated gamblers. Smiles held Ben back. "You're right, we're gonna need some privacy for this." He took a second to get his bearings, then pulled a one-eighty toward a long hallway of shops. "The business center. C'mon."

Ben huffed and followed him.

Smiles had spent a healthy part of the afternoon at the business center, and it had been completely empty. The ringing of the slot machines faded as he retraced his steps from earlier—halfway down the row of shops to Fox Creek's bare-bones "Business Suite," a windowless room with a fax machine, copier, and desktop computers for hotel guests. Smiles dipped his card key into the lock and entered.

Just like earlier, the room was barren. Ben followed Smiles in, still sulking, and dropped into one of the plastic chairs. Smiles made sure the door was closed before joining him by the computers. "Cheer up, man. I got it all figured out."

"Smiles, let's just get a coffee," Ben said. "There's nothing to figure out. You can't, like, fix this."

"No, no, that's where you're wrong. Look, you've been totally freaked out, and I can see why. You've got this dangerous thing, and you don't want it getting into the wrong hands, right?"

Ben nodded unenthusiastically.

"Just listen," Smiles said. "Tell me: Why don't you just give the thing to the government?"

Ben sparked to life at that. "'Cause then they'd know I have it, Smiles. That makes me dangerous, too. Who knows what they'd do to me?"

"Right," Smiles said quickly, and he could see that Ben was surprised he'd thought it out even this far. Ben probably thought Smiles's big idea was just handing his algorithm over to the government, but it was so much better than that. "Look, here's what you're going to do. You *are* going to give the government your algorithm. But you're going to do it anonymously—through me. They'll never even know who you are. And you're not just going to give it to them, Ben. You're going to *sell* it to them."

Selling it—that was the revelation Smiles had had at the blackjack table. It had come to him after listening to Erin talk about how the government would pay big bucks for just one stupid prime number. It was all upside: Ben would get paid, and he wouldn't have the entire weight of his discovery on his shoulders for the rest of his life. And if Smiles helped Ben pull it off, it would only be fair for him to get a taste of the action. It would be *his own way*.

And they wouldn't have to worry about it messing with Alyce Systems, either. The government knew how to keep this kind of stuff secret. That's what the guy at the microphone had said that morning—the NSA was like a black hole, keeping as much information about encryption to itself as possible.

If they pulled it off, the payday could be huge. The Clay Institute was putting up $1 million for a solution to the Riemann Hypothesis, and Ben's discovery was way more valuable than that. Smiles had done some research and found more than one organization offering hundreds of thousands of dollars to anyone who discovered a really large prime number. That much for a single prime number, and Ben had the key to all of them! Plus, those organizations didn't have the resources of the government, which had offered $25 million for Osama bin Laden.

So yeah, if they did this right, Ben was in for a payday. And Smiles could save his dad's company from becoming obsolete.

He felt like the businessman in the generic poster on the wall, celebrating some executive triumph with a fist raised in the air. The actual dude in the poster was probably just an out-of-work actor. His suit didn't fit and his cell phone was the size of a brick. Still, the poster said SUCCESS, and Smiles felt it in his bones.

Ben had that look he got when he turned inward, thinking furiously, twirling the mighty gears of his brain. Still, he wasn't rejecting the idea outright. Smiles leaned in for the kill.

"It's perfect, right? We put your algorithm in safe hands, we keep you anonymous, and we get you paid. You totally deserve it. I mean, you started this whole thing trying to get that million-dollar prize, right?"

Ben's shoulders lifted and fell. Smiles counted it as a yes.

"The point is, you've made this incredible discovery, and you deserve something for it. And selling it to the government is the best way to keep it safe. To keep *you* safe, too."

"Smiles . . . your plan . . . it wouldn't exactly be a simple thing to do. They're going to be able to figure out who I am."

"No, listen, I've thought about this." And the crazy thing was, he had. It was amazing how far ahead he'd been thinking today. "Here's what's gonna happen. You're supposed to meet with those NASA guys—"

"*NSA* guys. They aren't astronauts."

"Right. But you're supposed to give them your article, right?"

"Yeah, tonight. At the student reception." Ben checked his watch. "But it's in twenty minutes and I don't even want to go anymore."

"Forget that for a second. Look, I'm going to do the

hard part. I'm going to set up a meeting with them tomorrow to prove your algorithm is the real deal. I've already reserved a separate hotel room for that."

That was the favor he'd asked of Erin: to reserve a room under her fake ID. If Smiles had been less careful, he might have put it under Harold Bottomsworth IV, but there was always the possibility they could trace that back to him. He couldn't explain what it was all about, but she was cool with it—she seemed to like the intrigue.

Ben chewed it over. "But where would we even put the money? They can trace that, too, you know."

This was Smiles's trump card. Mr. Hunt had told him once how easy it was to set up a Swiss bank account. He said you could do it with one ten-minute phone call. It actually hadn't been that easy. Smiles had spent two hours on the Internet and had to call the Credit Suisse information line three different times, but he'd gotten it done.

"It's a numbered account. Untraceable." He flashed a scrap of paper with the account details he'd scrawled down earlier and waggled his eyebrows. "Whaddaya think?"

Ben cracked a few knuckles on his left hand. The popping sounds came sharp but hollow through the white noise of the room. He needed one final push before he caved.

"Think about when you were trying to solve that problem," Smiles said. "What did you want that money for? Why was it so important to you?"

A long moment lingered before Ben replied. When he did, he spoke so softly, Smiles could barely hear him.

"I just wanted to be great at math."

A sheen of moisture had covered Ben's eyes. You didn't cry about wanting to be great at math. No, there was a different reason he'd wanted that money. A sensitive one.

Smiles was grasping for a new angle on the situation when Ben looked him in the eye. "You were serious before, about that being your mom?"

"Uh, yeah." Not exactly the topic Smiles wanted to explore at the moment.

"Why'd she leave you?"

Ben looked too interested in all this to shrug him off. "I don't know, really. I mailed her a letter when I was little, and she sent it back unopened. After that I pretty much wrote her off—just kind of blocked it out. I used to get the drift that she was, like, disturbed, but I don't even know where I got that from. My dad never talks about her. It's one of those things that you just sort of know is off-limits."

It was painful, but it wasn't hard to tell Ben any of this. Maybe his mother meant less to him now that he'd seen her. He didn't have to wonder anymore; he could just be mad.

"My mom's disturbed," Ben said out of nowhere, and now the tears were thicker in his eyes.

"Yeah?"

"Or depressed, I guess. Stays in her bed, doesn't really eat. Like that, you know?"

Smiles didn't have much experience with depression, but he nodded anyway.

"She's in Boston?" Smiles didn't even know. He was suddenly overpowered by guilt. The truth was, he'd lost touch with most of his friends from Kingsley since getting kicked out, and Ben was probably his closest friend in the world. Maybe that was why it was easy to talk to him about his own mother.

Ben was nodding. "I didn't want to leave home, but they said I should go. Her and my uncle Jim. He's not actually my uncle, he's just a friend of hers who's around all the time. He looks after her pretty good."

Ben was playing with his thumbs, a confessional mood thick in the room. Smiles felt a little sacrilegious to be wondering how to turn the conversation back to his plan. He decided he might have to ride this therapy session out.

"So she's always been like that?" he asked.

"Not always, no."

The words came sharp from Ben's mouth, and right away Smiles knew he'd asked the wrong question. Something painful had happened to Ben's mom, and Smiles had stuck his finger straight into the wound. Ben's face colored at the memory. His chest heaved below the loose folds of his shirt.

Ben turned to him and said, "Ask for seventy-five million."

Smiles put his hand out, and they shook.

"Let's go," he said. "We've got some work to do before that reception."

MELANIE FOUND IT on the frayed edges of Jamaica Plain, on a short street near Egleston Square that had stubbornly resisted the hipster invasion taking over the neighborhood. Her GPS had directed her past a vegan bakery and no fewer than three wine bars on her way to the address in Tarasov's file. It sat in a depressing line of neglected homes, squeezed uncomfortably close together in a block-long pageant of chipped paint and warped siding.

Melanie passed the address slowly and pulled a U-turn at the end of the street. She stopped well short of Tarasov's address, across from a Spanish-language market with a bright green mural running along its side. The smiles of the Puerto Rican girls on the brickwork offered the only bit of cheer on the street. Melanie sat for a moment, drawing strength from their happy faces.

Her nerves were pointless, in all likelihood. Tarasov had been dead for more than fifteen years, and his HR file mentioned no family. The chances she would find anything of use here were slim indeed, but if she was going to learn anything about the message to Smiles, she needed a starting point. This was the only one she had. Maybe Tarasov had a roommate who stayed on. Maybe a neighbor would remember him.

A boy who could barely reach the pedals of his ten-speed swerved a drunken path down the street. She waited for him to pass before getting out and walking the sidewalk toward Tarasov's house. She chose the opposite side of the street, marking off each postage-stamp lawn in a matter of steps. The close quarters of the street suffocated her—Melanie could hear cooking sounds and the wail of a baby as she passed the houses one by one.

Tarasov's house looked like the others. Two stories tall with a deep front porch, it might have been majestic once. But now the porch bowed and its blue color had muddied with age. A severe crack split the concrete steps out front. The gap it left yawned wide and dark.

Directly across from it now, she noticed a set of wooden steps constructed at the side of the house. They led to a porch on the roof—a widow's walk, they called those things—with a gap-toothed wooden railing at its edge.

Melanie took a deep breath, drawing in the smell of empanadas, and stepped forward. She crossed the street and navigated the ruptured steps to the front door, which had a call box with two buzzers underneath. The house had been split into apartments, she realized, one for each level. Underneath the second buzzer, someone had taped a strip of paper with the resident's name. The print had faded to obscurity long ago, but the name wasn't long enough to be "Tarasov" anyway.

Melanie didn't remember an apartment number being in

the file, and her confidence faltered. Before it could fail her entirely, she pressed the first buzzer and waited. When no answer came, she pressed the second. A Hispanic woman bumped a grocery cart noisily over the sidewalk behind Melanie, who closed her eyes and hoped she didn't look suspicious. She breathed and tried each one again, hearing the electronic sound seep out through the thin walls of the house. Still no answer.

Fidgety and exposed on the porch, Melanie waited just a few more seconds before giving up. She crossed quickly to the other side of the street—hoping to get away from her failure as quickly as possible—and jogged a few steps for momentum back to her car. She took a last look back at the house and slowed, caught up by the sight of an older woman on the widow's walk, smoking a cigarette. She wore a shabby housedress but stood erect, surveying the street like a lost kingdom. Melanie flinched when the woman's eyes landed on her.

Melanie hadn't been doing anything wrong, or illegal anyway, but the weathered face of the woman made her feel like it. She stared down bitterly from the height of the roof. *"Go on!"* she yelled.

Melanie ducked her head and hurried to her car. She locked the doors as soon as she got inside, then checked herself in the rearview mirror. Her cheeks had blossomed red, and a strand of hair had slicked to her perspiring neck. As soon as her head stopped thrumming, Melanie berated herself for letting the old bat get to her like that.

Before starting up the car, she checked Andrei Tarasov's house a final time. The woman was gone, the house unlit against the darkening sky, and suddenly the entire weird episode began to feel like a dream.

She had just turned the ignition when somebody tapped on her window. The knock was light enough, but it struck the window right by her ear and she nearly jumped out of her seat. Gathering herself, she turned to see a pale, doughy man sink to a squat outside her car. He did a little rolling motion, asking her to put the window down, and Melanie was too off guard to refuse. His face didn't look too threatening, anyway.

"Hi there," he said.

"Yes, hello, can I help you?"

"Mind me asking what you were doing up at that house?" The man shifted, placing himself between Melanie and Andrei Tarasov's place. "Don't look up there, okay? Just look at me."

Melanie didn't answer right away—she wasn't about to tell a stranger her business, even if he was a cop. That's what he seemed like, anyway. The way he assumed authority over the conversation.

"Excuse me, but who are you, sir?"

As a rule, she avoided confrontation at all costs, so throwing it back at him like that made Melanie's stomach turn. Still, she knew it was the right thing—if he could have seen it, her dad would have been proud. Next he would have told her to get the hell out of there.

Melanie didn't do that yet. Whatever he was, the guy didn't seem physically dangerous. She could smell cherry cough drops on his breath.

"Miss, I am the man who has been conducting surveillance on that house for quite some time. And whether you know it or not, your presence here is jeopardizing a very long and expensive investigation." He flashed open his nylon jacket. Inside, a badge dangled from his neck.

"Investigation?"

He forced a smile across his lips (fake factor: off the charts), and a blue vein at his temple throbbed under the pressure. It contrasted sharply with his sickly white coloring. "I don't have a lot of time to be out in the street here, okay? You look like a nice young lady, in the wrong place at the wrong time, so I'm trying to handle this the simplest way I can here. But I do need to know if you have any more business at that house."

Melanie desperately wanted to know if this investigation had anything to do with Andrei Tarasov. At the same time, that seemed unlikely—and maybe she was fouling up some kind of drug sting. She hardly needed to be caught in the middle of something like that.

"No, officer, I was just on my way."

"And you're not coming back?"

Melanie shook her head and put the car in drive. The man patted the side of the car as he left, keeping his back to Tarasov's house the whole time. Melanie couldn't get to the highway fast enough. This was officially the dumbest idea she had ever had.

She wasn't ready to give up her investigation yet, though—she just needed to be smarter about it.

A CRYSTAL CHANDELIER hung from the ceiling of the cozy ballroom. It was big enough to hold maybe a hundred people, but there were fewer than that inside it now: a clump of twenty professors, an equal-sized huddle of students, and a few brave souls from each group daring to network with the other. Most of the professors had plastic stemware in their hands, courtesy of the bar in the corner. A few students were doing damage to the buffet of mini quiches and barbecue sliders. The food sat in silver trays on white-clothed tables under the chandelier, bisecting the room. A single row of chairs lined the walls, a last resort for the socially hopeless.

Smiles didn't belong here at all, but no one had looked twice at him on the way in. He had smiled generously to the girl at the door, wearing the orange lanyard he'd swiped from one of the cardboard boxes behind the registration table. He'd turned the blank name tag around the wrong way.

His plan was officially in motion, and it felt good. Tonight was the first step: identifying the NSA agent, and getting him—or her—interested.

By now, they were thirty minutes into the hour-long reception for the best and brightest math minds in the country. A bunch of universities were hosting the event, looking to woo high school whizzes into their math programs and college kids to their graduate schools. Apparently the NSA did some recruiting here, too—though they did it quietly, the way they liked to do everything else.

Ben had given Smiles this background while they'd scrambled to prepare for this moment. Ben's role here would be easy enough. He'd gone into the reception ahead of Smiles, fifteen minutes ago. All he had to do was give the NSA agent his article as planned, and then hang around long enough to ensure Smiles knew who the agent was. They had placed the article in a bright red folder to make it stand out, but Smiles didn't see anyone carrying a red folder, and he didn't see Ben.

Smiles used a healthy portion of his available willpower to refrain from heading to the bar. He sauntered toward the food instead, checking every face he could on the way. The sliders were soggy, and there was no such thing as a good mini quiche. What was wrong with good old pizza rolls? Smiles shook his head as he slapped a few shrimp tarts on his plate and reminded himself he wasn't there for the food.

Luckily, a few of the students hadn't dressed up. He didn't look quite as out of place as he could have in his plain white T-shirt, the classiest piece of clothing he'd brought on the trip. He was bobbing his head for a better angle into the collection of students when he heard a voice at his back.

"Aren't those delectable?"

Smiles wheeled to find a tall bald man with thin-frame glasses and a name tag with an intimidating number of colored ribbons hanging from it. It said: PETER WELSH, PH.D., CRYPTCON CHAIRMAN.

Oh, great. Smiles was talking to the head honcho of the entire conference.

"Peter," he said, extending a bony hand.

Smiles shook it and forced himself at ease. "Like I don't know who *you* are, Dr. Welsh."

The chairman guffawed and picked up a slider, taking it down in a bite. All the while, Smiles made a half-circle maneuver to get a better look at the attendees. The event was going to be breaking up soon, and Smiles needed to find the NSA agent fast.

"Well, you've got the advantage on me, then," the chairman said. "Tell me a little about yourself. I love hearing about our talented students. You're all so impressive."

"I'm Harold," Smiles said. "I just flew in, actually, but the conference looks great. Per usual. You put on such a great show."

Smiles was pretty pleased with himself. The chairman seemed to be eating out of his hand. The ribbons on his name tag fluttered as he leaned in conspiratorially, like they were old friends. "What's your area of interest, Harold?"

"Excuse me?"

Smiles had just spied Ben in the corner of the room. When their eyes met, Ben's went wide. Apparently, he knew who Smiles was talking to. His lips read: *What the . . . ?*

Smiles shrugged helplessly, then saw Ben direct his eyes to the far wall. There, in the same blue suit they'd seen him in earlier, was the guy they'd hidden from in the hallway. The copier salesman. He was holding a bright red folder in his hands, tossing his empty food plate away. Ben hadn't been paranoid after all—the guy was, in fact, the NSA agent. And now he was shaking hands with people, ready to leave.

"Your niche," the chairman said, demanding Smiles's attention. "Tell me what you're working on. I love to hear what you students are up to."

"Careful there. I could bore you all night with that one." Smiles hoped for a laugh that would get him off the hook, but the chairman only raised his eyebrows in anticipation as he polished off another slider. Smiles gulped. He summoned every bit of jargon he'd ever heard from Ben. "Well . . . there are these zeta functions, I'm sure you've heard about them. And I've also been dabbling in elliptical curves, those are good. I can't get enough of those, actually. It's a little complicated to explain, but—"

"Tell me where you're from, son." The chairman reached out and turned his name tag around, finding nothing.

"Like I said, fresh off the plane." In the distance, Smiles saw the NSA agent leaving the reception. If he got away, they'd lose any chance of making this work. Their plan hadn't even gotten started, and already it was crumbling around him. "Haven't gotten a proper name tag yet, but—"

"What school?" Something had definitely changed in the chairman's tone.

Smiles took a step toward the door. "I, uh . . . Berkeley." His mother's school was the first to pop into his mind. "But look, I should probably—"

"No, no, hold it right there," the chairman said, and

Smiles had no choice but to stay put. "Berkeley, you say?" Skepticism dripped from his voice, and Smiles had a terrible premonition of what was coming next. "You must be one of Professor Taft's favorites. Alice?"

Oh no. Smiles hadn't seen her, but there she was, emerging from a group of professors. Her dollish cheeks had been flush with wine, but they went pale at the sight of Smiles.

He did the only thing he could. He thrust his plate of shrimp tarts into the chairman's hand and said, "Sorry, Pete, I think I have food poisoning."

He dashed to the exit, never looking back.

⤩

Smiles had three choices: left, right, or straight ahead to the casino lobby. The NSA agent didn't appear in any of the hallways before him. Smiles quickly wrote off the one to the right. It led only to more conference rooms, and CRYPT-CON had to be wrapping up for the day. Straight ahead was a good possibility. The shops, Starbucks, and casino all lay in that direction. But the hallway to the left led to an elevator bank—the same one the agent had appeared from that morning. His room was up there, and maybe he was headed back to it now.

Smiles bolted to his left. If it wasn't the right choice, the plan was already up in smoke. There would be no chance of catching him, and even if Ben had a number for the guy, it wasn't likely Smiles could pull this off over the phone. He sprinted forward to the elevators. His ankle gave way as he made a ninety-degree turn at the elevator bank. As he hobbled forward, it appeared useless. There wasn't a soul waiting for the six elevators, three on each side of the small area. Just Smiles, a bowl of artificial flowers, and another confirmation that he was generally useless.

But then Smiles saw the green light ignited above one of the far elevators. Preparing to go up. The doors of the elevator began sliding closed. Quickly. Smiles stumbled forward and blindly thrust his hand between the door panels, just inches apart. They crunched together on his right hand, pinching his knuckles. After an excruciating moment, they pulled lazily apart.

From inside the elevator, the copier salesman eyed him with concern. His eyes were set deep into a hawklike face, and he wore a squared-off crew cut with edges much sharper than those of his travel-worn suit. For a moment, Smiles was too relieved to speak. But then he had to, because the doors were closing again. He jammed his hand against the doorstop and said, "Could I talk to you for a sec?"

It wasn't the best introduction. He was still out of breath from the run, and the guy was tense with suspicion.

"Talk to me?"

"If you would. Just a sec?" Smiles threw out his left hand to the little elevator area, like he was welcoming the guy into his home. "I just came from the student reception. I was hoping to catch you there."

The agent exited the elevator but wasn't happy about it. "Well, you missed me," he said, checking his watch, "and I actually have some things—"

"How much would a fast-factoring algorithm be worth

to you?" The aggressive approach was a gamble, but it felt right. Smiles had to seize control of this conversation, and quick.

The agent took a moment to absorb what he'd just heard, then laughed. "A lot. So would the Loch Ness monster and Santa Claus's home address. Unfortunately they don't exist." He circled around Smiles and pressed the call button for the elevator.

"It does exist, and I've got it. Can I prove it to you, or do you want to be the NSA agent who tried to turn away the most valuable information your agency will ever have?"

That last part got to him. Smiles had annoyed the guy, but also gotten his interest. "Two minutes," he said, holding up fingers in case the words didn't get through. "Where do you want to talk?"

"C'mon." Smiles led him back the way he'd come, praying that neither the chairman nor his mother would appear down the hallway. He opened the door inside the alcove that he and Ben had hidden in earlier. It led to a classroom-sized space with more chairs lining the walls. Smiles flicked the lights and closed the door behind them.

"Two minutes is all this will take," he said.

He and Ben had drawn up a script for this discussion, and so far Smiles had followed exactly none of it. But it was coming back to him now. From his back pocket, Smiles pulled some pages he and Ben had printed off the Internet at the business center. They listed the first five hundred prime numbers.

Smiles passed it over to the guy. "Could I ask your name?"

"Ken Gary. And yours?"

"Pick any two of those numbers, Mr. Gary. And don't show me."

Agent Gary squinted at him. "What is this, a magic trick?"

Ben said the agent would see the logic of the demonstration right away, and despite the guy's moaning, Ben was right. His interest was piqued.

"Pick the two numbers, multiply them together, and tell me what you get."

Multiplying the two numbers would create a public key—a gate key. If Ben's algorithm worked, using that public key alone he'd be able to identify the two prime numbers the agent had picked—the private key, the house key. It would be solid proof that they could defeat public-key encryption.

Smiles didn't even have to explain it to him. The agent pulled out his phone and opened a calculator app. Smiles turned away till the guy coughed, ready to show him the display.

Smiles copied the number into a text message on his own phone and prayed. Ben had written a quick program that would execute the algorithm on his computer. He called it a cipher. When he received the text, he was going to use the cipher and text back the two primes that the agent had picked. It was all in Ben's hands now, and if he was somehow wrong about his discovery, Smiles was going to look like the biggest ass in the world.

He pressed send and waited. The only delay, Ben told him, would be typing the number into his computer. Once he did that, the prime factors would spit right out.

The agent barely had time to check his watch before an incoming text bleeped onto Smiles's screen. It had two numbers in it.

"17 and 2203," Smiles said.

The agent crossed his arms, and Smiles knew that Ben had gotten it right. "Is this some parlor game? You have these memorized or something? You have them written down somewhere?"

"There are five hundred numbers on that page. That's two hundred and fifty thousand combinations. That's a lot to memorize, or write down."

"Who's on the other end of the phone?"

"My associate. He's just keeping the cipher safe." Smiles liked that. *Associate.* Pretty badass.

The agent inspected the pages, like there might be invisible ink on them or something. Smiles had his full attention now.

"Here's what's going to happen," Smiles said. "You're going to give me a line where I can reach you. Keep it open at eleven a.m. tomorrow. I'll tell you where to meet me."

"What happens when I meet you?" The guy was trying to sound amused, but it wasn't working.

"Bring ten public keys with you," Smiles said, getting back on script. "They can be a hundred digits, two hundred digits, however long you like. No parlor games, no magic. You choose the numbers. I'll produce the private keys for you in seconds."

The agent sighed and scribbled a number at the top of the pages Smiles had given him. He gestured to Smiles's phone. "How many people am I dealing with here?"

"Two. Just me and my associate."

"And you'll do the calculation in seconds?"

"Seconds."

"And then?"

"And then you'll have three hours to wire seventy-five million US dollars to a numbered account in exchange for the cipher."

A pause. "Seventy-five million?"

"You got it," Smiles said, and walked out.

TWO HOURS LATER, they were still giddy in the casino buffet. Smiles could hardly believe it had worked.

Of course, they still had a long way to go, and of course, his plan never would have worked so well if it weren't for Ben's little touches. Like the idea for how they could demonstrate the algorithm, with Ben keeping it safe in their room. Or how Ben had told Smiles to ask for seventy-five million *US* dollars. Like they needed to clarify that. Those kinds of things, they made all the difference.

Ben got up for another pass at the dessert spread, and Smiles looked out to a craps table swarmed by a bachelorette party. A girl in a white veil tossed the dice, cheered on by friends in identical blue T-shirts (TEAM LIZZIE) sucking down drinks from fluorescent cups. Smiles watched them and felt a desire to call Melanie. That always happened when he felt good about something. He couldn't do it now, though. It was past eleven o'clock already, and besides, she'd just broken up with him.

Then an even stranger feeling washed over him. For a second, it paralyzed him. Actually wanting to talk to his dad—it almost knocked him out right there at the table. It was a comfortable feeling—a great feeling—but it came from such a buried place that it stopped him cold. It felt like those odd occasions when he caught a whiff of macaroni and cheese and memories of Rose, his true mom, flooded through him out of nowhere.

Smiles extracted his cell and dialed the hospital. Shanti answered the line at the neuro-oncology unit. "Hey, what are you doing there so late?" he said.

"Wrapping up a long day, darling." He could hear her exhaustion. "How are you?"

"Not too bad. I left town for the weekend, but I was wondering if maybe my dad was still up?"

"That's sweet," Shanti said. "I know he'd love to hear from you, but honestly he had a sort of rough one and just got to sleep."

"Yeah, sure, okay." He wondered if it was worse than she was letting on. But then he bantered with Shanti awhile, and Ben brought a huge slice of cake back to the table, and he felt better.

Before he hung up, Smiles took a wedge of cake that Ben offered and told Shanti, "Hey, I'm having some birthday cake after all."

"Good, 'cause we finished yours in the break room tonight," Shanti said, and he could hear the smile in her voice. He clicked off and dove into the cake. He and Ben grinned stupidly at each other while they demolished the red velvet.

It tasted like triumph.

✕

She was sitting on the carpet by the door to their room. Still and defeated—like a room service tray put out for the night.

Her head hung down between her knees, her thin streaks of butterscotch hair sagging to the floor. He had given her his room number earlier, hoping that she'd ditch Zach and pay him a late-night visit. But something wasn't right here.

Smiles held Ben back. She hadn't seen them yet.

He knelt as he approached, wondering if maybe she'd just gone to sleep waiting for him.

"Erin?"

She sniffled, then slowly raised her head. Her hair fell back and he could see her face, beautiful even with the swollen red eyes that she turned to him.

"What happened?"

"Can I stay with you?"

Smiles liked the way she asked it right out—no big preamble, no need to explain herself. She'd been crying for hours, but she had steel inside her.

"Yeah, sure." Now they wouldn't be able to go over their plans tonight. Ben would have to deal with it, though— Smiles wasn't about to turn Erin away.

Ben just stood there staring down at them, failing to pick up the social cues that 99 percent of the population would have acted on by now. "Give us a sec, huh?" Smiles said from his crouch.

"Oh, yeah, okay."

Ben slipped into the room, and Smiles gave Erin a hand up. She had a hipster-ish messenger bag across her shoulder. You could barely see its green canvas through all the patches from jazz festivals and buttons about the virtues of biking (REAL GIRLS RIDE HARD, etc. etc.). The knit shoulder strap was biting into her delicate shoulder. Smiles eased it off her and down to the floor. They stood awkwardly close to each other for a second, with Smiles feeling protective of her in a way he never did with Melanie. Melanie never needed that. She was always ten steps ahead, charting a smooth course through life while he went off the map. Without thinking he wrapped Erin in a hug. She held him tight, desperately tight, crushing the air out of him until he got a slight high from lack of oxygen.

"He's a bastard," Erin said into his chest.

It probably wasn't right, but Smiles couldn't help thinking, *Jackpot.*

"God may not play dice with the universe, but something strange is going on with the prime numbers."

—Paul Erdös

SATURDAY

"I think I'll go to Boston
I think I'll start a new life
I think I'll start it over
Where no one knows my name."

—Augustana, "Boston"

THE FIRST HINT of sunrise peeked through her window just after six o'clock. Melanie never needed an alarm clock to wake up, least of all today. She'd been stirring since four thirty a.m. The pale radiance against her curtains was the only excuse she needed to hop out of bed and into the shower.

When she went downstairs, her dad was standing at the kitchen island with the *Boston Globe* splayed out on the marble countertop. There was something commanding in that stance, the way he surveyed the paper from above like a battlefield map. He saw her at the edge of the room as he sipped from his coffee mug.

"Early start," he said approvingly. "One for the road?"

"Yeah, thanks." She dropped her suitcase but didn't bother taking off the laptop case strapped over her shoulder. She wanted to get going.

Her dad gestured to the computer as he poured her a travel mug of coffee. "You're not planning on doing work up there, are you?" He was always worried she spent too much time on homework.

"Nah," Melanie said. "Just in case I need it for some-thing."

What that something might be, she didn't say. She hadn't even admitted it to herself yet.

Instead she flipped through the other paper on the counter, *The New York Times*, and tried to savor this moment with her dad. Every morning he read the *Globe*, the *Times*, and *The Wall Street Journal*. When she was little, her favorite part of the day had been sitting on his lap at the breakfast table, feeling the comfort of his terry-cloth robe as he read the news before heading out on his important busi-ness. Last year he'd bought her a monogrammed bathrobe for Christmas. It felt adult; it felt like a new chapter in their morning tradition.

But the Andrei Tarasov story had made her question ev-erything about her father. She didn't know what she would discover about him next, and this morning, this coffee to-gether, didn't feel like a new chapter. It felt like an ending.

She touched the plush robe and gave him a kiss on the cheek.

"Good-bye, Dad," she said.

✢

For an hour, she went through the motions of driving to Smith College.

Katie's expecting you.

It's rude to break plans at the last minute.

What if Dad found out?

The tug of guilt was just about the only thing keeping her on the Mass Pike toward Smith. And normally, guilt could make her do anything. But now it was competing with the unanswered questions about her dad. Questions about why he had kept the Tarasov suicide from her. And what it all might have to do with Alice's letter to Smiles.

She passed a sign announcing an exit in one mile. The symbols running at the bottom promised a gas station and restaurants. She had made this decision unconsciously last night, after being shooed away from Andrei Tarasov's house. But only now, as her car angled onto the off-ramp and slowly separated her from the highway, did she realize she was really going through with it.

She was just pulling off the Pike, but it struck her as a momentous event, as if she were somehow leaving the track that her life had been on for seventeen years. The Pike fell away to her left and the exit ramp rose to a desolate street running straight in both directions. The yellow line in the middle had nearly faded to nothing. It was seven o'clock in the morning, and life hadn't started here yet, wherever she was.

The red traffic light tilted in the morning breeze. It felt pointless to wait for it—like the apocalypse had come, the rules had gone out the window, and all the traffic lights and highway signs and road markings were nothing more than curiosities of a bygone age. Still, she waited at the vacant intersection for the ridiculously long light.

Melanie had never felt so alone, so untethered from her dad and Smiles and anything else that mattered. Sitting there at the empty intersection, waiting for the light, she began to cry.

Finally it clicked green. Melanie turned right arbitrarily,

and through her tears saw a coffee shop down the road. The kind of place that might have free wireless. She knew what she was going to do there: search Rose's email account for any more messages about Tarasov or the mystery letter from Alice, Smiles's birth mother.

She nosed her car into a parking space. The sunrise was in full flower now, glancing off the Camry's hood in indigos and pinks. She'd never done anything this irresponsible in her life. She was going to break her plans with Katie without telling her parents or even having the first clue of where she would stay tonight. This was crazy. But the beautiful dawn assured her it would be okay.

Maybe it was just her biorhythms, or stress. Either way, she seized the delirious confidence that came over her. Her heart lifted as she got out of the car. Her cheeks dried in the wind, and she laughed out loud in the parking lot, giddy in a way that only happened when she stayed up too late or studied for ten hours straight.

The coffee shop was lonely at this hour but filled with a consoling bakery smell. They had made it cozy, with low tables and soft chairs running the length of the shop. Melanie sat down and got out her phone. She was cutting herself loose from the world, and for that moment it felt like freedom.

"Katie, I'm really sorry, but something's come up."

ERIN WAS GONE.

They had stayed up late watching movies—Smiles and Erin on one bed, Ben on the other—and Smiles had a dim memory of drifting off during the climactic scene in *The Sting*, just before Robert Redford and Paul Newman tricked the fat cat from Chicago out of all his money. Smiles had seen *The Sting* before, during his movie-director phase. He hoped that he and Ben could be half as smooth as those guys in pulling off the sale of the cipher.

The sheets on Erin's side of the bed were rumpled pretty good, so Smiles figured she must have spent the night. But she hadn't woken him up or even left him a note.

Ben was toweling his hair dry in front of a mirror fogged with steam escaping from the bathroom. It was already nine thirty, and they had to get ready to do the call at eleven. So yeah, it probably wasn't such a bad thing that Erin wasn't around. Smiles had scored her phone number yesterday; he could track her down after they hit the jackpot.

"When did she leave?" Smiles asked Ben on his way to

the bathroom, unable to quite get her out of his mind.

"Gone when I got up," Ben said with a shrug. "She's really nice."

Smiles entered the shower, recalling what Erin had told him during the movie about her fight with Zach. It was all about money. Neither of them had much of it, and Zach had made a big deal about Erin gambling at the high-limit blackjack table. She had never told him about her GIMPS money, and apparently he didn't care that she was some kind of card-counting savant. They ended up in a shouting match in their room. That's when Erin had taken off.

Smiles was lathering up with purple shampoo from the hotel bottle when Ben's comment struck him as strange. Ben and Erin hadn't talked at all last night.

"What do you mean, she's really nice?" he called out a few minutes later, applying avocado-extract shaving cream to his face at the bathroom mirror. Ben hadn't answered by the time Smiles dressed and left the bathroom, smelling better than he had in days. He made a mental note to make sure Ben took home some of the hotel's fancy grooming products.

Now, Ben was typing away at the netbook he'd programmed the cipher into. It was the computer Smiles had given him from his dad's stash. "What do you mean, she's nice?" he said again.

"Nothing," Ben said. "We talked a little bit last night. You were asleep."

Hmmm, odd. Ben rarely talked to anyone. He wondered what it said about Ben's mental state that he'd engaged in a conversation with a girl he didn't know in the middle of the night.

"So what'd you talk about?"

"Umm, nothing." Ben was typing furiously now.

"You talked about something, dude."

"Smiles, I'm trying to make sure this thing—"

"Did you tell her about Melanie?"

"Nope. I'm checking the cipher here. The numbers are going to be huge, and we don't have that much time."

"Did you tell her about my dad?"

Smiles liked the fact that Erin didn't know his dad was Robert Smylie. Normally, he let that info slip within five minutes of meeting a hot chick. But he'd never mentioned it to Erin. It wasn't a conscious thing, but now he realized it wasn't an accident, either: He didn't want her to have a fake reason for liking him.

Still no answer from Ben. "Well, did you?"

"No, I didn't tell her about your dad, okay? Just let me finish, it's almost ten o'clock."

"Well, what did you talk about, then?"

Ben shoved back from the netbook and looked up.

"Not much. She's nice, that's all I meant. I was getting nervous about today is all, and maybe she could tell or something. We just talked. I'm not, like, trying to take her from you."

Smiles had to laugh at that one. Getting Ben a girlfriend was a dream, yes, but you had to start with training wheels. Not Erin. He was about to apologize for the grilling when Ben added in a dismissive voice, "We talked about the cipher."

"You what!?"

"She's not going to tell anyone."

"Hold on. Stop. Let me get this straight: *You told her about the cipher?*"

"I was nervous. I was starting to have a panic attack. She was awake, and really nice, and it just felt better to talk about it." Ben couldn't play it off that easy, and he knew it. He was like a puppy giving you upturned eyes with a puddle right there, stinking up the carpet. "She's not going to say anything," he insisted.

"Ben . . ." Smiles didn't know where to start. "What about all the paranoia? What about it being a nuclear bomb? Remember that stuff?"

"I know. I shouldn't have said anything, okay? But she's not going to do anything. She likes you. She doesn't know about our plan."

Ben was so naive, it was incredible. Smiles couldn't believe he had to explain this to him. "Dude, she could have taken your notebook last night."

Ben pulled it out of his bag. "It's right here."

"She could have copied it. Did you lock your bag last night?"

"I guess not," he said slowly. "What . . . You think she stole it?"

Smiles didn't know what he thought, except that they only had an hour to go before they tried to sell Ben's cipher, and now they had a whole new complication going on. "We've got to find her," Smiles said. "We've got to find her and keep her with us all morning, till we get this thing done."

"I'm sorry," Ben said, defeated. "I shouldn't have said anything, you're right."

"Forget it. We just gotta be smart."

Smiles was getting out his phone to call Erin when a knock sounded at the door. He held up a warning finger to Ben. "Stay there," he whispered.

Smiles tiptoed to the door, nervous in a way familiar to him from trips to the director's office at Kingsley Prep. This could be Ben's bad decision coming back to haunt them already.

He looked through the peephole and exhaled: Erin.

She was smiling. Too innocent to be up to anything.

When he opened the door, she was holding up a brown bag. "Went for bagels. You guys hungry?"

She walked past him into the room, plunked the bagels down on the dresser, and observed the complicated silence between Ben and Smiles. "What's the deal?"

Ben closed his netbook. "Smiles thinks you're a spy or something."

"Forget him," Smiles said. "Look, it's a long story, but you've gotta stick with us this morning."

MELANIE DIDN'T WANT to open it.

She'd gotten through Rose's email account without finding any new messages about Tarasov or Alice's letter. But then, double-checking the "sent items" folder, she spotted another message to mhuntJD@gmail.com. Melanie had sent hundreds of emails to that address. It was her dad's.

The email had a blank subject line. Melanie ate the last spoonful of her blueberry yogurt, which she'd only ordered because the guy behind the counter had been giving her the hairy eyeball. She scraped the bottom of the plastic cup and set it down.

"Please be nothing," she whispered to no one, and clicked open the message.

Rose Carlisle
To: Marshall Hunt <mhuntJD@gmail.com>
Bcc: Henry Worth <profhworth@northeastern.edu>
Thursday, May 12 9:38:03 AM
Re:

_____

Marshall,

You didn't return my call yesterday—I hope you don't think I'm going to drop this. Something needs to be done. I have verified Andrei's material, and it completely checks out. We need to make this right.

Call me. Let's figure this out.

Rose

For a moment, Melanie couldn't move. Rose had died not a month after sending that email. Her brakes had failed on a drive in the country. Rose always drove too fast, and she hadn't been able to make a raised turn. They found her in a ditch twenty feet below the road, dead on impact. It was accepted as a tragic accident—but it was the kind of thing that could have been engineered as well, couldn't it?

She slammed her computer shut, drawing another stare from the guy behind the counter. He was around her age, with thick blond hair, dark eyes, and amazing skin. He was the kind of put-together guy she fantasized about when Smiles got on her nerves. He kept staring.

"*What!?*" Melanie shouted, surprising herself.

The guy edged toward the back—probably getting a manager to deal with the psycho chick with the yogurt. She gathered up her stuff and got out of there before she could make it any worse.

She blazed back on the Pike the way she had come, although she knew she couldn't go back to Weston tonight. Her palms were slick against the steering wheel as she moved through the weekend traffic. She was going too fast and didn't care.

Planning would calm her down a bit. First, she needed somewhere to sleep. The answer came to her instantly: Mr. Smylie's cabin at Squam Lake. She'd been up there a million times with Smiles, and she knew they kept the key hidden in a fake rock by the back door. Nobody would know she'd been there.

It was going to take a long time to drive to Squam Lake, way up in New Hampshire, but she could use the time to think. Her pulse slackened as she settled in behind a sports car cruising down the passing lane. If anybody got a speeding ticket, it was going to be him.

She reviewed what she knew: Rose had come upon some important information about Andrei Tarasov. Information that she had "verified"—whatever that meant—and that her dad apparently didn't want to deal with. In the email, Rose told her dad that they needed to "make this right." Within a month, Rose had died in a car accident.

Melanie tried to blink away the thought that her dad could have somehow orchestrated Rose's death. But she couldn't ignore it: Both Andrei Tarasov and Rose were dead, and her dad was mixed up in their secrets somehow. If Melanie could find that letter from Smiles's birth mom, Alice, she was sure it would explain everything.

She cracked the window, drying the sweat beading on her forehead.

The strangest part of the email was the bcc line, to profhworth@northeastern.edu. Melanie didn't recognize the name associated with the address—Henry Worth—but at the moment he was her only lead. She had to find out what he knew and why Rose had copied him secretly on her email.

The sports car darted ahead and Melanie pulled into the right-hand lane, less frantic now that she had the semblance of a plan. She picked up her cell and dialed Smiles. It didn't matter anymore that they had broken up; he deserved to know this information.

No answer. She held the cell to her mouth and launched into a message. About halfway through she realized she was rambling and probably sounded hysterical. Melanie cringed and said, "I'm just stressed out about this, and, well, I guess this Henry Worth guy is all I have to go on right now. His email address is from Northeastern, so that's a start. I hope I can find out what was in that letter from your mother. I think that letter has all the answers to everything. I . . . I . . ."

Melanie wanted to tell Smiles that she missed him. It was hard to say if she actually missed him or if it was just that reflex she had—the reflex to make him feel special and wanted.

"I . . . I m—Just call. It's important. Okay? Okay."

Melanie made herself hang up.

She was about to toss the phone aside, but on impulse she flipped through the address book again. Melanie had stored Jenna Brooke's phone number there months ago. She'd never actually dialed it before, but Jenna was the only person who knew anything about Andrei Tarasov.

"Hey, Melanie!" Jenna's voice crackled over the line.

"Jenna? Hey. What are you up to today?"

"I don't know. Bobby Teague's having people over tonight.

Might be lame, though. You know Bobby and those lacrosse guys. I don't think they got the memo that the metrosexual look is—"

"Jenna?"

"Yeah?"

"Sorry to cut you off. It's sort of a long story, but I'm on my way to Squam Lake for the night. It'd be nice to have a friend along if you want to come."

"Seriously?" Jenna's voice rang with excitement—and below it, a note of worry. "Are you okay?"

"I don't know—I'll tell you about it when I see you. You're the only one I *can* tell, actually. You're the only one this would make sense to."

The line went silent for a moment. "I'm packing now," Jenna said. She was all business, and Melanie sensed her unquestioning eagerness to help. Would Melanie have acted the same way if Jenna called out of the blue with a strange emotional emergency? "Whatever it is, it'll be all right. Just come get me."

"Thanks, Jenna."

Melanie couldn't be sure, but she thought she might like the girl.

THE ELEVATOR CHIMED, the doors parted, and Smiles stepped out onto the seventh floor.

He'd left Ben and Erin back in the room a minute ago. Now he followed a sign to his left, toward the second room he'd reserved using Erin's ID. That's where he would perform the demonstration. Smiles would call Ben with numbers from the NSA agents—they would be too long for a text message this time—and Ben would use the cipher again to generate the private keys. It would prove definitively that they had the key to every online secret in the world.

And then, they would get $75 million two hours later.

This is it, Smiles told himself.

He made another turn and found room 781 just past a stairwell. He was reaching for the card key in his back pocket when a door cracked open, puncturing the silence of the hall. Smiles flinched violently, but it was just a maid, three rooms down, wheeling out a room-service tray. Smiles stilled himself, recovering from the shock. He didn't know exactly what he'd been afraid of.

It's gonna be cool. It's gonna be cool.

He sunk the card key into the door. The light of the cloudless day was streaming down the corridor, but once Smiles stepped inside the room it felt like dusk. Comforters were drawn tight over the beds, pristine as glass on Squam Lake. The heavy curtains blotted out the sunlight. The utter calm of the space felt eerie, but Smiles knew it was only the nerves whirling through his chest.

The alarm clock on the nightstand read 10:51. *Nine minutes. Focus, Smiles.*

He stared into the mirror over the dresser, aiming for a pose of confidence and power. Instead, he looked like a kid refusing to smile for his class portrait. Smiles was good at lying to himself, though, and this was just the time for it. He kept staring and thought, *You're ready for this. You're a badass. You're going to get that money for Ben . . . and yourself. This is* your *thing, and you're ready for it.*

As he stared at himself, gearing himself up, somehow his own voice transformed into his mom's. It came to him every once in a while, a little bird in his ear:

You can do it. You can do anything, and doing this will help your friend in a major way. I mean, that's why you're doing it, right? To help Ben? Not because it's a harebrained scheme to earn a false sense of worth and get over your daddy issues, I would hope. Right? Right? Hello?

The opening bars of "I'm Shipping Up to Boston" rocketed through the room. Just his ringtone. Just Melanie. Smiles pushed his heart back down from his throat and sent the call to voice mail. He really could have used a Xanax or something.

Smiles cracked the curtains and a splinter of light cut across the carpet. It didn't do much to dispel the haunted feeling of the room. He flicked the television on for background noise, but the financial news channel that came up was teasing a report about the Alyce Systems IPO. Smiles muted it.

Sizing up the brightened space, he figured he would sit behind the desk. If the agent wanted to sit across from him, he would have to settle for a seat on the edge of the bed. It would be uncomfortable. That's the kind of thing Mr. Hunt would think about—a little curveball to give you a psychological edge in a negotiation. Smiles was beginning to suspect he was a natural at it.

10:54. Six minutes to go.

Smiles pulled out his cell and dialed Ben. "I'm about to call them. You ready?"

"Yeah yeah," Ben said, but his voice wavered. "Smiles, I've had a bad feeling about this since last night."

"Stop with the negative vibes, okay? We're gonna get you that money." He thought about bringing up the matter of his cut (a fifty-fifty split sounded about right), but decided this might not be the best time.

"Yeah, okay," Ben said, and then his voice got low. "You really think it's a good idea to keep Erin here? What if something happens?"

"Nothing's going to happen. Just keep it together." Smiles heard a mumble of assent that didn't instill much confidence. "All right, then. The next time I call you, the agents are going to be here. Have that computer humming."

He clicked off and checked the clock: 10:56.

Screw it. Smiles pulled the agent's number from his pocket and dialed from the desk phone, figuring that calling early was actually a smart idea—another way to keep him off balance.

A voice answered on the first ring. "Yeah."

"Room 781," Smiles said. "Cedar Tower. Be here in ten minutes." He hung up before the guy could respond.

First step over, Smiles thought.

Ten minutes, tops, until the guy arrived. *In a couple hours, you'll have the money.*

Psyching himself up, he ran his palms over the smooth expanse of the desk. It made him think of the desk in his dad's office—a huge glass thing he kept obsessively clean of papers. Smiles had never seen a speck of clutter on it, just his clean-lined computer monitor and a glass tray underneath for stowing his keyboard. That desk had a way of freaking Smiles out. When you sat across from him, there was nothing to draw his attention from you, no buffer from his glare—which, in Smiles's case, was usually a disappointed one.

Modern Boston had done a puff piece on his dad once, and they made a huge deal out of the desk. CLEAN DESK, CLEAR MIND, it had said on the front of the magazine. The cover was a loving photograph of his dad with his feet propped up on the huge plane of glass.

Smiles rarely visited his dad at the office. The only time he'd been there in the last few years was the awful day he had to tell him about getting kicked out of Kingsley. Sitting in the too-bright light of the office, nothing but that sterile sheet of glass between them, he felt like a patient about to enter a ten-hour surgery.

Smiles spit out his story about Darby Fisher's weed and waited for a reaction. He expected anger. Possibly shouting. Best-case scenario, there'd be talk of a lawsuit over Kingsley's strict no-tolerance policy. What he got was much worse. His dad just lowered his head, nodding. He looked like he was about to laugh.

That's when Smiles realized his dad had written him off. Seeing the acceptance in his eyes, not even the slightest distress . . . it couldn't have hurt more.

Smiles felt the sting of it all over again. He jabbed at the remote, unmuting the station, but now they were knee-deep in the Alyce Systems report. He couldn't get away from it. "Even from his hospital bed," said a deep-voiced anchor standing pointlessly before the Alyce Systems logo, "the famously micromanagerial Robert Smylie is exercising tight control over the run-up to his company's IPO. It's a highly orchestrated process, and as we've seen with other tech players, a bad first-day performance can set a negative tone and have a huge effect on—"

The knock came then. Smiles shut the station off and walked to the door, wishing he'd stuck to his pep talk in front of the mirror.

The man he saw in the peephole wasn't the agent from the day before. He had cropped blond hair and a dark suit with a pocket square peeking out. Nothing fancy, but a contrast to the copier salesman. They'd gone up the food chain for this one.

Smiles opened the door, and the guy waddled in without a word. He was maybe in his forties, and somewhere along the way he'd gone soft around the middle. He had the kind of pale skin that verged on transparent. A blue vein ran visibly down his temple like something buried under ice. He might not get raves from the doctor's office, but there was something authoritative in the guy's manner. Yeah, they'd brought in the heavyweight to do the deal.

"Cole," he said, flashing an NSA ID. He stepped forward, still holding out his credential, glancing about the room to ensure they were alone.

It seemed like Smiles should check the ID, so he did. It said EDWARD COLE, with his picture in the corner opposite an NSA seal. A bar code ran along the bottom.

"Thanks for coming." Smiles released the ID and shook the guy's hand. To his surprise, he felt himself growing cool and poised, the way Melanie looked before her cross-country races.

"Let's do this at the desk," he said, and walked to his prearranged spot behind it. As Smiles hoped, the guy looked around uncertainly before taking a seat on the bed. He tried to sit up straight, but kept sinking into the mattress. Smiles was eating it up.

"I've been briefed," Cole said, struggling to maintain his dignity on the flowery comforter. "But I'll tell you right off, I'm skeptical."

"That's fine. I would be, too." Smiles toyed with a pen on the desk, just to put on a little show. He figured he should give the guy his money's worth. "But you've brought your own public keys. There's no way for us to rig this. There shouldn't be any doubt after that."

Cole allowed a nod. "No, not if it works." He'd brought a thin leather folder with him. He moved the folder to his lap and rested his hands on it with a light touch.

"So . . . should we get to it?" Smiles said.

"Just one thing first," Cole said with a raised finger. "Who's the partner?"

Smiles wondered if they'd ask. But he reminded himself that they didn't know anything about Ben. As far as the agents knew, Smiles was the math genius and Ben was just his assistant.

"Not important," Smiles said dismissively. "He's helping with the demonstration, that's it."

Cole eyed Smiles closely. Before he could snoop any further about Ben, Smiles decided to cut him off. "And *your* partner?" Smiles said. "Where's he?"

Cole cracked a smile. "Seventy-five mil doesn't come from petty cash. He's taking care of the financial arrangements, in the unlikely event that we need to act on them."

"That's what I like to hear," Smiles said. "Now . . . shall we dance?"

Cheesy, perhaps, but Smiles couldn't help it—he was feeling awfully good. The guy rolled his eyes, pulled a sheet from the folder, and handed it across the desk. The page had five typewritten numbers on it, all but one so long they spilled onto multiple lines.

Smiles held the sheet up. "We said you could bring ten numbers."

"Appreciated," Cole said in a condescending way. "But if you can produce the prime factors to those, that will be more than ample proof." He twisted a cough drop from its wrapper, plopped it in his mouth, and sucked at it like a fish. Smiles got hit with a blast of cherry-scented vapors.

He picked up the phone, making sure Cole wasn't watching his hands as he dialed the room below. Ben picked up on the first ring.

"He's there already?" he said without any introduction. Ben was using his freaked-out voice, which Smiles was getting pretty familiar with by now.

Smiles didn't let any reaction cross his face. "Yes, we're ready," he said calmly. "I have five numbers in total. If you're set, I'll begin."

"Fine, okay, go ahead," Ben said.

Even though the cipher had worked the day before, Smiles felt a brush of nerves. Maybe it wouldn't work with bigger numbers. Smiles wondered what kind of trouble he could be in if this blew up in their faces. Was there some kind of federal law you broke when you tried to get $75 million out of the government with a bogus cipher?

Smiles held the page before him, aware of the agent's watchful eyes. He cleared his throat and read the first five digits of the first number.

"Eight, nine, six, zero, four . . ." Smiles paused for breath, and across the phone line Ben repeated the numbers back to him. It established a rhythm, making the tedious work of reading the number easier. Smiles marked his place with the pen and paused every five digits for Ben to confirm them.

Finally, after what seemed like ten minutes of work, he had only two digits left.

". . . three, nine." Smiles sighed.

"Three, nine," Ben said. "That's it?"

"That's the complete first number, yes." Smiles heard the tiniest click of a computer key across the line.

"Okay, ready for the private keys?"

Smiles clenched a fist in celebration beneath the desk. Ben had taken less than a second to produce the private keys. Smiles made sure Cole saw the pleasure on his face and said, "Yes, please go ahead with the results."

They repeated the process in reverse, with Ben reading two numbers back to Smiles in five-digit chunks. Thankfully they were relatively short.

They went through the next three numbers the same way. It took a while, but they got into a groove, and for minutes at a time Smiles forgot Cole was even in the room. Every once in a while, his eye caught the guy shifting on the bed. At some point, Smiles saw him get up and commandeer a bottle of water from the mini fridge.

"Make it two," Smiles said with a smile. He enjoyed watching Cole come back and serve him, like he was his personal waiter or something.

The water cooled his throat, which had been getting dry from the constant reading of numbers. By that point they had reached the final one, which was shorter than the others. Smiles breezed through it like a victory lap.

". . . seven, three, one, one. And that's all she wrote," Smiles said. He cracked his knuckles with satisfaction—

another little show for Cole in anticipation of getting the last two private keys. Ben wasn't saying anything back, though.

"Seven, three, one, one, did you get that?"

"*Yes I got it*. But . . . I don't know . . . It's not . . ." Smiles could hear a pronounced clatter at Ben's keyboard.

His heart skipped a few beats. Ben kept murmuring in frustration, and Smiles felt like he was staring into a canyon, about to get pushed off the ledge. He suddenly realized how much of himself he'd put into this project.

Cole circled over to the desk, vulturelike.

"Repeat the number, please," Smiles said to Ben. It was a stalling device; he knew Ben had copied the number right.

"Something's screwed up here." Ben's voice was hovering on the edge of sanity. "I don't know what's happening. I can't explain it, but I'm not getting anything here. I'm sorry, Smiles, I don't know what's going on, but—"

"Yes, I see," Smiles said firmly. "Thank you. I'll call if we need anything else." He hung the phone up peacefully and turned his eyes to Cole, still circling over the desk. "If you'll have a seat, I have the results."

Cole sat down on the bed and Smiles passed the page across. He had written the private keys beneath each number, leaving the space under the last number blank.

"Something's missing here," Cole said with some relish. He un-twirled another cough drop and popped it into his mouth.

"Yes. There's a problem with your number. Perhaps you copied it incorrectly."

Cole chuckled. "Okay then. Let's see about the others."

He pulled a second page from his folder, no doubt containing the private keys for each of the five numbers. Withdrawing a pen from his suit, he methodically compared the numbers Smiles had provided to the true private keys. The cough drop made little clicking sounds in his mouth as he went.

He didn't know why Cole was even going through the exercise. Smiles had made a show of staying calm, trying to pass off the screw-up with the final number on the NSA. The fact was, though, they hadn't come up with anything. There was no way the government was forking over millions of dollars for a half-working cipher. Maybe Cole was just torturing him, putting him in his place for making such an outrageous demand. Or maybe he was buying time, trying to figure out whether to arrest him.

Cole closed the folder and stuffed the pen back in his suit. His hand came back out with a mobile phone in it.

Smiles felt a jolt of panic as the guy tapped away. "Who are you calling?" he said as Cole returned the device to his jacket pocket.

Cole ignored the question.

"Impressive," he said. "Now, where would you like the money delivered?"

COLE SHOOK SMILES'S hand on his way out. He had the Swiss account information tucked away in his leather folder. In exactly one hour, he was coming back. Smiles would confirm the money was in the account, and then hand over the cipher.

"The last number was just a test," Cole said, halfway out the door. "We wanted to see what would happen if we gave you a number that wasn't the product of two primes."

Just a head game by the feds, that's all it was. If that's what they needed to do to make themselves feel better about handing over $75 million, Smiles was all for it. He watched Cole leave and let himself exhale. He pushed the door closed, leaned his back against it, and slunk to the floor in a state of utter bliss.

A laugh bubbled up from his insides. Ben had done it after all. Smiles had done it.

After an extended internal celebration, he raised up and looked at himself in the mirror. Standing taller now, a glow on his face. "You did it," he said.

It wasn't Melanie he wanted to talk to now, or his father. It was his mom, and not the one at the conference. "I did it, Mom," he said to the mirror, and waited for her imagined reply.

Congrats, baby. That's a crapload of money you just made. For doing . . . what again? Selling Ben's work? And wanting a big slice of it for yourself? Almost sounds like one of those shortcuts to success your dad has always warned you against. You know what feels better than a crapload of money? Devoting yourself to something, using the talents God gave you. You've got a lot of them, Smiles, you're gonna find that out someday.

Sometimes she could be kinda blunt. "You're harshing my high, Mom."

Oh fine. I'm happy for you, baby, I am. Go on and celebrate—Ben's waiting for you down there.

She didn't have to tell him twice. He let his joy carry him out of the room.

⨯

He took the stairs down to the fifth floor, burst into the hallway, and jogged down to their room.

"Yo, Ben!" he said, knocking on the door. "Good news, my friend!"

Smiles didn't have to worry about keeping anything from Erin. They'd been pretty much forced to fill her in on the basics that morning, telling her everything except the amount of money they were getting from the government. It was the only way they could get her to stick around without seeming too creepy. Smiles bounced on the balls of his feet, waiting for one of them to get the door.

No one came. *Maybe they turned on the TV and can't hear me*, Smiles thought as he hopped outside the door, looking like a fool and not caring one bit.

"Yo, Ben, c'mon man!"

He pounded on the door some more, until he realized he had his own key. The light at the doorknob turned green as he pressed the card key down and barged into the room.

"Hey, man, we did it!"

Smiles stopped. Before the door closed behind him, his heart had sunk to the floor. All of Ben's stuff was gone. His clothes, his netbook, his army bag with the combination lock. Most of Smiles's things were still there, but someone had rifled through them pretty good. The few clothes he'd brought—a pair of jeans, his Red Sox boxers, and a couple of T-shirts—had been dumped out on a bed. His duffel bag had been turned inside out and thrown on the floor.

Ben was really nervous about something bad happening. Maybe he decided to clear out of the room early.

Smiles couldn't fool himself, though. Ben would have called if he'd left the room for some reason. He checked his phone to be sure, but saw only the missed call from Melanie.

Smiles backed away from the bed, feeling an instinct that he shouldn't touch anything. Still, he had to press a hand to the wallpaper for balance. He felt like he had a few months before, when he'd signed up for a one-year gym membership and spent five minutes on a treadmill—dizzy and hot and clammy with sweat.

Smiles checked the closet at the front of the room, just to make sure Ben hadn't stowed his stuff in there. The metal hangers clanged against one another as he yanked the door open, finding nothing. Next he checked the bathroom, which had been emptied out and wiped clean. Anything that wasn't nailed down was gone—all of the shampoo bottles, the towels, the little glass by the sink. Smiles could smell something more powerful than your average bathroom cleaner, and from the stinging in his eyes he suspected it was bleach.

Between the fumes and the fear building inside him, Smiles almost blacked out. He stepped out of the bathroom, put his hands on his knees, and tried to breathe. He could only get so much air into his lungs. On the far side of the room, the air conditioner blew into the curtains.

His phone rang in his hand, and Smiles answered it almost before "I'm Shipping Up to Boston" could start. The line was ragged with static. "Smiles! Look out the win—"

Ben's voice trailed away, and then a terrible scratching sound came across the line. Smiles was already yanking the curtains apart. Below in the parking lot, he saw Cole stomping on Ben's phone. Somehow, Ben had grabbed it and made the call. It must have been difficult, because Cole and the other NSA agent, Gary, were carrying him roughly by the armpits.

They were taking him away.

BEN HAD NO chance.

His feet pinwheeled above the asphalt as the two agents whisked him from the casino. They flanked him tightly, handling him with ease. In his free hand, Gary held a sagging black trash bag, which from the angle of his shoulders appeared heavier than Ben. It probably contained Ben's stuff and the items from the bathroom. Even with the lumpy Cole at one side, the agents were plenty strong enough to carry Ben a clear foot off the ground.

Smiles could see now that they were headed for a black minivan. Ben's hands had been bound behind him. He jerked his neck around, shouting a call for help that Smiles couldn't hear.

Smiles pulled at the window latch but knew it was welded shut. He banged on the glass but knew the sound wouldn't reach them. He prayed someone would intervene, but there were no witnesses in the lot.

"Hey!" Smiles shouted into the glass. It barely vibrated as he pounded on the window. He kept at it, but it was only making his fists sore and his arms burn. The agents were about to get away. Smiles had never felt so helpless.

Gary slid open the minivan door, let Cole toss Ben inside, then slammed the door shut. The agents glanced briefly around the lot and got inside. Cole fixed a pair of dark glasses over his eyes and spoke harshly into the rearview mirror.

Smiles hoped that somehow Ben would string the conversation out.

He charged out of the room, heading downstairs.

⨍

He took the stairs two at a time. The stairwell was positioned at the end of the hallway, so now he had to backtrack toward the casino lobby to get out to the parking lot. He ran down the row of retail stores for people itching to blow money on overpriced sunglasses and celebrity-endorsed jeans. He took the length of it in full stride, darting right and left to avoid sixty-year-old women in plastic sandals and velour warm-ups, window-shopping for Prada and Gucci. Husbands and wives saw him coming and scooted out of his path.

Only now did Smiles begin to realize, as the chimes of the casino grew louder in his ears, how dumb the whole plan had been—how obvious it must have been to the agents that Ben had the cipher. He was the genius Gary had come to meet at the casino, after all. The agents must have been watching them all night, laughing at their amateur ways. Smiles felt his face get hot with embarrassment as the hallway opened up to the lobby.

He dodged around a CRYPTCON information table,

slipped across the marble floor of the entrance, and crashed open the doors to the parking lot. A wave of warm air blew him back. Smiles pushed through it and sprinted across the driveway in the direction of the van. A valet shouted as he crossed inches in front of a Jetta, but Smiles was in no mood to listen. He pressed on despite the protests of his lungs, which weren't used to this kind of thing.

It was a three-hundred-yard trek to the minivan's parking spot, but Smiles didn't have to go that far. He stopped fifty yards short and bent over, chest heaving. His legs had turned to spaghetti. A drop of sweat fell from his forehead, darkening the asphalt.

The parking space was empty. Ben was long gone.

✕

Smiles gulped oxygen as he plodded back to the casino. The valet gave him a dirty look as he walked the stone path to the main entrance. Smiles was used to getting those looks— he'd seen them on teachers and coaches and other adults he'd let down in one way or another over the years. After a while they all melded together into one great glower of disappointment, and now Smiles felt like he deserved it. If it were physically possible to give himself a dirty look, he would have.

The conditioned air of the casino did little to relieve him. The manic sounds from the slot machines hurt his head, reminding him that he needed to get going—to do something to fix this situation he'd created. But what?

Smiles toyed with the phone in his pocket. The logical

step was to call the police. He hadn't done that yet, and he knew why: He was clinging to some stupid, dying hope that he could still rectify things.

Just feet away from him, people were winning jackpots for doing nothing more than pulling the arm of a slot machine. Meanwhile, Ben had worked on something real, something actually worth a fortune. And then Smiles got involved, and it had turned into a nightmare.

Smiles stopped, gritted his teeth, and entered 911. For once in his life he didn't want to give up, but Ben's life might be in danger. He pressed "send."

"Emergency services, where are you located?"

The 911 operator sounded like a harried mother, demanding to know why he was out past curfew. Smiles opened his mouth but nothing came out. It had been a mistake to call from his cell. He was dealing with powerful people here. People with unlimited budgets. People who had taken Ben against his will and wiped any trace of him from the hotel. They would do anything to keep this thing from going public, and if they ever checked the records of this call, they could track it back to him.

"Where are you located? Are you in danger, caller?"

He was preparing to speak when he saw the CRYPTCON information table and was struck by a thought: *Maybe my mother could help.*

~

It made a lot of sense, if you thought about it. She would know how the NSA operated, but she wasn't too chummy with them, if all that talk about Never Say Anything and No Such Agency was any indication. Plus, if anybody in the world owed Smiles a favor, it was her.

He ran to the information table, manned by a willowy guy with greasy hair that offered a potential solution to the domestic oil supply problem. He marked a page in his book as Smiles approached.

"Can you tell me where Professor Taft is?" Smiles asked. Another drop of sweat fell from his face, this time onto the cover of the book, *The Blackjack Bible*. Smiles smeared it off with the bottom of his T-shirt and smiled innocently.

After a long moment lamenting the damage done to his reference material, the guy picked up a printout and said, "She's starting in room 132 in five minutes." His eyes stared at the spot on Smiles's chest where an orange lanyard should have hung. "Are you registered?"

"Sort of," Smiles said, and dashed down the hallway to the conference area.

He turned the corner where Erin had given him the eye the day before, then started scanning the conference rooms. Each had a plastic square by its entrance, identifying it with a number that could be read in braille below. The theater where they'd held the opening session was 130. Two doors down, Smiles burst into a much smaller room, with chairs for maybe forty people and nothing more elaborate than a table with a microphone on it at the front.

His mother sat behind it, flipping through blue index cards as the full room of people settled into their seats. Some seemed to recognize him from the opening session.

Whispers circulated in the room as he approached Alice.

Her lips settled in an emotionless line at the sight of him. Her throat clenched, the only signal of her distress, before she leaned into the microphone. "We'll get started in one moment," she said, and led Smiles out of the room without a word. The murmurs grew as he left.

Out in the hall, his mother got some distance from the room before turning back to him. She yanked at the sleeves of her blazer, composing herself. "We have a lot to talk about, but I'm sorry, this isn't an ideal time for a conversation." Her voice was flat—the voice from the phone. "Or an ideal place," she added.

She obviously knew who he was. And Smiles realized then that she thought he was stalking her—that he'd come to Fox Creek for the very purpose of confronting her.

"Look," he said, "I honestly didn't even know you would be at this thing. That was, like, a total coincidence. And I'm sorry about interrupting your lecture." His guest appearance at the student mixer couldn't have helped, either, but he dropped it.

She watched him like she was posing for a painting: motionless, eyes as dead as her voice. Smiles felt the anger rise within him.

"Anyway, something really bad has happened to my friend, and—"

"I'm sorry, but we just can't do this now. I have to get to this session." She checked her watch. "I'm already late."

"I need your help here," Smiles pleaded. He couldn't believe she wouldn't give him five minutes. "There's no one else I can go to. I mean, you know things about the NSA, right?"

She held up her hand. "Look, maybe we can set a time to talk. Calling you, that was a mistake. Still, I know there are things that we should, or that *I* should, explain." For a brief moment she had turned into a human being. "But let's not make this"—her eyes tracked a few conference stragglers passing them in the hall—"a matter of public consumption. And for now I'm quite late, and this conference is very important."

"I'm not important?" Even after not hearing from her his whole life, he could hardly believe this.

"That's not what I said. It's just a case of very poor timing, and I really need to go."

Was he supposed to wait another eighteen years, when it might be more convenient for her? Smiles remembered the opening session—the man with the mustache going on and on about her bravery. She had risked getting tossed in jail to protect one of her students, but when it came to her son, she couldn't give him the time of day.

"You're my *mother*. I'm in a bad situation, and I'm asking for your *help*."

"I can't, not now."

That was all she said before she marched back toward the conference room, swiping at her eye.

⁂

Smiles stumbled back down the hallway, gut-punched by the conversation. He walked in a daze to the lobby, where the stores he had run past just minutes ago shot off down a hallway to his left. At the mouth of it was Starbucks. Its seats spilled into the lobby.

And there, in one of the green chairs, sat Erin.

"SMILES!" SHE YELLED. Her arm waved for his attention.

Smiles trotted over, floating across the lobby like he was being pulled on a life preserver. In the rush of events he had almost forgotten about her. Now he had someone to get answers from—even if she did have an ass of a boyfriend, and even if that boyfriend was sitting right across from her in another muscle shirt. He drank from a gigantic cup filled with some kind of frilly drink. Strands of chocolate topping crisscrossed the foam just so.

"Hey, what happened to you?" Smiles said to Erin. "Where'd you go?"

Erin threw a cautious glance at Zach before answering. Probably smart to be careful, but Smiles was beyond that. He needed as much information as he could get.

"Ben sent me down here," she said. "Did he ask you to come get me?"

"Come get you? No. Listen, just tell me what happened. It's really important."

"Smiles . . ." Erin had her messenger bag over her shoulder again. She ducked under the strap, put it on her seat, and stood close enough to whisper.

"What's going on?" Zach yelped.

"Don't worry about it." It felt good to vent his anger—especially on that guy. He wondered why Erin had even been sitting with him, after their fight the night before.

"Actually, I *am* worried about it," Zach said.

He sounded like the kind of guy who could have done the I-know-you-are-but-what-am-I routine for hours without losing interest. It was about the last thing that Smiles needed.

Erin placed a warning hand on Smiles's arm.

"Just sit there and enjoy your cocoa," he said.

That did it. Zach's chair toppled behind him as he rose. "You want to do this?"

"I do," Smiles said. "And yet I'm busy. Rain check?"

The other customers were noticing now, peeling their eyes from laptops and cell phones. Erin pushed Smiles gently away, extending her other arm to keep Zach at bay.

"Don't get into it with him, okay?"

Smiled edged away, far enough to talk without Zach hearing. "They took Ben this morning. I need to know what you saw."

"They *took* him? What do you mean?"

"I mean they took him. They frog-marched him out of here. They didn't give us a dime and they took Ben and the cipher. This is real, and Ben's in trouble."

As he said it, Smiles realized he didn't have any more time to waste. He needed to get to a phone that couldn't be traced to him immediately. The business center would do.

Erin was shaking her head, trying to absorb it. "He was so nervous this morning. He told me to—"

"I gotta call the police now," Smiles said. "Will you be here?"

Erin looked between Smiles and Zach, struggling with the choice. "Smiles . . ."

He didn't wait for the rest of it.

He raced down the hallway, turning past the Gucci store and into the darkened nook that led to the business center. As usual, it was empty. As usual, there was something fake and pitiful about its flimsy reproduction of office life. No wonder people preferred the luxury stores. The man in the SUCCESS poster looked happy as ever, but this time he seemed to be mocking Smiles, ready to strike him over the head with his enormous cell phone.

Smiles grabbed some Kleenex by the coffeemaker. He used one tissue to pick up the receiver, and another to protect his finger as he dialed 911.

"Emergency services, where are you located?" A man this time, equally harried.

"I'm at the Fox Creek casino, but that's not really—"

The pounding stopped him. The door had a rectangular window set into it, and on the other side Erin was flailing away. He dropped the phone and opened the door.

"What is it?"

She paused before she spoke, breathless from effort.

"Smiles, I have the cipher. I have the only copy."

"YOU HAVE THE cipher?"

"Yeah. The only copy. If those agents took Ben, they don't have it."

Smiles couldn't make sense of her words. "How'd *you* get it?"

Erin eyed the phone lying on the carpet. "Who were you calling?"

"911. Erin, I don't get it . . ."

He was picturing Ben, so crazy and paranoid and yet so trusting. Smiles thought he was ridiculous for keeping his bag locked up. And yet when he got scared the night before, he spilled everything to Erin. Smiles could understand why. There was something true in her honey-colored eyes, something about the scar on her cheek that said life would hurt you but it would be okay. If it turned out she had stolen Ben's algorithm, Smiles was never going to have faith in anyone again.

Erin crossed the room and hung up the phone. She returned to Smiles and took his hands. She stood upright before him in her white sundress; her hands warmed his from underneath. Stripped of her messenger bag, with a wisp of golden hair falling across her forehead, she looked like a spring bride. She was calming him down, and it was working magnificently.

"Tell me what happened," he said. "We need to do something quick."

"I know." She underlined her words, letting him know she understood the urgency. It was the voice of the warm bath, the one that did everything but tuck him in bed. She drew him back to the chairs by the computer terminals.

"I didn't know what to say out there. With people around and Zach—"

"Just tell me," Smiles said. "Forget Zach."

Her eyes softened. She curled her fingers tight into his. "Okay, here's what happened. I was there in the room while you guys tested the cipher. When the last number didn't work, Ben flipped out. I know you were on the phone, but in person it was scary. He went nuts, Smiles."

"I can sorta imagine," Smiles said, thinking of Ben's display at the opening session. "He has Asperger's, you know?"

"I didn't, but yeah, I can see it," she said. "So after you hung up, he wigged. I'm not sure if it was the fact that the last number didn't work or he was just nervous about the whole thing in general. Anyway, he stored the cipher on a thumb drive and deleted the memory from his netbook. He gave me the thumb drive and the page from his notebook and told me to go downstairs. I tried to tell him it'd be okay, to stick to your plan. But he was sure something was off, and he didn't want anybody getting that thing."

Smiles nodded. Erin might have been thrown by Ben's actions, but they made perfect sense. Ben had it in his brain that something was going to go wrong. The kid had a stubborn way about him, and once he got something fixed in his head, it took a jackhammer to dislodge it.

"It all seemed crazy to me, but in a way I wasn't worried about it because the algorithm didn't even work."

Smiles didn't bother correcting her for the moment. Against the wall, a printer whirred to life and began spitting out pages. The room filled with the smell of toner.

"He wanted to be a hundred percent sure things were cool before he gave anybody the algorithm. So the deal was, I was supposed to hang down here until he knew things were kosher. He was going to call me if you guys needed it for the exchange. But he never called. I wasn't really expecting him to, either, to be honest."

"Because you thought it didn't work," Smiles said.

"Right. Wait, what? It *did* work?"

"Yeah. The last number was just a test."

Erin's mouth fell open. "Oh my God. A fast-factoring algorithm . . ."

"They played us," Smiles said. "They had us the whole time. After we tested the algorithm, the NSA agent sent a text on his phone. The other agent must have been waiting for the signal. By the time I got back to the room, they'd taken him. And that room . . . you could almost feel what had happened in there. They wiped the place down with *bleach*."

"No trace of Ben . . ." Erin said.

"Yeah. Or the agents. Who knows what they're going to do to him." Ben was in that van right now. They were bouncing over roads and Ben was tied up in a seat, sweating it out. Probably rocking back and forth with worry. No one in the world knew where he was except those two agents. No one even knew he was in trouble except Smiles and Erin.

"I convinced him to do it," Smiles said. The confession felt good, and then it poured out of him. "I thought I had this great plan, which now seems like the stupidest thing in the world. I don't know if Ben even wanted to do it. I kind of forced it on him."

He leaned back, but Erin locked her fingers around his. "You guys did it together."

Smiles shook his head. He didn't want her to make this easy on him. He'd happily take that from anyone else— Melanie made things easy on him all the time—but not Erin. "You don't know about me, but I'm actually a pretty major screwup—"

"Smiles, shut up for a second, okay?" She gave him a crooked smile. "I've gotta tell you something. I'm actually the screwup here." The printer shut off behind her. Only after it wheezed to a halt did he notice the absence of the sound. The room was fresh with silence.

"I know who you are," Erin said.

Smiles blinked. "Like, metaphysically?"

"I know you're Robert Smylie's son."

"What? How did you—"

"Zach figured it out." She shrugged, sorry to even say the name. Smiles was sorry, too. He was done thinking about that guy. "He looks stupid, but he's not. I actually met him at the University of Maine. I was taking a class on linear algebra that they don't have at my high school. He was this macho ROTC guy, seemed like the only normal human there." She shook her head, getting back on track. "Anyway, he's been a nut about Alyce Systems for a long time, even before all the IPO stuff. He's read your dad's business book, like, five times."

Smiles had a copy somewhere. It was called *The Transparent Innovator*, all about how good values and clean living lead to business breakthroughs. His dad's desk was on the cover of that thing, too. Smiles remembered now: His copy had gotten ruined when somebody left a cold beer sitting on it all afternoon.

"You know how the book has those pictures in the middle of it?"

Smiles shook his head. "I've never opened it."

"Anyway, there are pictures of your dad starting Alyce in his garage and stuff. Family pictures, too. You're in a couple of them. Zach thought he recognized you from them. He searched on the Internet last night and found some Facebook pictures of you. So he knows."

"Okay, fine, it's not important—"

"Hold on, that's not the worst part." Her head sank. Smiles wasn't sure he had the patience for this. "Zach found me at Starbucks this morning. And I guess we started to make up. I mean, you were really sweet last night, but I didn't even know if I'd see—"

"It's okay."

"Smiles, I told him about the cipher. I thought it didn't work. I didn't say all that much, though." She was pleading with him. "I just said these guys thought they'd discovered a fast-factoring algorithm but it turned out to be a bust."

"Look, it's fine. Forget that. What are we gonna do about Ben?"

She nodded, pulling his hands onto her lap. "This is what I'm thinking. For one, we could go to the police— call 911 like you were doing. But aren't you afraid of that? I mean, do you know how powerful the NSA is? They're going to deny it, and would the police really believe your story over two federal agents?"

"Yeah." Smiles had been thinking the same thing. And there was another reason he couldn't go to the police, too— one he hadn't thought of earlier. "There's no way I can take this to anybody. If it gets out that there's a fast-factoring algorithm, my dad's whole company is in jeopardy. Especially right now, right before the IPO." It hit him like a bar of lead.

"True," Erin said. She tapped her fingernail against a front tooth. "I keep going back to that bleach. They were getting rid of evidence. They're calculated, and they must be worried about you. It's almost like when Ben turns up missing . . . they'll want you to get the blame."

Smiles hadn't even considered that. The guy at the desk had seen them register together. And there were probably cameras all over the hotel and casino.

"So what do I do?" He was really asking. He knew Erin was way smarter than him. Melanie was smarter than him, too, but only in the sense that she could ace some history test that Smiles didn't care about. There was something savvy about Erin—something that let her see life like a chessboard. The way Smiles wanted to be when he thought of himself in that SUCCESS poster.

"Smiles, tell me why you wanted to sell that cipher."

For a second, the answer didn't come to him.

"It couldn't have been the money, right? You must have tons of money."

"Probably not as much as you think," Smiles said. "But . . . no. I guess you're right. That's not exactly it."

"So why then?" Her voice was soft but weighted with meaning. It slipped from her lips to his ears. It went inside his head and pulled the answer out with it.

Smiles said it as best he could. "I've never done anything important in my life. I've never done a single thing that matters. This felt like it mattered a lot."

She was grinning when he looked back up at her. "Yeah, that makes sense. Smiles, it might be risky, but I think there's a way out of all this for you."

"Tell me."

"We sell it to them again," she said. "And this time we don't just get the money back. We get the money and Ben."

Something swelled inside Smiles. "Yeah? Will you help me? Are you up for it?"

"You know I am." She was saying something more, and it made his imagination dance.

"If we do this, we have to stick together," he said. "We have to stay together every second till it's done."

"We will."

Smiles couldn't have held himself back if he'd wanted to. But he didn't want to, and neither did Erin. In one graceful hop she was in his chair. The lightness of her body fell into his, her laugh soared high in the air, her hair tickled his neck.

Their lips met with a wild energy.

MELANIE SMELLED PINE and knew they were close.

The scent of the trees had been etched in her mind during childhood weekends up at Squam Lake. Her family came up to the Smylies' cabin every Fourth of July and Labor Day. The dads would pair off and head out on the boat, the moms would pair off and have drinks on the deck. Melanie and Smiles would swim out to the floating dock, a tiny wooden platform that had seemed like its own world. Then she and Smiles had paired off for real, and they would come up here alone in the winter, spending nights snuggled under a quilt by the fire.

Melanie rolled her window down. "God, I love this air." It was always a bit cooler at Squam Lake—cooler and clearer and always with a hint of pine.

Jenna followed suit, rolling down her own window and breathing in.

"Wow, nice." Melanie wondered if Jenna was just humoring her and decided it didn't matter.

Her company had settled Melanie down even while she

explained the gory details of Andrei Tarasov's suicide on the Smylies' front lawn. Jenna hadn't broken in with her usual commentary on whatever stray thing happened to float, butterfly-like, into her brain. Instead she sat in the passenger seat for the two-hour ride, nodding encouragement while Melanie went on. She'd explained how, years after Tarasov's death, he had become the subject of odd emails between Smiles's stepmom, Rose, and his birth mother, Alice, who had abandoned him when he was two. It all had something to do with a letter that Alice had left for Smiles to read when he turned eighteen.

"Holy crap, Mel," Jenna said at one point. "I *knew* it was going to be about the Russian guy. I didn't want to say anything, but it was so weird that you'd stolen his file. Anyway, keep going . . ."

Something about Jenna's naked fascination won Melanie over. She was lapping up the story with the same titillated delight with which Melanie purchased copies of *Us Weekly* more frequently than she cared to admit. She let her guard down and told Jenna about her expedition to Tarasov's old house and getting warned away by the pale cop with the cherry-cough-drop breath.

"Strange," Jenna said, and that about summed up Melanie's feelings on the subject as well.

Then she got to the most disturbing part, the part that had been consuming her since the start of this whole thing. She told Jenna about Rose's emails to her dad. The first one, while he was in Saint-Tropez, and then the second one shortly before the car accident that killed Rose. Melanie watched Jenna closely. She held off any suggestion that her dad might have been involved in Rose's death, wanting to see if Jenna would draw the connection.

"But you don't . . ." Jenna stopped herself, turning away and taking in their first glimpse of Squam Lake through the trees. The last bits of afternoon sun sparkled on the water.

"Don't what?"

"Nothing."

So yes, she had made the connection. And Melanie hadn't even mentioned that her dad was an expert mechanic, spending countless weekend hours underneath his Aston Martin, oiling up his Maybach. Fraying a brake line would probably be nothing to him.

"I remember that accident," Jenna said from far away.

Rose's death had been the talk of Kingsley for a few days last spring. Melanie had gone to the funeral in a nine-hundred-dollar dress she bought at Neiman Marcus for the occasion, and which had felt tainted ever since. The next day at Kingsley, Melanie faced a siege of questions about the accident, the funeral, and most importantly whether anybody famous had shown up. She resented the attention, knowing people were only curious because Rose's death happened to tangentially involve Mr. Smylie. But by the end of the week, everyone at school had moved on, and Melanie wanted to scream: *That's it? Don't you want to hear about the white lilies at the wake? Don't you want to know what the governor said? Don't you care about Rose anymore?*

"You've *got* to be joking," Jenna said. She was leaning

forward in her seat, the better to stare up the length of the driveway. Her eyes had grown to the size of softballs. "You said *cabin*, Mel, not *palace*."

"It's pretty swank, huh?" Melanie had forgotten what it was like to see the Smylies' place for the first time.

Jenna was right: *Cabin* didn't do it justice. *Fortress* was more like it, if a fortress could be clean and modern and inviting. A wide concrete chimney anchored the right side of the house, surrounded by boxy configurations of glass and wood. One of the box shapes—Mr. Smylie's office—jutted forward, hovering in midair over the driveway and the three-car garage beneath it. The bed of pine needles covering the drive softened their approach. Melanie parked in front of the garage doors and turned to Jenna, whose eye condition looked permanent at this point.

"This is nothing. Wait till you see the Pollock."

✗

Jenna didn't care about the Pollock.

Melanie showed it to her right off the bat—a massive, ugly, gorgeous thing that the great Jackson Pollock had painted in his trademark abstract style. The painting hung high on the living-room wall, which rose to a vaulted ceiling striped with wooden beams. Even up there, the painting drew the eye with its crazy splotches of gray and blue and orange. They suggested some messy but beautiful drama that Melanie wished, somehow, she could experience herself one day. If somebody painted her life, it would be pure impressionism: soft, orderly, muted.

The painting held her like a magnet as it always did, long after Jenna got bored and went up the spiral staircase to explore.

"You have *got* to be joking," her voice boomed from the second floor. "A claw-foot tub? A *claw-foot tub*!?"

Melanie smirked and waited in the kitchen. She raided the pantry and came away with ramen noodles and an unopened bag of cookies, hopefully still good. By the time the water was boiling, Jenna had come back downstairs, breathless and yammering about the wonders she'd seen: the fireplace in the master bedroom, the oak-paneled walls, the view of the lake. And of course the claw-foot tub. Melanie let Jenna get it out of her system and pushed a bowl of ramen across the distressed-wood table.

"Crap, and a Viking stove, too," Jenna said as she took in the kitchen. She managed a bite of her noodles before she continued. "I can't believe the way you live, Mel," she said, waving at the house like a game-show hostess showing off a prize.

The statement probably would have annoyed Melanie a few days ago, but now she almost wanted to hug Jenna. She sat across from Melanie in a summer sweater with little knobs from the hanger sticking up at her shoulders. Jenna had probably tossed the outfit together in a rush, pulling the special sweater from deep in her closet. There was something sweet about it that touched Melanie—like Jenna was interviewing to be her friend.

"This is how the Smylies live, not me," Melanie said.

"Oh, come on."

Melanie looked up from the table. "Okay, fine," she said after a second, and they both cracked up.

Emboldened, Jenna leaned in conspiratorially. "If I said something really bitchy, could you, like, not hold it against me?"

This oughta be good, Melanie thought. "Yeah, sure."

"You know everyone's jealous of you. Pretty, smart, everything else. I mean, I know I am. I blabber nonstop around you like you're some crush." Jenna swirled her fork through her noodles, suddenly shy. "But, you know, I've always sorta wondered why you don't have more friends."

It was a bit of a blow, hearing that from Jenna. But it wasn't unfair—Melanie was always a bit off by herself. "I don't know. I guess I've spent a lot of time doing what other people want me to do, and other people don't fill out your social calendar for you."

Jenna pushed her bowl away. "I'm such an idiot. You invite me up here and I'm, like, psychoanalyzing you. Here, hold on a second, let me just train a bunch of lights on you and give you the third degree, okay?"

Melanie laughed despite herself.

"I think I left my waterboarding supplies out in the car." Jenna was on a roll now. "Mind if I bust those out later and torture you properly?"

Melanie spat out some of the water she'd been drinking. It was hard to say whether she actually found Jenna funny or if it was just the relief of escaping her own thoughts. It was nice to stop obsessing about car crashes and suicides for a minute.

"I'm actually really glad you came," Melanie said.

"Me, too. So . . . what are you going to do about Smiles and this bizarro letter?"

"Let's figure it out later." Melanie suddenly felt the long morning catching up to her. "I'm gonna crash for a half hour if you don't mind. The lake is super pretty right now if you want to go down for a walk."

"Sure, I'll be fine," Jenna said, and then her eyes brightened. "Oh my God, would you care if I took a bath in that tub?"

"Go for it."

Before the words were out of Melanie's mouth, Jenna was hurtling up the spiral staircase, overnight bag in hand.

⤴

As soon as Melanie lay down on the sofa, she knew it was pointless. Her dad called it being "too tired to sleep." It happened to him after late nights at the office. He'd come home and go through a whole wind-down ritual that usually involved Red Sox highlights and a glass or two of Cabernet; only then could he go to bed. Melanie would sometimes hear his heavy footsteps on the stairs in the middle of the night, and the sound of them would comfort her like a blanket.

She tossed the quilt off herself, crossed the zebra-hide rug of the living room, and returned to the kitchen for a glass of water. Through the window above the sink, the lake shimmered in the sunset. She had an idle thought about swimming to the floating dock alone for once, seeing how the world looked out there without Smiles at her side. She checked her phone out of habit, but he'd never called back.

She took the long way back to the living room, looking in on the lonely rooms of the house with the sounds of the tub filling audible from upstairs. Mr. Smylie's office had always seemed too important to enter. She stood at the doorway and remembered the last time the families had been up here together. Mr. Smylie had spent a lot of time in this office, finishing his book, *The Transparent Innovator*. The title was scrawled on a cardboard box on a chaise longue directly across from Melanie, next to an oversize globe.

It felt wrong to cross the threshold, but underneath the book's title, the box said *Pictures*. That was too much for her to resist. She tiptoed across the floor, plunked down on the chaise, and pried open the box flaps. Inside were three copies of the manuscript with varying amounts of red pen scrawled across them. Melanie flipped one open at random and smoothed her hand across a heavily marked page, amazed as always by Mr. Smylie's clean penmanship. His writing was like the fake handwriting on advertisements: pleasing to the eye, startlingly clear.

She pulled the manuscripts out and found three sets of pictures underneath. Each set was enclosed with a sheet of paper and bound up in rubber bands. The first sheet said *Final Cut*, the second said *Maybe*, and the last said *No*.

The maybes were the biggest group. Melanie unwrapped them and laughed out loud at a picture of her dad with long hair. His face was plump and boyish, his hair grown out in an awful grunge look, complete with flannel shirt. She flipped through pictures of Mr. Smylie—giving a business talk, pushing a five-year-old Smiles on his bike, unveiling the Alyce logo outside the company headquarters—and stopped on another picture of her dad. It had been taken in a Harvard dorm. He was playing a game of foosball with Mr. Smylie, twisting his then-thin body as he made a shot. It wasn't how young he looked that surprised her, or even how athletic he'd been. It was the joy on his face.

Melanie didn't think she'd ever seen him so genuinely happy. It might as well have been another person in that picture, and it reminded her again that she didn't really know her dad.

She put it away quickly, her good mood broken. She was stuffing the pictures back in the box when the small group of *No* pictures slipped from her hand and spilled onto the floor.

Melanie went to pick them up and gasped. Andrei Tarasov was looking up at her.

THERE WAS NO mistaking it—she remembered Tarasov's milky coloring and jet-black hair from the photo she'd seen in the HR file. He stood in an academic-looking hallway in a short-sleeved business shirt, nervous eyes staring into the camera. Two older men stood at his sides. On his right was Mr. Smylie, and on his left an even older man with one hand around Tarasov and the other holding a pipe. They all stood together at a half-open door to a professor's office.

The nameplate on it said WORTH.

✗

"Hello?" The voice was frail but good-humored, like his face.

Melanie had to collect herself. She had dialed the number that appeared in Northeastern's online directory, but hadn't really expected to get anybody on the line.

"Hello. Is this Professor Worth?"

"That's me," he said jovially. "I sure hope so, anyway."

His laugh descended into a series of hacking coughs.

"Are you okay, sir?"

"Quite, quite," Professor Worth said. "Just the old body giving out, nothing to be alarmed at. What can I do for you, dear?"

Melanie liked him already. "Well, sir, my name is Melanie Hunt and I, well . . ."

She was still crafting her approach, wishing she'd planned this out a bit more, when Professor Worth picked up the thread. "That wouldn't be Hunt as in Marshall Hunt?"

"Yes, actually. You know him, then?"

"Oh, certainly." More coughing.

Melanie had brought the three pictures from the *No* group out to the kitchen table with her. She thumbed through them, waiting for the professor to recover. "Are you sure you're okay?"

"It's nothing, child, just the standard convulsions. It's good for me, reminds me I'm alive. For the moment. What can I do for you, Ms. Hunt?"

"I'd like to talk to you, sir, if that's possible." It would be better to do this in person. Melanie did a quick mental review of her schedule for the next week and decided the world wouldn't end if she skipped a few classes. She had never actually done that before, but if anything called for it, this did. "Would you have any time to see me on Monday?" When he didn't answer she added, "It's very important, sir."

"My dear girl," Professor Worth said after a pause, "my schedule is entirely free on Monday. I have precious little to amuse me in my old age, and there's nothing I'd enjoy more than spending a few minutes in the company of a promising young woman. And you sound very promising indeed."

From the corner of her eye, Melanie saw Jenna bound down the spiral stairs and prance to the kitchen. Melanie held up a finger, doing her best to convey with her facial expression that she was talking to a charming-but-possibly-deranged math professor.

"Oh, well, thank you, Professor."

"My door shall be open and you are free to come at your leisure on Monday afternoon."

"That's great, I—"

"But I must advise you to think about something." His voice got stronger with the warning. "I have to assume, being the intelligent and inquisitive young woman you sound like, that you might want to ask this decrepit old man about some ancient history involving your father. Am I right, dear?"

"Actually, yes, you are."

"Has he been a good father to you? May I ask you that?"

Melanie had turned cold. There was something creepy about this, something that made her want to end the call. Still, she answered, "He has, yes."

"Indulge me, my dear. With age comes wisdom. And hear me when I say this: Sometimes it's best not to turn over every rock in a person's life. Especially if they've treated you well. If they have fed you and clothed you and provided you a comfortable life that you enjoy, one you would not wish to see compromised. So think hard before you come to see me. But if you do, know that my door will be open and your company welcomed by an old man."

"Okay, thank you, then." Melanie could barely talk anymore.

She hung up the phone like it was hot.

MELANIE DIDN'T KISS him like this. Not at all.

There was something hungry about it, something that made Smiles feel more desired than he'd ever been in his life. Erin gripped the scruff of his neck and pulled him toward her. Her lips were soft and yielding, her murmurs a hum of delight.

They had both been starving for each other, and the passion of it almost knocked Smiles out. The closest thing he could compare the feeling to was stealing drinks from his dad's liquor stash back in seventh grade—the feeling of having so much fun that you knew it had to be wrong.

He was losing himself in it all when the doorknob turned with a chunky metal sound. A woman in a blazer entered and walked briskly to the printer, giving them a cutting stare on her way. Smiles and Erin snuck an embarrassed look at each other as she eased off his lap.

The woman bustled to the printer and grabbed the waiting pages. "This is a *business center*," she said on her way out. The door closed, and then their laughter shattered the silence.

They couldn't enjoy the moment too long, though. "We need to set this up and get out of here," Smiles said.

Erin nodded. "Right."

✗

"Hello again," Smiles said. They had stayed in the business center for the call. Erin was watching the door.

"Who is this?" a smooth voice said. It was Cole, the one in charge.

"You know who it is," Smiles said. "Missing something?"

Cole didn't respond. Smiles gave Erin a thumbs-up.

"I think we probably have all we need." His voice dipped a few degrees, more threatening now. He was talking about Ben, of course, and it sent an unwelcome tingle through Smiles.

"I'd be surprised if that's the case. I think you'll find your passenger to be pretty stubborn. If you think you're going to get anything out of him, you'll be waiting for a long time."

Again Cole didn't respond. Smiles listened for sounds in the background, anything to suggest whether the agents were still in the minivan, and if so where they were headed.

"You're lucky, though," Smiles continued.

"Oh yeah, how's that?"

"I shouldn't be willing to do this. But I'm going to offer you another chance to get the cipher."

Smiles listened to the silence, and this time it was delicious. If the agents had any other options, they wouldn't be bothering with him. But Ben must have been holding out, not telling them a thing.

"Is there some kind of proposal here?" Cole said.

"Well, in light of recent events, the price has gone up." Erin shot him a look, but Smiles was feeling it. He had these guys. "It's going to cost you one hundred million now, and of course I'm going to need my associate back. Unharmed."

"He hasn't been touched," Cole said in a tone somewhere between bored and offended. "Where and when?"

Smiles knew they had to move. They'd be sitting ducks if they stayed at the casino. The first place that came to his mind was the Alyce Systems headquarters. "Tomorrow morning, ten o'clock, the corner of Water Street and Congress in Boston."

Smiles hung up before Cole could answer.

He closed his eyes, relieved, and felt a kiss on his cheek. "Got a little greedy, did you?"

Smiles shrugged, unable to hide his satisfaction with himself. "Let's get out of here."

For the first time since he'd found Ben gone, he felt on top of things. It was like he'd broken the surface of the water after being under for an hour.

He and Erin walked to the door. Before Smiles opened it, he asked, "You've got the cipher?"

"Yeah." Erin's hand reached across the spaghetti strap of her dress, grasping at the tan flesh of her shoulder where she normally carried her messenger bag. The panic in her eyes told him everything.

"You didn't leave—"

"With Zach," she said.

Together, they bolted from the business center and back down to Starbucks. Smiles scanned the tables three times over, but it was useless.

Zach was gone, and he had taken her bag with him.

"WE'RE REALLY SCREWED, huh?"

Smiles nodded. In fourteen hours they were supposed to give the agents the cipher, and they had no idea where it was. They bounced over a dark road in the Infiniti, searching for a safe place to hole up for the night.

"Try him again," Smiles said.

Erin barely got her phone to her ear before shaking her head. "Still turned off."

They had been trying his Zach's cell without luck since finding his hotel room predictably empty. They had burned away the afternoon at the Starbucks, hoping he might return. They both knew he wouldn't, though, and set out on the road a half hour ago. The sunlight was dying as the road before them narrowed, closed in by greenery and stands advertising sweet corn and strawberries. During the day, it might have been pretty. Smiles flicked on his lights, trying not to panic.

"There we go," Erin said, pointing into the distance.

It was called the Old Lantern, and it would have to do. They parked in a gravel lot, serenaded by bugs as they walked to a small office behind a tired screen door. It slammed shut behind them on nonexistent springs.

They checked in with a woman sporting fluorescent orange fingernails that matched her tube top. Smiles passed over his credit card and listened to the bleating of the crickets through the window screens. They sounded like a giant insistent clock, ticking off the seconds until their morning date with the government agents. Smiles didn't want to imagine what would happen to Ben if they didn't get the cipher by then.

The woman processed the transaction silently, keeping a good three-quarters of her attention fixed on a fuzzy broadcast of Anderson Cooper coming through a television fixed high on the office wall. She handed the keys over with a parting shot: "Pool's not open for another month, so don't even ask."

Maybe it was the power of suggestion, but Smiles and Erin headed right to the pool after dumping their bags and grabbing two Cokes from the vending machine. They sat with their legs dangling over the gutters, airborne in the dry bowl of the empty pool. The gunmetal concrete, spotted with round lights, made the far side of the pool look like a submarine.

Erin cracked her soda and unzipped the hoodie she'd thrown on in the car.

Smiles pointed to a NO SKINNY DIPPING sign. "Better keep your shirt on," he said.

"You should be so lucky," Erin said, and they laughed softly.

The situation had gotten too serious for any joking

beyond that. Smiles tried not to dwell on the increasing like-lihood that they weren't going to have the cipher anytime soon. He settled back and watched the crescent moon.

Ten minutes later their Cokes were gone and the crickets were still going at it. Erin had made a pillow of her hoodie and was lying on the pool deck. Her short T-shirt revealed a band of flat stomach, enough to distract Smiles from the troubles pressing down on him. A muted chime sounded from within Erin's hoodie and she sprang upright.

"Your phone?"

She pulled her legs from the pool and twisted her atten-tion to the hoodie. She dug through one pocket, then the other, and came out with her cell.

"It's Zach," she said, and then answered it on speaker-phone. "Hey," she snapped.

Her eyes shimmered with anger, and for a second, Smiles couldn't resist noticing how beautiful she was.

"Guess what I got?" Zach's voice said into the night.

"Where are you?"

"Oh, what, you want it back? Is your new man with you, 'cause it sounds like I'm on speaker." Erin threw Smiles a frustrated look. "I'll take that as a yes, and it's a good thing, actually. He should hear this."

"Just tell us where you are," Erin said.

"Hey, let me finish my thought here. You're always interrupting. Hey, Smiles—that's, like, your little nickname, right? That's something you should know about Erin. She always cuts you off before you get a sentence out. It's super annoying, man, you're gonna get really tired of it quick. Just, like, beware, is all I'm saying."

The guy was feeling his oats. There was nothing to do but let him circle around to the point eventually. But Smiles didn't like the overflowing confidence in his voice. If Zach knew as much about math as Erin said, he'd know just how valuable the thing in his possession was.

"So, anyway, man, kudos to you. I checked out what you got on that thumb drive. I mean, I can hardly believe this thing. A fast-factoring algorithm? Are you shitting me?"

Erin was gritting her teeth. "Look, just tell us where—"

"Oh my God! There she goes again! I swear, Smiles, that's gonna grate on you in, like, two-point-five seconds. You gotta nip that shit in the bud."

Erin's mouth drew tight. Above them, clouds drifted across the moon like lace.

"So aaaanyway, here's the score. I don't have a lot of money like you, man. I don't gamble in the high-roller section, know what I mean? But this thing in my hands is worth a lot of money. Like, *a lot*. And also, Alyce Systems would go up the second this thing became public. Which, I mean, I don't want *that* to happen."

A terrible, crushing feeling overcame Smiles then. It was far worse than he'd thought. He listened, waiting for the hammer to fall.

"So alls I'm asking is a measly ten million. Which, like, check between your sofa cushions and you'll get more than that. Otherwise, what I'm gonna do is post this on the Internet, and you can watch your dad's IPO go down the toilet."

Erin reached for Smiles. She knew how much was on the line—she knew Smiles would happily turn over whatever he had to keep this from getting out and ruining his dad's company. But he had to shake his head. He didn't have $10 million. All he had was the $50,000 check he'd gotten from Mr. Hunt.

"Zach, this is stupid. You're not getting ten million—"

"You guys talk it over. Weigh the costs and benefits, all that kind of stuff. See what you come up with. If I don't get ten million by Monday, this thing is going worldwide."

Then the line went dead, and Erin buried her head in Smiles's chest. There was nothing to say, and Smiles couldn't talk anyway. He watched the moon, wondering how he managed to screw up every single thing in his life. And now he'd put Alyce Systems itself in jeopardy. It was unthinkable. A shame like he'd never known penetrated his entire being.

"This is all my fault," Erin said. She grabbed up her hoodie and pulled it tight to her chest, one sleeve drooping to the ground. "I'm the one who told him about the cipher. He never would have known."

Smiles pulled her to him by her hoodie. "We're in this together."

"Smiles, I hate to say this, but he'll do it. He really will. He's crazy."

"I'm starting to pick that up."

"Do you want to call your dad?" Erin said, cringing. "And, like, warn him or something?"

"No." Smiles couldn't even think about that.

"But I mean, unless you have ten million dollars . . ." A car passed on the distant road. A line of shadow passed over her face, leaving it clear and bright in its wake.

"Yeah, I know. I know. I know."

He repeated it again and again. He stared into the gray pool, contemplating the mildewed drain at the bottom. If it had been full, he might have considered drowning himself there. Because he couldn't tell his dad, and he didn't have ten million dollars . . .

Smiles turned to Erin. He didn't have ten million dollars, but he had something else. They could get the cipher out of Zach's hands and turn around and sell it for ten times that. And get Ben back.

He almost smiled.

"Tell him we'll do it for seven," he said. "Seven million."

It'll be a bargain.

IT WAS TOO warm for flannel sheets.

They must have never changed them out for the spring, with Mr. Smylie being so sick for the last few months. Melanie didn't mind, though; the flannel sheets in in the bedroom she and Smiles used to sleep in reminded her of the winter nights they'd spent at the cabin together.

Jenna had set up in the master bedroom, where they'd roasted s'mores in the fireplace and talked the night away. Melanie had told Jenna about Professor Worth's comments, but not how much they'd frightened her. The further down this path she went, the more likely it seemed that her dad was involved in Rose's death. Her dad . . . a murderer? She pushed away the thought. She pushed and pushed, but it weighed on her as Jenna skipped on to other topics of her choosing: whether her boobs were too big to go with a strapless prom dress, the best graduation parties, and what college guys would be like.

College guys. Melanie had never put much thought into them. She was forever clinging to Smiles—and still doing it now, she realized, as she huddled in his bed without him even there.

She had brought a lantern with her to make the room cozier. She struck a match, lit the wick, and watched the warm light casting on the walls. She and Smiles loved setting up the lantern, but it didn't have the same effect tonight.

You can't live in a scrapbook, Melanie told herself as her cell went off.

Her heart quickened at the thought that it might be Smiles, but it was her dad again. He'd called three different times while she and Jenna were talking. Checking in on her trip to Smith College, she had figured, but now all the calls were starting to worry her even more. Had he somehow found out that she never made it to Katie's? Could he possibly know what she was up to—and was he trying to stop her?

She put down the phone without answering, wishing she could break it against the wall.

The three photos she'd taken from Mr. Smylie's office lay on the nightstand. The first was the shot of the three men: Andrei Tarasov, Mr. Smylie, and Professor Worth. She'd also taken a picture of her dad in his grunge phase for laughs, but nothing seemed funny anymore. The third picture she hadn't figured out yet.

Melanie bunched the pillows under her head and held the third picture in the flickering light. Tarasov and Mr. Smylie were in this one, too. It was a happy scene of a picnic, and there were two people in the picture with them: a gorgeous woman with olive skin and a small child. The woman was bouncing the baby on her knee, smiling in the direction of Tarasov and Mr. Smylie with a look you would give to the love of your life.

The baby had a toy truck in his hand. Melanie couldn't make out his face; only half of it showed in the aging, curling picture.

Melanie couldn't help wondering if the baby was Smiles.

Of course you can't, Mel. Everything comes back to him for you.

"The mathematician is entirely free, within
the limits of his imagination, to construct
what worlds he pleases."
—John William Navin Sullivan,
Aspects of Science

SUNDAY

"I was gambling in Havana
I took a little risk
Send lawyers, guns, and money
Dad, get me out of this."
—Warren Zevon,
"Lawyers, Guns and Money"

SMILES SHIFTED IN the driver's seat as they exited the freeway. The saggy bed in the hotel room hadn't exactly done wonders for his back. He probably would have done better to sleep in the Infiniti, which offered all the lumbar support one could ever desire. As if to prove the point, Erin was crashed out in the warm embrace of the black leather passenger's seat beside him, snoring away.

Smiles wanted to get to the meeting point early, which had unfortunately meant getting up before seven o'clock for the second time this weekend—easily some kind of record. He made a mental note never to schedule a meeting before eleven o'clock again in his life.

The GPS dumped him onto Atlantic Avenue. They were deep into the city now, but it still felt like Sunday morning. Leaves were filling out the trees on the Rose Kennedy Greenway, and a long formation of bikers pedaled across the intersection ahead of him, undisturbed by traffic. Smiles hung a left on Pearl and shut off the navigation; he knew where he was going now.

The office buildings grew taller with each block, casting the Infiniti in shadow and dropping the temperature a few degrees, as he drove toward the heart of downtown and the Alyce Systems headquarters.

He saw the sculpture first—the two keys of the Alyce Systems logo. It made him think again of the explanation of his dad's encryption system. The gate and the door, public keys and private keys. The dashboard clock said they had a half hour before the meeting, where Smiles was supposed to get Ben in exchange for the cipher.

That wasn't going to happen this morning—but amazingly, getting Ben back didn't even seem like his biggest problem at the moment. First, they needed to get the cipher from Zach and ensure that Alyce Systems didn't come crumbling down right before the IPO. And in order to do *that*, they needed to get their hands on Smiles's trust fund. *First things first*, Smiles told himself before he passed out from the pressure.

Zach had agreed to the $7 million price, so now the only problem was accessing his trust money. Smiles didn't have the first clue how he was going to do that yet; he wasn't supposed to get all of it until he turned twenty-five.

He could just make out the sculpture down the narrow corridor of Water Street. It loomed larger with each block, until he got to the wide intersection with Congress Street and could see it in its full majesty. Directly behind the sculpture, the mirrored tower of the Alyce Systems headquarters rose even higher, reflecting back the imposing bronze logo and the soaring office buildings around it.

Smiles didn't wake Erin up. He slowed through the irregular intersection, where three different streets came together. Seeing no sign of the agents, he took one-way streets in a circuit around the triangular park at Post Office Square. The tip of the park formed one wedge of the intersection, and as Smiles returned to it he tucked the Infiniti into a parking space that offered a decent view of the crossroads.

He turned the radio on low, and obviously the first thing that came on was a newsbreak about Alyce Systems. They were counting down the hours until ten a.m. on Tuesday, when the company would begin trading. The reporter was talking about how last-minute leaks could have a big effect on the all-important opening-day trading. "This has been a very well-choreographed process for Alyce so far, and you'd expect nothing less from Robert Smylie. Even with questions swirling about his health, he retains a firm grasp on his company and any information that gets released. It will be interesting to see if that holds up for the next crucial forty-eight hours."

That's putting it mildly, Smiles thought. He snapped off the radio, suddenly starving. Unfortunately, he wasn't about to find a hot dog cart in operation at nine forty-five on a weekend—the coffee shop across the street would have to do. Five minutes later, he returned to the car with two steaming coffees and Danish-type things to get them through the morning.

The smell of the coffee roused Erin. She mumbled a thank-you as he passed one to her, enjoying the eye-rubbing routine that was apparently a major part of Erin's waking-up process.

"So, um, run this quote-unquote plan by me again," she said.

"First we're going to make sure they have Ben in one piece. Then we're going to go up there." He pointed to the heights of the Alyce Systems office building.

"To get your money?"

"To try, anyway."

"You're a little light on details, champ."

"We'll flesh it out as we go along."

"Sounds brilliant. What could possibly go wrong?"

Smiles touched her knee, nodding to the plaza. Agent Cole was strolling up in front of the key sculpture. The little dot in his cheek was undoubtedly a cherry cough drop. In his dark-sunglasses-and-suit combo, he might as well have been wearing a sandwich board that said FEDERAL AGENT ON DUTY.

Smiles whipped out his phone and Cole's number, which he'd kept on a scrap of hotel stationery since arranging the demonstration. Erin grabbed his hand before he could punch it in. "Star-six-seven first, to block it," she said.

Why didn't he think of this stuff? Smiles nodded and started over. Ten seconds later, Cole looked curiously at his pocket. He extracted his mobile, cocked his head at the blocked ID, and put it to his ear.

"That you?" he said, scouring the intersection. When his eyes swept past the Infiniti, Smiles and Erin shrunk down.

"Let me see that he's okay," Smiles said.

Cole did a 360-degree turn, looking slightly ridiculous now in his search for the caller. "Bring the cipher and you'll see him," he finally answered.

"You'll get it. Right now, I need to see he isn't hurt."

Cole's head levered skyward in annoyance. Smiles could feel Erin looking on at his side, her presence comforting and electric at the same time.

"The kid's never been better in his life," Cole said. "We want one thing, that's all we care about."

"You could have had it at the casino."

Cole leaned against a light post at the corner, relaxing into the conversation now. "We didn't know what you were about. We had to cover our bases."

"Cover your bases? Is that a euphemism for kidnapping?"

"Are you going to show up or not?" Cole said. "The kid's fine. He slept in a five-star hotel last night, if that'll ease your worries."

Smiles was weighing his next move when Cole craned his neck along Congress Street. His eyes fixed on something, then continued surveying. Smiles turned to the spot, and just as he saw it Erin's hand tightened over his knee. In a distant parking spot on Congress, Ben was sitting in the passenger's seat of an unmarked car, the other agent behind the wheel.

Ben looked fine, maybe even better than normal. His biggest care in the world seemed to be choosing what to select from the Dunkin' Donuts box on the dashboard. Next to him, the other agent—Gary—was offering him an orange juice. Ben shook his head and started in on a bear claw.

Cole was right. These guys might be dangerous, but they weren't violent—they were rational and after only one thing. Ben would be all right for another day. Smiles sure hoped so, anyway.

"Still there?" Cole said.

"The Prudential Center, tomorrow at four," Smiles said, and clicked off.

THE ELEVATOR WAS whisking them to the thirty-fourth floor at a pretty good clip, and a distinct about-to-puke feeling was overtaking Smiles. It wasn't motion sickness exactly; it was more the thought of telling Erin about Melanie. That was the last thing he wanted to do, but they were about to talk to Mr. Hunt, and the topic of his daughter was sure to come up. Didn't he have enough problems to deal with?

It was Sunday morning, and the lobby of the building—a cavernous space with long shafts of sunlight angling down through its glass entrance—had been empty when they arrived. The black-veined marble of the white lobby floor wore a glossy shine, buffed to perfection by a janitor at a stand-up polishing machine. The only two people in the football-field-sized lobby had been the janitor and the security guard, who hadn't recognized Smiles and didn't seem overly impressed when he dropped his name.

"We're here to see Mr. Hunt," Smiles had said, while the security guard conducted a microscopic examination of their IDs. *Dude missed his calling as a bouncer*, Smiles had thought, before the guard finally opened a directory, picked up a red phone, and dialed upstairs.

Weekend or not, Smiles knew that with the IPO just two days away, Mr. Hunt would be in.

He must have picked up, too, because after a short conversation the guard had brought them to the executive elevator bank, inserted a security card, and sent them on their speeding way to the top floor. The thing was hurtling skyward so fast, Smiles thought he might actually catch air when it stopped. Instead, he experienced only the queasy anticipation of coming clean about Melanie.

Erin must have read something on his face. "You'll figure something out," she said as they stepped off the elevator. She thought he was worried about how he was going to get his $7 million, which was a pretty big problem in its own right.

Smiles gave in and turned to her. "So, uh, look, there's something I should probably—"

"Oh, boy."

"What?"

"I know that tone of voice," she said with a sidelong stare. "It pairs well with breakups and talk of other girls who've stolen your heart. Why don't you save this episode of *True Confessions* for later? You've got a job to do here."

Smiles couldn't help it. He kissed her. "Let's do it," he said, and walked decisively down the corridor. When they made the turn at the end of the hall, they could see the sizable shadow of Mr. Hunt behind the frosted glass of his office.

"That him?" Erin said as they approached.

Smiles nodded. "Cross your fingers."

Mr. Hunt always heard him coming, but today Smiles had to knock. There was no booming greeting, either, just a tired hand waving them inside. The forced smile on his face was ragged. You rarely caught him with his tie loosened and sleeves rolled up, as they were today. And never with the stubble that peppered his cheeks. Seeing the bags under his eyes, Smiles wondered if he'd been up all night preparing for the IPO.

"C'mon in," Mr. Hunt said. He stayed put behind his desk and gestured lazily to the chairs in front of it.

"This is Erin," Smiles said as they sat down. Then he added, just to fill the prolonged moment in which Mr. Hunt stared blankly at her, "A friend of mine."

It wasn't like Mr. Hunt to be unfriendly, but he acknowledged Erin with only a brief dip of his head. "I'm glad you're here, actually," he said to Smiles. "I wanted to ask you if you'd seen Melanie this weekend."

Of course—she had to come up right out of the gate. From the corner of his eye, Smiles saw a rueful smile cross Erin's face. "Yeah, uh, well actually, things didn't go so great the last time I saw her. But that was Thursday night."

"And you haven't heard from her since?"

"Nope," Smiles said. He didn't really want to dive into this subject, but these questions seemed a little odd. "Wasn't she going to Brown this weekend?"

"Smith College."

"Right, right." Smiles totally should have known that— Melanie had been talking about it for weeks.

"I got a call from her friend up there. Apparently she didn't make it." Mr. Hunt pinched at his eyes, and Smiles could now understand the source of his stress. "It's fine. I was a senior once—she's probably just with friends from school." Mr. Hunt didn't believe it for a second, and neither did Smiles. It wasn't like Melanie to take off without telling anyone.

Before he could consider it further, two businessmen swept into the office without knocking, one of them heaving a giant stack of documents. They stopped short at the sight of Smiles and Erin.

"Should we come back?" the guy with the documents said. He was almost lost behind them.

"Just five minutes." Mr. Hunt watched them go, then rolled his eyes for Smiles. "Investment bankers. Those people don't come cheap, let me tell you. Anyway, what brings you downtown?"

"Well, it's actually kind of an emergency. It's about my trust." Mr. Hunt's head reared backward at that, a line creasing his forehead. "If I, uh, hypothetically, needed to get all of the money in my trust fund now—like, immediately— would there be any way to do that?"

Mr. Hunt's eyebrows rose in growing disbelief as Smiles asked the question. "That's quite a request. And it doesn't sound too hypothetical."

"Yeah, umm, I guess it's not."

"Well, if we're talking about your money, that's a private matter." His eyes bounced to Erin and back.

"Oh, she's cool, Mr.—"

"It's fine," Erin said, already up and headed for the door. She left with a small wave.

He swiveled back around to find Mr. Hunt giving him a look. "You move pretty fast."

Oh boy. "Yeah, about that . . . It's not really . . . I mean, we hardly even . . ."

Smiles was fumbling so badly that apparently even Mr. Hunt took pity. "I'm giving you a hard time. You aren't married—you're a teenager."

"Yeah, but I mean, I'd never want to hurt Melanie or anything. Did she tell you she broke up with me on Thursday night?"

Mr. Hunt rolled his shoulders. "She hasn't been telling me a lot lately. Anyway, you're family to me, no matter what's going on with Melanie." That distracted look was on his face again, and Smiles wondered again what could have led Melanie to go off without telling him—and where exactly she would go. "But as for your question, the answer's easy: no."

"No way at all? There aren't any exceptions? Or some kind of loophole?"

Mr. Hunt just laughed. "No, there's no magic loophole. What in the world are you asking this for, anyway?"

There was no way Smiles was going to explain it all. Even if Mr. Hunt believed him, it would just drag another person into the whole thing. "Look," Smiles said, "I know how crazy this must sound, but all I can say is that it's incredibly urgent that I get that money. It's, like, a life-and-death-type situation."

"A life-and-death situation that has nothing to do with Melanie, I hope."

Smiles shook his head. "I'm serious, she officially hates my guts. She doesn't want to be anywhere near me."

Mr. Hunt grabbed a Diet Pepsi from the mini fridge under his desk. He pulled the can open with a sharp crack, shooting a fine mist into the air. "Don't take offense to this, but I don't think I even want to know what you've gotten yourself into. It's immaterial to your question, in any case. The terms of the trust are clear. You get the defined allowances until you're twenty-five, at which time you get the balance."

So the answer was clear enough—no chance—but Smiles couldn't accept defeat yet. With a glance to the front of the office, he could make out Erin sitting in the hallway, her back a dark shadow against the frosted glass. She believed in him, anyway. She was the only one who knew how much rode on this conversation—the future of Alyce Systems, the safety of Ben. He couldn't let it drop.

"There has to be a way, doesn't there?"

"No." It was a quick answer, with a touch of exasperation. "A trust is a contract, Smiles. You can't get around its terms just because you want to very badly. I mean, of course . . ."

"Of course what?"

Mr. Hunt closed his eyes, like a man who had just

opened a can of worms. Smiles felt his pulse surge. He could only hope that his $7 million was lying somewhere beneath those worms.

"Of course what?" he insisted.

"Well, a trust *is* a contract, and you have to follow the terms that are written. But like any contract, those terms can be changed."

"Changed to give me all of my money right now?"

Mr. Hunt shrugged unhappily. This was it.

"How do we change it?" Smiles said.

"*You* can't change it. Your dad would have to."

"Okay, whatever—how does my dad change it?"

Mr. Hunt held the can of Diet Pepsi to his forehead. "Your dad is in the hospital. Your dad is seriously ill—I'm sure I don't have to remind you."

"I have to do this, Mr. Hunt. How does my dad change the trust?"

Mr. Hunt checked his watch. "Smiles, I have some things I really need to attend to this afternoon, not to mention things being crazy with the IPO. Could we—"

"Just tell me and I'll go." Smiles stood at the desk. A battle of wills was going on, and after a few moments a light went out in Mr. Hunt's eyes and Smiles knew he'd won. He might have Melanie to thank for that—the stress of her weekend jaunt had obviously sapped all of Mr. Hunt's strength.

Mr. Hunt broke off the stare and turned to the mahogany drawers built into the bookshelves with the Celtics basketball and his model cars. He returned to the desk with a stapled document that Smiles could see was his trust agreement. Mr. Hunt flipped through to the back, where his dad's original signature appeared in blue ink.

He scoured the pages, marked a particular clause with his finger, and wheeled his chair over to his computer. Shaking his head in disgust, Mr. Hunt typed rapid-fire into his computer for a short while and then clicked his mouse decisively. A single page spat from a printer behind him. Mr. Hunt retrieved it, then held the page to his chest before handing it over.

"You remember, I hope, our conversation before. Your dad has given everything to his charities. There's no more money for you after this, period."

Smiles nodded—anything to get on with it.

"Don't think the IPO is going to change anything, either," Mr. Hunt said. "There's been a lot of talk about people getting rich when Alyce goes public, but son, I'm telling you this for your own good: You aren't one of them. Your father still has a majority of the voting shares in the company, but none of those is yours—now or when your dad dies. He wants you to be your own man."

Smiles absorbed the hurt. Mr. Hunt was doing this intentionally—reminding him what a nothing he was so he'd cling to his trust fund. Still, it didn't make it any less true. If Alyce survived the next two days, Smiles was going to be cut out of it for good.

"I understand." Smiles reached for the page, but Mr. Hunt clutched it tighter.

"If you won't consider yourself, think of your dad. The

last thing he needs is the kind of trauma that asking him to sign this would cause him. On both a financial and personal level, I'm advising you that it's a mistake you'd regret for a very long time."

"Can I have it now?" Smiles said.

⤝

Erin read it on their way to the elevators. It was only a few lines long, with a space for his dad's signature at the bottom. Smiles didn't really care about the details. He'd taken a glance and seen enough legal mumbo jumbo ("This amendment shall supersede any and all prior conflicting provisions, including but not limited to" *yada yada yada*) to convince him that it would get the job done.

Erin flicked the page as Smiles pressed the elevator button.

"You did it."

Smiles couldn't quite match her excitement. Mr. Hunt's speech had turned him sour.

"I still gotta get my dad to sign the thing," he said.

"One step at a time," she said.

Smiles nodded. "So, uh, listen. Shoulda told you this before." He pointed back toward Mr. Hunt's office. "His daughter is sorta my girlfriend. Ex-girlfriend. She broke—"

"Smiles."

The elevator arrived right as she interrupted him. Its doors slid open, inviting them in. Neither of them moved.

"What?"

"I don't care." Erin took two long steps to him, until

she was looking up from right under his chin. She looked like the pixie he'd seen at the casino reception desk—the girl with the starfish scar, the honey-colored eyes. The heat seeker. The girl he couldn't believe was talking to him.

"It's you and me now," she said. "Screw everybody else."

They made out the whole way down.

SMILES COULDN'T BRING himself to do it, not just yet. The page was right in his back pocket, but he couldn't make himself pull it out and ask his dad to sign it.

Smiles had taken his regular seat at his dad's bedside, the one by the picture of his mom. It was the only part of this visit going according to script—everything else was terribly wrong. In the two days Smiles had been away, his dad's complexion had faded to a shocking, ashen gray. He wasn't even listening to his classical music anymore. Worst of all was the fact that his dad had turned into a different person. The ball of emotion collecting in Smiles's throat felt like it was going to choke him.

It had started as soon as he stepped into the room five minutes ago. Before he could even say hello, his dad had bellowed, *"About time! Where have you been?"*

Smiles halted, trembling inside. Shanti had warned him it was a bad day, but he hadn't been prepared. Not for the person in the hospital bed—the rageful man inhabiting the body of his calm, collected dad.

"Sorry," Smiles had mumbled, and walked carefully to his seat. His dad had a right to be upset—Smiles probably should have checked in a few more times over the weekend—but he'd never been one to yell. *Don't take it personally,* Smiles told himself. *It's the cancer—changing his brain, affecting his mood.* The doctors had told him this could happen, but so far the scariest effect Smiles had witnessed was the memory loss. This was something different, and it didn't matter whether he'd been warned by the doctors or not—it shook him.

As Smiles began explaining that he'd taken a last-minute trip with a friend (he left out the casino part), his dad suddenly seemed to remember himself. The anger leaked out of his eyes, replaced with confusion . . . and then shame. He covered his face and began to shudder.

As his dad wept into his hands, Smiles checked Erin in the hallway. He was glad he'd left her out there—things were screwed up plenty without adding anything else into the mix. She mouthed the words, *You okay?*

He nodded a yes and felt more in control of himself. Going to the foot of his dad's bed, he spun through the vast collection of classical music on his dad's iPod.

At the front of the room, the green-screen setup had grown more elaborate. A glass podium with a microphone had been placed over an X of duct tape on the floor. A glass panel faced the podium, and at the edge of the setup were three oversize monitors. Smiles assumed the panel was a teleprompter, and he worried that the pressure of the IPO was doing all of this to his dad's brain. If Zach leaked the cipher before Smiles could stop him, what would that do to his dad?

Smiles turned back to the iPod and chose a random symphony heavy on the violins. By the time he got back to his seat, the music had brought his dad around a little bit.

"Oh, thank you," his dad said, finally emerging from behind his hands. "I don't know where that came from."

He hung his head in embarrassment, turning Smiles's world upside down. Smiles was the messed-up one; his dad was the one with his crap together. It had always been that way, and Smiles realized now that he'd liked it like that.

"Dad, it's all right. I know that's not you." Smiles cringed inside—another moronic bedside platitude. They were all that seemed to come out of his mouth around here.

"You've had problems, but you're a good son. You don't deserve any of this." Smiles didn't even know what he was talking about—the cancer, his mom dying, or maybe all of it. Tears welled at the corners of his dad's eyes, and Smiles wished it would all stop. This was almost worse than getting yelled at. This Overly Emotional Dad was no more his own father than the one who'd barked at him when he entered.

Smiles shifted in his seat and felt the folded page from Mr. Hunt's office crinkle in his pocket. He had to get his dad to sign it, but it didn't feel right just yet. All Smiles cared about now was protecting Alyce Systems, but it still felt somehow like he was taking advantage of the man before

He tried to draw strength from the image of his mom. In the picture, she carried a flute of champagne in her hand.

She was holding it out for balance, laughing inside a ring of flower girls she'd been leading in a dance. Her eyes were drawn to creases by the huge smile on her face. It was a black-and-white photo, and Smiles knew from her exhaustive cataloging of the family albums that if he turned it over he would find a handwritten description on the back. *Robert and Rose's wedding day*, it would say in her big chunky handwriting. Or *Rose dancing with flower girls*. Or *Rose, your mom, gone from the world but never your heart.*

Smiles found himself wishing for a last glimpse of her brilliant green eyes. He wished he could hear the encouragement she would give him now.

Get over yourself and get your dad to sign that thing. He's having a bad day—we've all had them, cancer or not. You need to do this to save Alyce Systems. And to save your friend. I mean, forget how you got into this. Forget that you started all this as a shortcut path to self-respect, and that it got your friend kidnapped and put the entire company in jeopardy. Even though I sorta warned you about that. I mean, I did. So listen to your mom: What's important right now is that you save your dad's company. Just get him to sign the thing.

Smiles shook his head free—it hadn't helped quite as much as he thought it would.

His dad was mumbling to himself now. He'd gone from angry to sentimental to whatever this third stage was. Confused? Incoherent? Smiles only knew that he had to get out of this room before he lost his own mind. "You're a good son," he heard his dad say amid a stream of babble.

Smiles didn't know what to do, until a last uninvited comment from his mom sounded in his head: *Being honest is the best gift you can give to someone.* It was a motto of sorts; she'd used it on him several times when she knew he'd lied about something.

Smiles suddenly felt centered. He knew what was getting in the way of asking his dad this last favor—he had to cleanse himself first. He held his dad's hand.

"Dad, I . . ." Smiles cleared his throat. A cool glass of water would help at this particular moment, he thought. That or maybe some appropriate words on the teleprompter. "I'm actually not a very good son, you know," he said. "Or I haven't been, anyway."

His dad's face went still, and Smiles became a torrent of confessions. How he'd gone on spring break to Cancun instead of lacrosse camp; how he used to drive his dad's car when he was out of town; how the weed that got him kicked out of Kingsley Prep hadn't just been Darby Fisher's—half of it had been his own. How he couldn't stand living in Weston because he always felt nervous around his dad. How he'd never loved him the way he should. "I'm not smart enough to figure myself out, but I've always resented you. That's terrible, I know, and it's not your fault at all."

Had he understood any of it? Smiles wasn't sure until his dad shook his head. "Doesn't matter," he said softly.

"Dad," Smiles said, gripping his hand firmly now, ready to do what he'd come for. "There's something else I want to tell you." He gave him the background in broad strokes: Ben's discovery, and the danger his algorithm presented to his dad's encryption method. His dad listened passively, his concentration straying. Smiles forged on, determined.

"I can't explain all the details," he said, gliding over the small matter of Ben's kidnapping and Zach holding the cipher for ransom. "But I've got a chance to put everything right." He retrieved the page from his pocket and looked directly at his father, something he rarely did. "I need you to sign this."

Smiles laid the page on the blanket over his dad's legs. Slapping at his pockets, he realized he'd forgotten to bring a pen. But then Erin appeared at his side, Bic in hand. "Thanks," Smiles whispered, and she retreated as quickly as she'd come.

His dad's eyes followed her out of the room. "Melanie?"

Smiles nodded awkwardly. It felt like he was betraying Melanie, Erin, and his father with a single move of his neck. But there was no time to get into his love life now. He raised the pen.

His dad didn't take it. For a long minute, he held the page in his good hand and read it over again. Or did an impression of reading it over—it was hard to tell what was registering anymore. At last he turned his head up and motioned for the pen.

"You read the letter, then?" he said. "You got the package?"

The letter he'd asked Mr. Hunt to destroy, the package that may or may not even exist. Smiles swallowed around the lump in his throat. "Yeah."

The feeling of betrayal sunk deeper into his heart. *It's*

the only way to get through this, Smiles told himself. *Let him think you got her letter. You don't want to read anything from her anyway, and you don't have time for a talk about memory loss.*

"I named the company after her, you know?"

"Yeah, Dad. That was nice."

The scars of their conversations hadn't healed, and Smiles felt them fresh all over again. *It's better left alone*, she had said. *It's a case of bad timing*, she had said. *It's better left alone. I'll have to end this call now.* He didn't want to think about her anymore. He had a mom, and she was beautiful—she was laughing in a ring of flower girls at his side.

"People do their best," his dad said. "They do their best and they make terrible mistakes."

Then he signed the page.

MELANIE WAS HAVING more fun than she'd had in weeks. Jenna had convinced her to go swimming, even though the lake wouldn't be comfortably warm for another month. They got dressed in T-shirts and running shorts, raced across the lawn to the water's edge, and leapt in before they could change their minds. The bracing water had literally taken Melanie's breath away. She had to tread water for a good minute until her chest relaxed enough to get a decent lungful of air.

And then, after the shock had passed through her system, it was great. Jenna dog-paddled out, smiling despite the violent chatter of her teeth. Her lips had turned three different shades of purple already. As she took a last stroke toward Melanie, she cackled and tossed a string of algae off her arm.

"Holy crap is this gorgeous," Jenna said with shortened breath, twirling to take in the sun-dappled, tree-lined beauty of Squam Lake. She was a surprisingly good swimmer, treading water with practiced ease while Melanie bobbed up and down with each sloppy kick of her legs. "Any sand-bars out here?" Jenna said.

There were. "That way," Melanie said.

Jenna made it out first, standing waist-deep by the time Melanie arrived. The air was still, the sky cloudless. The lake mirrored back the lofty trees along the shoreline and powder-blue sky above. It was the kind of beauty that shut you up and made you stare at it.

The sun had dried their arms by the time they decided to head for shore. Jenna dove from the sandbar but Melanie held back, extending the moment. She used to feel like this when she and Smiles swam to the floating dock—wishing she could freeze time, halt the turn of the Earth and hold off her return to the world. It was more pronounced today, because going back meant diving into the mystery of Smiles's letter again. Into the mystery of her father.

Melanie hadn't made much progress on her investigation, and she'd found it easy to give in when Jenna suggested they go swimming instead of doing more research on Professor Worth, who remained her single lead. Only the thought of the hot tub got her to push off and plunge back into the cold water.

They had started up the hot tub the night before (Jenna insisted), and now Melanie was glad for it. It was set into the deck behind Mr. Smylie's house, and steam wafted from the gurgling water as they dipped in. It always felt best after you'd earned it—after a long run or a swim in the lake. Melanie closed her eyes and sunk to her chin, finding a good spot against a jet. The water smelled faintly of chlorine, but beneath it she could still smell the pine trees.

"This is the life," Jenna said. She let her legs float out from underneath her and wriggled her purple-painted toes when they broke the surface.

Melanie was on the verge of saying something cheesy about Jenna being a good friend when they both heard a *tinking* sound from the direction of the house.

Melanie was struck with a sudden fear that Mr. Smylie had been released from the hospital and decided to come up to the cabin to recoup. It would be so embarrassing if he found her there without Smiles—she and Jenna had basically broken in to the place. Or maybe some real robbers had come, she thought, and she would be responsible for having left the house open and unattended.

Tink, tink, tink. Louder now.

The thoughts whirled through her mind, spinning her into a frenzy, as she half stood in the hot tub and scanned the back of the house for the source of the sound. Sunlight glanced off the windows, obscuring them in glare. But it was unmistakable when she saw it, and it was worse than any of her imaginings.

"Mel, is that—?"

"Yes."

Yes it was. The air had gone out of her again, more forcefully than it had when she dove into the water. It was her dad at the kitchen window, rapping on it with a key, looking as angry as she'd ever seen him.

"WE SHOULDN'T STAY here too long," Smiles said as he shut the door to his apartment.

Erin walked into the kitchen, accidentally kicking over a collection of Cap'n Crunch boxes Smiles had left by the garbage can. A stray crunchberry rolled over the tiles and lodged under the refrigerator. Erin perched on the kitchen counter, looking beneath the overhead cabinets to the living room. "You're right, we shouldn't—this place is a sty."

"I meant because the agents could track us here. They might know my name by now, and Ben lives right next door."

"I know, I was kidding. Sort of. You've heard of maids, right? For a small price they come to your place and clean up this matter called dirt, which you seem to have—"

"Hilarious." Smiles could feel his cheeks redden as he rummaged through the front closet for fish food. He wished he had something more substantial for the dragon eel, but the best he could come up with were some algae discs and shrimp pellets.

Erin kept at it while he made his way around the tanks.

"I mean, you could even do it yourself. You'd have to become familiar with these things called sponges, and also a whole variety of cleaning products, but that would come. It may seem intimidating at first, but it's nothing beyond your ability to—"

"You should totally show me," Smiles called out as he watched a shrimp pellet sway to the bottom of his hundred-gallon tank. The dragon eel didn't move for it; he was still in hibernation mode. "Really show me how to do it right, you know, since I'm not familiar with these advanced concepts you're talking about. I'll take notes and stuff."

He was speaking loud enough for her to hear in the kitchen, but as he watched the dragon eel huddle among the rocks he felt Erin's hands slither around his stomach. Smiles turned in her arms.

"My bedroom's quite a bit cleaner, you know."

"You don't say?"

"Immaculate. You should see it."

Erin backed away, toying with him. "So what's with the fish, anyway?"

Smiles wasn't sure why, but something in her voice made him uneasy. "I don't know. I like looking at 'em. Don't you?"

"I just thought people lost interest in aquariums around eighth grade. I mean, you do realize that fish are meant to roam large bodies of water, not this little prison cell here?" Her hand caressed the glass, like she was trying to soothe them. "You're like a fish warden, that's what you are."

Smiles had absolutely no idea if she was serious or not. "I always thought they had it pretty good," he said feebly.

"Good? These guys are trapped."

Smiles should have known by now: Putting a move on a girl by the fish tank never worked out for him.

"Well, I suppose we could debate fish justice all day," Erin said, "but don't you have a phone call to make?"

He did. Smiles needed to get in touch with the dude at the bank who handled the trust, to get everything set for tomorrow. Luckily, the guy's name was on the papers Smiles received from Mr. Hunt on Thursday—they couldn't have gotten lost that quickly. Smiles picked the phone up off the carpet.

"Give me ten minutes," he said, hoping she'd get over her fish issue by the time he returned.

The hardest part about the call was finding the papers Mr. Hunt had given him. After that, it went amazingly well. The bank dude's name was Nicholas Perry, and he had a mobile contact on his business card, which Smiles found after a thorough ransacking of his bedroom. (Only after a mental reenactment of Thursday afternoon did Smiles realize he'd crashed on his bed with the papers in his hand, leading him to their hiding place between his comforter and the wall.)

Mr. Perry was at his three-year-old son's birthday party, which might have explained why he asked only a few distracted questions of Smiles before telling him the transaction wouldn't pose too much of a problem. It was fine if he wanted to come by early, Mr. Perry said over a chorus of kazoos. The bank opened at nine.

Smiles clicked off the phone and fell back on the bed,

hardly able to believe what he was on the verge of doing. Just last night he'd been faced with an impossible task, and by ten a.m. tomorrow he was going to have accomplished it. He stared at the ceiling with an unknown thrill in his heart, until he realized he shouldn't be feeling this good until the IPO went off okay and Ben was back in safe hands.

Erin knocked softly on the door and peeked her head in. "How goes it on the trust-fund front?" she said with a dash of tension lingering in her voice.

"All set for tomorrow." He lifted his hand in a What-can-I-say? kind of way.

"Hmm. Color me impressed." Erin looked the room over. "I'm afraid you oversold the cleanliness of your private quarters. And I think you're right—we need to get going. Any thoughts on where?"

It came to Smiles right away—it was perfect. "We've got a place on Squam Lake. No one will be there."

The hot tub will make everything better, Smiles thought.

IF THIS COULD be any more humiliating, Melanie wasn't sure how. She and Jenna trudged from the hot tub to the mudroom at the back of the house, where her dad waited with his arms crossed over his chest.

They didn't even have towels to cover themselves. They had to make their way in full view of him, wearing only their soaked shirts and shorts. Melanie could only imagine what he thought of this picture; they must have looked like they'd been holding their own private wet T-shirt competition. Or like they'd been off on some secret lesbian holiday.

Her dad held the door open as they walked to the cabin, wood chips clinging to their bare, wet feet. His mouth was a tight slash of anger.

"Get cleaned up and meet me in the kitchen," he said, and marched inside.

At least they'd left towels for themselves in the mud-room. Melanie tossed one to Jenna and grabbed the other for herself.

"This is really bad, huh?" Jenna whispered.

Melanie could only nod. Her brain was simultaneously

going a hundred miles an hour and unable to function. It was spinning in place—that's what it was doing.

Somehow, her dad had found out that she never made it up to Smith College. Melanie thought she was in the clear after checking in with Katie, but she should have known it would get back to her parents somehow. That explained all the calls last night. And now that he'd shown up, it was easy to see how he'd tracked her down. It wasn't even a matter of tracking—it was just logic. He knew the Smylies' cabin was one of her favorite places in the world. He knew she had access to the key. It would be the most obvious place to check for her.

And if he knew all that, he might know all the rest— that she'd been looking into the mystery letter, and Rose's death, and her dad's involvement in all of it.

Melanie hadn't been thinking straight at all these past few days.

She dried her hair as best she could, then wondered for a long time what to do about her basically transparent T-shirt. She settled on taking it off and wrapping the long towel below her armpits. Jenna followed suit.

"So he's, like, super mad? On a scale of one to ten, would you—"

"Oh, it's a ten," Melanie said. "I've never done anything like this before."

"I'll just tell him about my homecoming experience this year." Jenna smirked. "You'll look like the picture of maturity by comparison."

Melanie couldn't even muster a laugh, but she was more

thankful for Jenna than ever. "Time to face it," she said.

Her dad was sitting at the head of the kitchen table. He turned off his phone—a sure sign of the apocalypse—and used both hands to point at the chairs beside him. Melanie shrunk into her designated seat and summoned the courage to meet her dad's eyes. "Does Jenna have to be here? I'm the one who brought—"

"That's a yes, at least until I get some questions answered."

In the brief silence that followed, Melanie half hoped Jenna would start in with her homecoming story. Instead, her dad placed his elbows heavily on the table.

"You asked me," he said pointedly to Melanie, "about a former employee of Alyce the other morning."

Melanie held her head, rubbing her temples. This was the worst-case scenario. This wasn't just going to be about Melanie going off on her own for the weekend. It was about Andrei Tarasov, and whatever her dad had to do with him. The fact that he wasn't using Tarasov's name scared her all the more.

"I have a feeling this trip of yours has something to do with that question."

Melanie nodded, feeling small.

"Okay. And Jenna, do you know anything about this former employee?"

Melanie wanted to save her from the inquisition, but any hope that she could control the situation was long gone. Jenna shrugged. "Barely. I mean, neither of us knows very much at all."

"Well, what *do* you know about him?" He was directing the question at Melanie now. "Let's start there."

Her dad's careful wording was freaking Melanie out—he didn't want to say any more about Tarasov than he had to, so he was establishing the limits of their knowledge first. It was like some kind of lawyer's trick: figuring out the other side's evidence so you could fit your own story around it.

A small part of Melanie became angry with him—for lying to her about Tarasov in the first place, for causing her so much stress over the last few days, and for the possibility that he'd had something to do with the sudden death of Smiles's stepmom. And for the way he was treating her now. There was no kindness in his eyes, nothing parental in his voice. Looking at him, she saw only a man trying to save himself.

The seed of anger took root, and she decided not to spare him any details. "Well, we know that when I asked you about Andrei Tarasov—that's his name, you know—you lied about not remembering him. We know that because he died on Mr. Smylie's front lawn. Shot in the head, probably by himself, but who knows? I don't. Either way, it's not something you'd really forget."

Jenna eyes were nearly popping out of her head. They screamed at Melanie, *Umm, what exactly are you doing?*

Her dad retracted from the table and wiped at the sides of his mouth. He was furious. "You should be careful about what you're saying," he said, but the warning only grated further on her nerves. "Anything else?"

"Actually, yes," Melanie said, and saw Jenna shut her eyes in terror. "I know that Mr. Smylie's wife—Rose—

was in touch with you about something to do with Andrei Tarasov. Apparently you were putting her off for some reason. But then she suddenly died before she could do anything about it."

"Enough," her dad said sharply. He held his words for a moment, taking labored breaths through his nostrils. *He's going to have that heart attack after all*, Melanie thought.

"And you came here why?" he said at last.

"When I found all this out, I was pretty upset." Melanie tried to keep her tone even. "So I started looking into it. Why would my own dad lie to me about Andrei Tarasov, and Rose? I couldn't get it out of my head. Still can't, actually." Her dad didn't react. "I'm not going to Smith anyway, so I decided to ask Jenna up here to figure it out."

"It was more just a fun girls' weekend, really," Jenna said airily, scrunching her nose.

"And I don't suppose your parents know where you are, either?"

"They, uh, know I'm with Melanie, but they might sorta think we're at your house."

"We'll deal with that," he said, and Jenna cast a stone-faced look at the table. Melanie would really have to make this up to her someday. "For now," her dad said, "why don't you tell me what you've found out?"

"Nothing." It was true. Melanie's lame attempts at digging into the mystery had gotten her nowhere. She'd gotten warned off by a cop, looked at some pictures, and talked to a senile professor—that was about it. Scratch private investigator from her list of career options.

"Okay, then." Her dad had calmed down a little. He rose from the table and poured himself a glass of water from the refrigerator, looking out at the crisp spring day that had been ripped away from Melanie. Neither she nor Jenna dared to move from the table.

"You didn't find out anything because there's nothing to find out." Her dad sipped from his water, dragging his attention back from the lake. "Nothing except a sad story that would have been better left buried. But since the two of you haven't been able to leave it alone, I'll tell you."

"Dad, Jenna isn't really the one who—"

"She's not as much to blame as you, I know. But you're both here, and you're both going to keep what I say to yourselves. Right?"

Melanie murmured her agreement along with Jenna, getting her first inkling that this investigation may have been a colossal life mistake. Her dad drummed his fingers on the distressed wood of the table, finding a starting point for the story.

"Andrei was an extremely talented mathematician. A brilliant young man," her dad said. "He came to the United States and studied under Mr. Smylie at Harvard. And when Mr. Smylie received a government grant for a research project on encryption, he selected Andrei to help him. A great honor for any graduate student, that was. And do you know how Andrei repaid it?"

They found out that Tarasov had been stealing research and handing it over to the Russian government. Jenna's words from Friday's lunch played back to Melanie. "He spied for the Russians on the research project," she said with a blossoming sense of shame.

"Well, you know more than you said you did," her dad said. "He betrayed our country, and he betrayed Mr. Smylie in a very personal way. It could have ruined Mr. Smylie's career—would have, really, if his reputation hadn't been so good to begin with."

Melanie tightened the towel around her. She hadn't once thought of Mr. Smylie's feelings in this whole thing—the great Mr. Smylie, who revolutionized computers and was such a decent man on top of it all. *And for her next act, Melanie Hunt will dig needlessly into the secret past of Mahatma Gandhi.*

"Andrei was stopped, but it was all kept quiet. The government doesn't like to advertise that it has been spied on. He was deported, and if that had been all that happened, it would have been bad enough." Mr. Hunt seemed to be enjoying the reverent embarrassment on the faces of Melanie and Jenna. "But it got worse. A few years later, after Mr. Smylie started Alyce Systems, Andrei snuck back into the United States illegally under a new name, Tarasov, and got himself hired as a low-level programmer at Alyce."

A tiny gasp escaped from Jenna's mouth.

"But why?" Melanie said.

Her dad toyed with his empty glass. The moisture sang as he traced a finger around the rim. "He knew that Mr. Smylie was the one who discovered his spying, and he became obsessed with him. That happens to people, unfortunately. Something goes wrong in their life, and instead of addressing their own problems, they fixate on something external to them. For Andrei, that something was Mr. Smylie. It was very sad, and very scary for Mr. Smylie. We didn't realize he was working at Alyce until he shot himself on Mr. Smylie's front lawn. His way, I suppose, of making some kind of confused statement."

Jenna wore the solemn look of a funeralgoer. Melanie probably did, too. She couldn't help asking: "Dad, what was Rose doing asking you about Andrei?"

He shook his head. "That's the saddest part. At the very end, he was making elaborate claims about the great work he was doing and how he deserved to be running the company. It was all part of his unraveling. The first one to pay any attention to it was Mr. Smylie's first wife, Alice. You never knew her, but she was a soft-hearted person then. The kind of person who would try to understand a man like Andrei, even though there was nothing to understand. Of course the suicide right on their front lawn was extremely traumatic for them. She didn't respond well. I'm not a doctor, so I don't know if it'd be right to call her reaction a breakdown, but she left Mr. Smylie after that. Which, of course, only deepened the wounds that Andrei had inflicted."

"Oh, God," Jenna said, and then realized she'd spoken aloud. "So that's why you never talk about him, then?"

Mr. Hunt nodded. "To Mr. Smylie, Andrei represents the darkest time in his career and the failure of his first marriage all wrapped into one." Turning to Melanie, he said, "To answer your question, I think Rose learned about it from Alice. Though why Alice would want to stir up that trouble, I have no idea. And no, I wasn't eager to deal with it again."

"Of course," Melanie said. She would have apologized, but nothing she could say would even scratch at the depths of her embarrassment.

That happens to people, unfortunately. Something goes wrong in their life, and instead of addressing their own problems, they fixate on something external to them. Her dad had been talking about Tarasov, but he might as well have been talking about Melanie. Breaking up with Smiles was too much for her to deal with, so she had distracted herself by constructing a conspiracy theory with her dad at the center. It had nothing to do with anything except her own misplaced energy. Her time would have been better spent on UFO sightings. At least that way, she wouldn't have hurt her dad so much. A minute ago, she had been on the verge of accusing him of murder. Melanie wondered if, somewhere, there was a fast-moving bus that she could step in front of.

"Time to go," her dad said. "Get your things and I'll meet you out front. And Jenna, we're going to call your parents."

They made for the bedrooms on the spiral staircase, which no longer enthralled them the way it had when they'd arrived. Melanie apologized profusely to Jenna as they packed.

"It's okay, Mel," Jenna said, jamming clothes into her bag. "Glad we got all the real dirt, anyway. What a story."

"My God, you're nice," Melanie said.

She felt like she was defiling Mr. Smylie's house with her

mere presence in it. She couldn't wait to get out of the place. They bounded down the stairs with the Pollack in full view. *Happy now, Mel? Your life is as messy as that painting.*

They locked up and handed her dad the key on the front porch. Melanie was about to tell him about its hiding place out back when a car pulled up and her life got even messier.

It was Smiles. And he was with a girl.

"WHAT THE . . ."

Smiles had seen some odd things in the past couple of days, but the sight of Mr. Hunt, Melanie, and some bug-eyed chick standing together at the front of his dad's cabin had to be right up there. Highly unexpected, anyway. Not to mention awkward.

An encounter with Mr. Hunt was going to be uncomfortable enough after the way they'd left things at his office. The presence of Melanie, though, took it to another level. Smiles's flight instinct kicked in, but he'd pulled too far down the driveway to back out now. He shut off the engine in defeat. Erin stared through the windshield. "Is that Mr. Hunt?"

"Yep."

"So which one's your ex-girlfriend?"

"Give me some credit," Smiles said. "On the left."

"Hmm. Hottie. You reconsidering?"

It wasn't really Smiles's choice to reconsider—Melanie had been the one to break up with him—but he didn't point out that technicality. Instead he watched as Mr. Hunt directed the girls to Melanie's car, and then started walking to the Infiniti.

Erin cleared her throat. "This is where you say, 'No, are you crazy? Not in a million years.'"

"C'mon," Smiles said. "Let's see what's going on here."

He heard Erin sigh as he got out of the car. She joined him against the hood as Mr. Hunt approached. He was wearing aviator shades and a frown, both of which made his shuffle out to the Infiniti more imposing than it otherwise might have been. When he arrived, he held out a single key on a plastic chain with the Harvard shield. It was the key they kept in the fake rock out back. As soon as Smiles reached out his hand, Mr. Hunt dropped it and turned for his own car, all without a single word. It was pretty anticlimactic.

Melanie's taillights brightened first, then Mr. Hunt's. He drove a Bentley with white leather seats and an exterior blue color that was probably called something like Sapphire Dreams. It started up like distant thunder.

Smiles lurched toward the Bentley, his chance for an explanation escaping. "Mr. Hunt, wait. What are you doing here? What's going on!?"

Mr. Hunt ignored him. The Bentley slipped away, and Melanie followed. Smiles caught her eyes as she backed out. They were empty. A corner of her mouth turned up, but it wasn't a smile—she was holding off a cry.

"Mel, wait! What's the deal?"

Erin held him back by the shoulder. "Let 'em go, Smiles."

He did.

⨯

At least Operation Hot Tub was working. They had scraped together a dinner of hard pretzels and gourmet mustard and spent most of the night on the deck. At full dark Smiles told her it'd be a shame to let a good hot tub go to waste, and Erin had gone for it.

She dipped her shoulders under the water, giving him eyes with unfathomable sex appeal. Still, she kept to the opposite side of the hot tub, holding her distance. "So you know how I said I have a big ego?"

"Yeah."

"That's one fault. There's another one you should probably be aware of. I'm pretty good with the old self-sabotage routine. When I start thinking I might really like somebody? I start finding problems that aren't there. Like, just for instance, maybe criticizing their perfectly healthy and actually kind of adorable interest in domesticated fish."

"Ahhhh. Good, 'cause I like them."

"Right. So maybe if you could just wipe that episode from the record books? Or file it under Erin's Endearing Quirks or something?"

"Done," he said. "Any more faults I should know about?"

She pondered the stars theatrically. "Nope. Other than that, I am perfection."

"Just as I thought," he said, and then they were kissing. Eventually she pushed away from him with her feet.

"You never answered me earlier," she said.

"What?"

"About that girl. Wish you were still with her?"

"Nah," Smiles said. And actually, he didn't. Which was kind of weird. He'd known Melanie forever, lusted after her for almost as long. He wasn't feeling the need to be with her anymore, though, and Erin was the reason. She stretched her arms out along the lip of the hot tub. Her hair pooled at her shoulders, waving in the bubbling water.

"So why am I the lucky one? I want to hear it. Flatter me." She blinked her eyes at him, playing cute.

"Uh, you know, I'm not really good at talking about this stuff. I mean, why does anybody like anybody? You can't put it in words. You just do."

"Well, try. Because that last answer isn't doing much for me." She flicked water from her fingertips at him.

Smiles looked up at the stars, brighter out here than they ever were in Boston. The stars at Squam Lake always reminded him of the laser light show he'd gone to the first time he got truly stoned. He was feeling that kind of disoriented now. He was definitely into this girl, and if he wanted things to keep going well, he probably should give her some kind of answer.

"Okay, well, it's sort of hard to be with Melanie. It's, like, work. Not because she's high maintenance or anything. She's just this *perfect girl*, so it feels extra-bad if you're not winning the Nobel Peace Prize or something. It's different with you. You're . . ." Smiles reached for the rest of the sentence, realizing he'd painted himself into a corner.

"Far from perfect? Deeply flawed? Perhaps this is where we should review the meaning of 'flatter.' Would that be helpful?"

At least she was smiling. "Hey, I warned you I'd be bad at this," he said.

"Not *this* bad."

"Well, I always like to exceed expectations." Smiles pushed off from the wall and moved gently across the water. He grasped her hands and Erin pulled to the edge of the seat, their bodies half floating close to each other beneath the wisps of steam. "Okay, here goes," he said. "You know how I said I was a screwup? I meant that. I got kicked out of school last fall and pretty much have no clue where my life is going. My plans last for about twenty minutes each. Know why I can't settle on anything?"

Erin waited to hear it.

"Because the only thing that I've ever really wanted to do was to run my dad's company. It's been stuck in my head since I was little. It seems pretty dumb now, 'cause I don't know anything about computers or encryption or any of that. But it's all I could ever seriously imagine myself doing."

"So why don't you—"

Smiles shook his head. "I'm not gonna, like, go to college and, you know, cut to a *Rocky* montage of me studying up at night and turning into a brain. I'm not smart like that, but that doesn't even matter. The point is, I've had that idea fixed in my mind since I could walk. And I've always held on to a sliver of it. But when we were in Mr. Hunt's office, he told me it's not happening. For sure. None of my dad's stock is going to me—none of it. I'm not going to have anything to do with the company at all."

Erin rubbed her hand along his arm, but Smiles didn't

need to be soothed. "I'm not telling you for sympathy. I've known for a long time that my dad doesn't trust me like that—this just makes it official. I'm telling you because I *can*. If I said this to Melanie, it would just make me feel worse.

"I don't feel judged by you, understand?" he said. "I don't feel like you're waiting for me to screw up. I don't know how that sounds to you, but for me it's pretty awesome."

Erin nudged off the seat and hugged him. She whispered in his ear, "Oh, Smiles, you just exceeded my expectations."

⨯

She was waiting for him in the master bedroom. Smiles had stayed down in the kitchen, insisting on cleaning up their plates before they went to bed. Better to do it now than early tomorrow morning, when they'd have to get on the road to the bank. That's what he'd said, and it was true. But he was also thinking of Melanie's strange appearance at the cabin, and all those calls she'd left on his phone. Something real was happening with Erin tonight, and Smiles had a feeling that he owed it to Melanie to hear her out before things went any further.

He put the last dish away and dialed voice mail, cringing inside. A string of messages in which Melanie stated her desperate case for getting back together weren't going to make fun listening. He shouldn't have been worried; in the three voice mails she'd left, she hadn't brought up their relationship once.

Instead, Smiles listened gape-jawed as Melanie's static-ridden voice told him what she'd been up to the last couple of days. The girl had gone nuts. First, she had *broken into his mom's email account* and found some old messages to both his birth mother and Mr. Hunt. They all had to do with the letter Smiles was supposed to get on his eighteenth birthday and/or some ex-Alyce employee named Andrei Tarasov, who had *shot himself on Smiles's front lawn* years ago. Because all of that wasn't bizarre enough, Melanie had contacted some professor at Northeastern and was planning to skip school to meet him on Monday. In the meantime, she had decided to *go AWOL and hole up at his dad's cabin for the weekend* while she tried to figure it all out. Unbelievable.

The skipping class part, actually, might have been the strangest of all.

A grin crossed Smiles's face. He had to hand it to Melanie—it sounded like she'd stirred up a bunch of trouble. Not that he could begin to grasp what it all meant. It was definitely weird that Smiles had never heard about this guy who offed himself, but that sounded like ancient history. Plus, through Melanie's frantic voice mails, it was difficult to draw any connection between the guy and the letter from his mom. Which Mr. Hunt had destroyed, anyway.

He'd looked pretty pissed off when he handed Smiles the keys to the cabin. That scene at the front of the house made more sense now; Melanie and her friend were being involuntarily returned from their weekend frolic as detectives/runaways.

Smiles's finger hovered over the phone, readying to call Melanie. What was the use, though? She'd broken up with

"A single idea—the sudden flash of a thought—may be worth a million dollars."

—Robert Collier

MONDAY

"Money often costs too much."

—Ralph Waldo Emerson

ANOTHER DAY, ANOTHER absurdly early start. The early wake-ups were getting ridiculous, but Smiles didn't see any way around it. If they had any delays along the way, they were going to have to haul ass to get Ben by four o'clock. First they had to go to Boston to get the money, then backtrack an hour north to York, Maine, where Zach had demanded they meet for the cipher exchange. ("He stays close to home," Erin had said. "That trip to Fox Creek might as well have been a European vacation.") Then back downtown to the Prudential Center to meet the agents and Ben. If Smiles managed to pull this off, he was going to sleep for a month.

The number of details Smiles had to keep straight had almost overwhelmed him. First thing after getting up, he'd sat down at the kitchen table and written out a list with phone numbers and meeting times for Zach, the agents, and Mr. Perry (the banker dude); his Swiss bank account details; and whatever other scraps of information might come in handy. The exercise calmed him down enough to close up the cabin pretty well as the sun rose over the lake.

Now they were cruising south on I–93, and thankfully Erin was staying awake for the ride. Smiles never thought it would be possible, but he might have gotten his fill of driving the Infiniti at this point.

"Do you realize what Ben did?" Erin said, cracking her window on a gray stretch of highway past Concord. "To a mathematician, solving the Riemann Hypothesis is like finding the cure for cancer. And Ben's discovery, it's almost more of a breakthrough than that. I'm not exaggerating to make a point. That's the best actual comparison I can think of."

"You know," Smiles said, "I don't think I actually *do* realize what Ben did. I mean, I can't really appreciate it. It's like telling someone from Mongolia that somebody broke Joe DiMaggio's hitting streak. They're not going to get it, no matter how hard they try."

"Who's Joe DiMaggio?"

Smiles turned in disbelief, but she'd made a pistol of her finger and was pointing it at him.

"Anyway," Smiles said, "not appreciating the brilliant people in my life is something I seem to excel at, so it's par for the course."

Erin took his hand, and they drove in silence for ten miles before she said, "He's in bad shape, huh?"

"Yeah. Worst he's ever been."

Erin turned sideways and played her finger along his ear. "Well, you know, I'm incredibly brilliant, and you seem to appreciate me."

The good feeling lasted all the way to the bank.

✕

The whole procedure lasted only half an hour. They parked in a downtown structure and crossed the street to Third Boston Bank, the exterior of which had round gray columns of a reassuring thickness. It was one of those old banks, with its name actually etched into the stone and a long double row of wooden desks opposite the brass teller windows. The desks were filled with people in business suits who would have been right at home in a library, considering the obvious effort they made to stay quiet. Someone's desk phone went off, and the ringer sounded like a sonar pulse from a submarine movie. Chewing gum probably got you fired on the spot.

The sound of Erin's flip-flops echoed through the tall open space, which didn't have any other customers in it yet. Smiles and Erin had been the first, arriving just as a security guard was unlocking the double doors at the front of the bank. A reed-thin man looked up at the *thwack*ing sound of Erin's footsteps, and Smiles saw the name PERRY on his gold name tag.

"Mr. Perry?"

"Yes. You would be Mr. Smylie, then?"

Smiles almost said no. "Uh, yeah, but everybody calls me Smiles."

Nicholas Perry found that extremely amusing. "Okay, then," he said, with a smile still frozen on his face. "Let's have a seat and see what we can do for you, *Smiles*." The guy couldn't get past the idea that some human beings have nicknames.

They followed him to a desk in the back row, away

from the bank entrance. Smiles wondered if they intentionally kept Nicholas Perry as far from the public as possible. "Now, you said you have an amendment of some kind, allowing you access to the full trust?"

"Uh, right." Smiles panicked for a second, but luckily he was wearing the same pants from yesterday and still had it in his back pocket. He had folded the page into quarters, and it held the curve of his butt cheek as he dropped it on the desk.

Mr. Perry picked it up gingerly, humming as he examined it. "Yes, well, I made some inquires about this after your call yesterday. To Mr. Hunt, of course, and then to your father." Smiles wondered if that was normal. He tried to imagine Nicholas Perry conducting his high-level financial queries while Junior blew out his three candles and opened his presents. "They seemed to know about this arrangement, and your father verified that he had signed the addendum. Third Boston is very proud to have your father's business, I should add." Mr. Perry suddenly turned grave. "We're all very sorry about his condition."

It was nice of him and everything, but what do you say to that? Thanks?

"Thanks," Smiles said.

Mr. Perry nodded and hid behind the page again. Finally, he slapped it down onto his desk blotter, raised his eyebrows, and said, "So you want the whole amount, then?"

"Uh, that's right."

"Okay, well since you called yesterday, I came in early to get things moving. Let's see where we are with the check. One moment."

Mr. Perry got up and scurried to a door that said SAFE DEPOSITS. He punched a code in a keypad and darted inside when the door clicked open.

"That's it?" Smiles said to Erin. "I figured they'd, like, want my fingerprints or something."

"I do believe that's your guilty conscience speaking," she said. "You're not here on a trespassing charge—you're here to get your own money." Erin rested her flip-flops on the desk and leaned her head back, taking in the impossibly tall ceiling.

Smiles snuck a glimpse of the tight curves of her body, ill-hidden beneath her T-shirt and jean shorts. He wondered how a girl with legs like that could really be so into math. "So you actually like that math stuff, huh?"

"And that," Erin said, pointing to him, "is your chauvinist pig speaking."

She may have had a point. Smiles grabbed a Third Boston pen from Mr. Perry's collection, just for something to do. Erin released her feet and the front legs of her chair dropped to the floor. "It's pretty easy to get excited about math, actually. Especially codes."

Smiles hummed noncommittally.

"Think about having an idea like Ben had—how exciting it would be. Or your dad," she said. "He's sitting there one day, and then all of a sudden he's figured out how to do asymmetrical encryption over the Internet. Your dad is a freaking genius, Smiles."

And Smiles had put that genius at risk. For now, he could only pray that he'd get the cipher back before Zach could bring down Alyce with it.

Mr. Perry returned with a smile three counties wide. "Success," he said, and flopped a large file folder on his desk. Inside it was a copy of the trust. Mr. Perry fidgeted with the binding for a minute and fixed a copy of the amendment into the back. "Original's already being messengered to Mr. Hunt," he said, pleased with himself.

He set the folder aside, revealing underneath it a copy of *The Transparent Innovator*. "Now, Mr. Smylie—*Smiles*— I've been asked to make a request," he said cautiously. "It's from my colleagues, and you should by all means feel free to refuse. But we would be absolutely honored to have your father's signature on our bank copy of his book. Assuming, of course, that he's up to that kind of thing."

It was going to be less trouble just to take it, so Smiles did. "Sure, I can try," he said.

"That's wonderful. That's just wonderful. Everyone here has read it." Mr. Perry shook his head at his own ramblings. "Anyway, the pièce de résistance."

With great ceremony, Mr. Perry cleared his throat and detached a check from the page it had been printed on. Before handing it to Smiles, he passed him a single form with three marked places to sign. "There, there, and there, please," Mr. Perry said, indicating the signature lines with his pen and using his church voice.

When Smiles passed it back, Mr. Perry handed him the check. The final tally: $6,950,000.00. "It's an awfully pretty number," Mr. Perry was saying in the background. Smiles's eyes were feasting on the check, a tingling feeling in his head. It wasn't the full $7,000,000—Smiles had already gotten the first little payment—but Zach would just have to deal with that.

Erin was tapping lightly on his shoulder. "You okay there?"

He was very okay. He had done it.

"An absolute pleasure meeting you," Mr. Perry said to them. He rose and shook their hands. "You know what they say, right? Don't spend it all in one place."

SMILES WAS GOING to spend it all in one place. He was going to spend it at a lobster shack called Fran's Fish House on the outskirts of York, Maine. They had left the bank an hour ago, and now Smiles was parking the Infiniti on the street across from Fran's, Zach's meeting place of choice. He liked the clam chowder, Erin said.

They had passed through the city center five minutes ago to find themselves here, where the pretty resort spots gave way to ramshackle buildings failing the test of nature the salt air imposed on them. The red paint on Fran's Fish House had cracked years ago, revealing lifeless wood in a leopard-spot pattern. The overhead sign hung at a fifteen-degree angle that spoke of nor'easters past.

Smiles pulled the check from his back pocket and noted the time. "We've got ten minutes, right?"

"Yeah, he said ten thirty, but he probably got here early. Dude can be anal."

"All right, one sec." Smiles consulted the list of phone numbers he'd made back at the cabin, then dialed the agents.

If he was going to do this, he wanted to be sure it was set in stone.

Cole answered right away. "Yeah?"

"We're on for four o'clock," Smiles said. "Right?"

The guy exhaled. "Yeah. Like you said. Prudential Center, four o'clock. The food court. Do you need directions or something? Another confirmation or two? A wake-up call at three thirty?"

"Just have the money. And I want to talk to Ben first."

Another sigh, then silence.

"Good idea," Erin whispered, then peered toward Fran's for signs of Zach. Smiles congratulated himself: For once he'd thought of something first.

Eventually, Ben came to the phone. His voice sounded clear, normal.

"Smiles?"

"Hey man, how you holding up?"

"I, uh, okay, actually." His voice had dropped, and Smiles could sense the presence of the agents. Ben was being careful with his words, but there wasn't any hidden message in them. Maybe they really did have him coddled in five-star luxury.

"Smart of you not to talk," Smiles said. "Guess I shouldn't be surprised."

"Yeah, right, thanks."

Smiles nodded into the phone. He was suddenly nostalgic for all the afternoons he'd spent at Ben's place in the inflatable Budweiser chair, talking about nothing. "Sorry it took us an extra day to get all this together."

"It's okay," Ben said, and Smiles was relieved. Getting into the whole Zach situation probably wasn't the smartest thing to do right now.

"Anyway, I just wanted to make sure you're okay. We're going to get you. We're going to get that money for you, too."

"Yeah, good."

He sounded pleased, but he was still keeping a tight leash on his comments. It occurred to Smiles that this would be an ideal time to negotiate his split of the cash. Instead he said, "All right, bud. Hang on for five hours and you're going to be rich."

Smiles ended the call and turned to Erin. "Showtime."

⅄

Zach was polishing off a bowl of clam chowder when they slid into the booth across from him. He was sporting yet another muscle shirt. The guy had made a bad choice for his trademark look; his arms hadn't gotten any bigger since the last time they'd seen him.

Zach dropped his spoon into the bowl with a clatter and pushed it aside. For a suspended moment they all just sat there. Smiles was on the outside, Erin against the window. Underneath the table, she placed her hand reassuringly over his thigh. It must have been weird for her to be facing her ex-boyfriend like this, but she wasn't showing it.

"Beautiful place you've chosen," Smiles said, turning his eyes to the dirt-streaked windows. The sill was caked with bird crap. He couldn't tell whether the grimy lobster traps lining the walls were decorative or functional. A transistor radio playing the Red Sox pregame from the kitchen was the only other sign of life in the place.

"She never had a problem with it," Zach said.

"Yeah, well, tastes change."

"Do you want the cipher," Zach said, "or do you want to fight about a skirt?"

Erin rolled her eyes. "Please."

"I've got the girl already," Smiles said, and felt Erin pinch him lightly. "I came for the cipher." He held the folded check in front of him.

"A check?" Zach said suspiciously.

"It's written on the bank, clod," Erin said. "It's as good as cash. What'd you expect, we were going to come in here with duffel bags?"

Zach shrunk into himself for a second, aware that Erin was right. Smiles had to make himself frown to keep from cracking up.

Zach hoisted Erin's messenger bag onto the table. From inside, he produced a page from Ben's notebook and a small green thumb drive. Smiles remembered seeing the green drive sticking out of Ben's netbook—it appeared to be the genuine article. To prove it, Zach produced his own laptop from his side, fired it up, and placed the thumb drive inside. "Go ahead, see for yourself. I haven't touched a thing."

Erin swiveled the computer around and tapped on the trackpad. Smiles made a show of checking the screen, but he had no clue what he was looking for. He was gladder than ever to have Erin at his side.

"We're good," she said.

"Make it to cash," Zach said to Smiles. It didn't hit him what the guy was talking about until Erin pulled a pen from her bag and handed it to him.

"Yeah, right," Smiles said, wondering if either of them could sense his embarrassment for habitually forgetting to bring pens to occasions like these. He wrote *Pay to the order of CASH* on the back of the check and signed underneath.

After that it all went very fast. Erin grabbed up her bag and the page with the algorithm. Almost before she'd extracted the thumb drive and shut the computer, Zach had taken the laptop back and held his hand out for the check. Smiles gave it to him, and then he and Erin were out of the booth, out the door, not looking back.

They shut themselves inside the Infiniti and looked at each other.

Erin held the thumb drive out. "We got it. We actually got it."

"I kept waiting for something to go wrong," Smiles said. A laugh passed through him in a wave. He had just saved Alyce Systems. He was about to save Ben. He was about to get rich. "I can't believe it. You're my good luck charm."

"Let's get out of here," Erin said.

"Back to the cabin?"

"Yeah, it's still early—we'll have some time before we have to head back to Boston. I want to show you how lucky you are."

"MEET ME FOR lunch?"

Melanie had sent the text during physics. Jenna had a double lunch, and Melanie was hoping she would hold off and join her for the late period on the patio. It was a lot to ask of Jenna, who always seemed eager to eat as early as possible at Alyce. As usual, Melanie had found her own table out on the newly landscaped grounds behind the Kingsley Prep cafeteria; it didn't seem quite as pathetic to eat alone when you were outside.

It was mostly girls out there today, none of them seniors as far as Melanie could tell. They all wore Kingsley's tartan uniform: purple blazer, plaid skirt, gray kneesocks. The fit of their white shirts and the hang of their gold ties gave each girl a look of her own. Sun shone through the new leaves of the sugar maple trees at the edge of the patio area, which had been planted with great fanfare when Melanie was a freshman. The school had brought in some transcendentalist poet, a Kingsley alum of course, to dedicate the trees with an interminable piece about nature and education. "How

Walden Grows," he called it. It had all sounded very Oprah to Melanie.

She put her tuna sandwich down and opened her notebook to start another list. She wrote:

What I Learned
1.
2.
3.
4.

There had to be something useful to take from her weekend . . . but Melanie wasn't sure what. The empty spaces stared up at her until she sensed something on her left.

"Good luck with that," said Jenna, who was eyeballing the page over Melanie's shoulder.

"I know, right?" Melanie said as Jenna circled to the other side of the bench. "I thought the most humiliating episode of my life might come with some helpful insights, but I guess not."

"So does your dad still want to kill you?"

Not the best phrasing, perhaps, considering how close Melanie had come to accusing him of actual murder. She nodded. "He is not pleased. How'd it go for you?"

"Grounded," Jenna said casually. Her eyes followed a lanky guy dribbling a basketball over the patio, headed to the courts in the distance. "Would you look at that? No, that's wrong. He's a sophomore. That's robbing the cradle." Jenna was talking more to herself than Melanie. "Anyway, so did you hear from Smiles? Was that some new item with him?"

"No clue," Melanie said. "I haven't even thought about him that much since we saw him. Kinda weird."

Jenna was working at an orange, tossing bits of peel onto the table. "So you're not going to meet that Northeastern professor?"

Melanie shook her head. "No point."

"Well, you did take those CPR classes last year," Jenna said. "He might be in need of your assistance any moment."

Melanie laughed and looked at the sugar maple trees. "I'm letting it go."

Her cell rang then, and wouldn't you know: Smiles. "I think I'm letting a lot of things go," she said as she sent it to voice mail.

After lunch, she was going to get the "What I Learned" list out and write on the top line: *To be thankful for Jenna Brooke.*

SMILES STARED WITH half-lidded eyes at the wooden tim-bers lining the ceiling of the master bedroom. His mind had been blown. Three days ago, on his eighteenth birth-day, everything had been going so wrong. Now he'd almost made it all the way through the biggest challenge in his life, and in a few short hours he was going to come out on the other side. He was going to save Ben and his dad's company, and collect a fortune in the process. Not to mention Erin, asleep next to him, her soft breath tickling his neck. He didn't even know her three days ago.

Her eyes eased half-open, and she exhaled with the pleasant exhaustion of sleep. "Are we gassed up for the ride back?" she cooed.

The Infiniti had been low when they pulled in. "I'm on it," he said, slipping out from underneath her. "We got a half hour. I'll be back in twenty. Think about how you want to celebrate tonight."

"Mmmmm," Erin said, and rolled over.

Ten minutes later he pulled into the old Squam Lake gas station where his dad had always stopped before their trips back home. The owner sat in a rocking chair outside the beaten garage door of the repair shop. He was wearing the same coveralls Smiles had seen him in a thousand times before. It was familiar here—the twenty-year-old Coke machine, the view of the inlet across the road, the peculiar mix of smells from the gas station and hamburger stand next door. Smiles couldn't help it—it reminded him of Melanie.

They used to wave to each other from the back windows of their parents' cars as they fueled up. They used to stop here together when they came up by themselves, too. Melanie had made friends with the old man who ran the place.

Smiles grabbed his phone out of his pocket. The pump clicked off behind him, his tank full. Smiles didn't bother with it yet—first he owed Melanie a call. Yeah, she had broken up with him, but they had a history. It had been a rough weekend for her—the least Smiles could do was to call and check in, offer a friendly voice.

Straight to voice mail. He thought she'd be at lunch now, but then Smiles had never really gotten a good handle on her schedule. He didn't know what to say, so he hung up. At least she'd see his effort to reach out. It gave him tremendous satisfaction as he raced back to the cabin, feeling like he'd checked a final item off his to-do list.

It was fair to say that Smiles had never been happier in his life than he was when he entered the cabin and called up to Erin, his voice filled with great expectations for the things yet to come that day.

"Erin! Wakey wakey!"

But Erin didn't answer. Erin didn't answer because she was gone.

AT FIRST SMILES didn't feel panicked, or distressed, or terrified. What he felt most of all was *mystified.*

Fifteen minutes ago he had left her right in that bed.
And now she was just . . . not there. She wasn't anywhere.
He did a loop of the house, checked in every room. He'd
looked in the hot tub, in the lake. She had just . . . vanished?
Impossible, unless David Copperfield had dropped in and
pulled a fast one while he was up at the gas station.

He wasn't even worried that the agents had decided to
double up on their hostages. The thumb drive was right
there in Erin's bag. They wouldn't have left without grabbing the cipher. So where did she go? It was mystifying in
the extreme.

For the next ten minutes he went back through the house,
racking his brain for possible explanations for Erin's disap-
pearance. Maybe she went for a walk—girls had a thing for
walks—but she knew they were supposed to get going by
one thirty, and it was past that now. Maybe someone had an
emergency out on the road, and Erin had gone to help? But

you couldn't even hear the road from the house, much less when you were asleep. He couldn't come up with anything.

Smiles was going to have to leave without her in a minute. Standing at the top of the spiral stairs, tapping his head in frustration, he finally thought of her phone. Smiles had plugged her number into his phone when she first gave it to him. He pulled it up now, punched it, and closed his eyes. *"Please please please . . ."*

A high-pitched chime sounded in his ear, and an ethereal voice said, "The number you dialed has been disconnected. Thank you for choosing AT&T."

Smiles wanted to scream. Had he entered the number wrong? What was going on here?

He was going to be late for the exchange at the Prudential Center if he didn't get going, like, five minutes ago. But Smiles couldn't leave like this. He had fallen in love with her—he was sure of it now.

He went through the house a third time, this time opening cabinet and closet doors, as if Erin had maybe shrunk to pint-size while he'd been gone. It was ridiculous, but if he stood still his head was going to spontaneously combust.

In the guest bedroom where he and Melanie used to stay, he picked up the lantern that had been left on the bedside table. Melanie loved that thing—maybe she'd slept in this room when she'd come up to the cabin.

He plunked down the lantern and noticed, for the first time, the three old pictures lying beside it on the nightstand. He rifled through them—the first a shot of Mr. Hunt about a hundred and fifty pounds ago, wearing an embarrassingly nineties flannel shirt. He must have had a Kurt Cobain phase that Smiles didn't know about. The next was Smiles's dad in some kind of college hallway with two other men: one a younger guy with milky skin and questionable facial hair, the other an older professor type with crazed eyes. Smiles didn't know what to make of it.

The guy with the milky skin was in the last picture as well. He was chatting happily with Smiles's dad at some kind of picnic, observed by a knockout woman. She had a baby in her lap, and she was giving a steamy look to the milky-skinned guy.

Unfortunately, at some point Smiles was going to have to stop ogling the chick in the picture and try to figure out what was going on here, back in the present day. He tossed the pictures Frisbee-style onto the bed, where they landed facedown. Smiles saw some writing on the back of the last picture.

He read his mom's bubbly handwriting and almost blacked out:

Math Department Family Day—Robert with Andrei Eltsin, Darya Eltsin, and baby Benjamin.

A VERY STRANGE sensation was taking over Smiles's body.

The suicide case that Melanie had told him about, the guy who had killed himself on Smiles's front lawn—his first name was Andrei, Smiles was pretty sure about that. And he had a baby named Ben. Ben Eltsin.

Slowly, heavily, a giant gear engaged in Smiles's brain. It was like the thick door of a vault being shut. And then the clicks of the wheel being spun, and then only silence. Silence, and the terrible realization that you had been locked inside.

His hands shook as he pulled the page with the phone numbers from his pocket. His ears were hot. His brain was hot. He had fallen to his knees on the hardwood floor, upright against the bed.

He tried the number for the agents.

A high-pitched chime. An otherworldly voice: "The number you dialed has been disconnected. Thank you for choosing AT&T."

Smiles's mouth went dry.

Ben's cell had been destroyed in the casino parking lot. Smiles tried it anyway, frantic. "The number you dialed has been disconnected. Thank you for choosing AT&T."

Oh no oh no oh no no no no no no no no . . .

OH YEAH.

The cab turned and Ben saw the first real sign of home: Mercado Rosanna, the fixture on the corner of the tiny street he'd grown up on. The painted faces of the Puerto Rican girls on the mural smiled like they were in on it, too, like they were proud of him. *You did it, Ben. You did it.* He'd done the impossible, and he could hardly believe it.

He wanted to leap out of the cab. He'd ridden over with Russell, the two of them cooped up in the taxi liked they'd been cooped up in the hotel room for the last two days. He rolled down the window to take in the scent of empanadas. The smell pulled his smile wider as the cabbie advanced up the street. Ahead, Uncle Jim burst onto the porch. He shouted into the street, giving them a grand welcome.

Ben flew out, leaving Russell to pay the fare. He bounded up the cracked steps he'd walked a thousand times, crashed into Uncle Jim, and wrapped him tight. "We did it," he said. He said it once, and then couldn't stop until Uncle Jim pulled away and held him by the shoulders.

"I'm so proud of you," he said. "Who'd've thought you'd pull it off, with your Asperger's and all?"

They cracked up. Ben's closest experience with Asperger's was the hours of Internet research he'd put in, reading articles and watching YouTube videos of people who actually had it. He'd faked it all, just like he'd faked coming up with the fast-factoring algorithm. Just like Uncle Jim had faked being the NSA agent Ken Gary.

"Erin and Zach are coming with the check. Let's pay this guy, get 'im out of here."

"Yeah." Uncle Jim waved Russell in. "C'mon, c'mon, c'mon," he said, and ushered them upstairs to the apartment. Russell lumbered up the steps behind them. He was a friend of Uncle Jim's, and when Ben had laid out the plan, Uncle Jim had suggested Russell might make a decent candidate to play the second NSA agent, Cole. He had, but he wasn't nearly as good at poker. Ben had taken $450 off him over the last two days, which they'd spent at a downtown hotel to keep things authentic, Russell popping his cherry cough drops like candy the whole time. Uncle Jim had come back early to check on his mom, but Ben and Russell had only left the room once, on Sunday morning, to put on the show for Smiles. Other than that, it was a lot of room service, seven-card stud, and television.

But now Zach had the check in his hands. They'd gotten the call from him fifteen minutes ago. He'd just picked Erin up from Smiles's cabin—the last step of the plan, complete. There wasn't any need for appearances anymore.

They clustered giddily around the kitchen table, where

Uncle Jim poured two glasses of whiskey and another of ginger ale. Uncle Jim and Ben used to sit at the table, sometimes with his mom, playing long games of gin rummy. Ben sat there and played and listened to Uncle Jim's old stories about his lawless days, never knowing exactly how true they were. And then Ben got his big idea and thought, *I wonder if he'd want to help with a really big job?*

Russell shed his suit jacket and started in on his tie. "Get me out of these things," he said, flopping them over a chair. They had been careful about maintaining their roles, and for a second Ben had to remind himself that the guy wasn't an NSA agent in real life.

Real life.

It was a concept Ben had clung to for the long months he'd spent pretending to be someone else: a sixteen-year-old MIT student. Ben was actually eighteen in real life, just older than Smiles, but small and thin enough to pull it off. He wouldn't have to do it forever, he had told himself a million times. Someday, when Smiles believed in his character enough, and when the perfect moment came, they would pull the con. Months into the plan, Ben had tired of the role, almost lost his faith. But then the IPO came along, giving them the perfect bit of leverage to use against Smiles. When it was scheduled right after CRYPTCON—the ideal setting for their plan—Ben knew they could do it. And that, someday, he'd get back to *real life.*

Uncle Jim passed the drinks around. "All right, all right," he said, and raised a glass. "To Ben."

"To Ben!" they shouted, and then Ben had four hands thumping on his back.

"To you guys, too," he sputtered.

Russell drained his whiskey and poured another. "To us, then!"

"To us!" they all said, clinking glasses.

It went on like that for a while, and Ben was soaking up every second. Real life. At some point Russell pulled out his receipts from their hotel stay and Uncle Jim tallied up his expenses. He added it to the cut they'd promised Russell, throwing in a little extra for scaring off Smiles's girlfriend. That wasn't in the script until Ben's mom called, letting them know she was snooping around.

Ben took in the old apartment: the water stains on the ceiling, the slanting floor that could make you seasick. He had hated this place for so long—thought of it as a prison—but it wasn't so bad when you weren't trapped in it anymore. Pushed up against the living room wall were the entire contents of his apartment at the Pemberton—an old mattress, the card table, the folding chair, and the desk. Ben had given Uncle Jim the keys before he left for Fox Creek.

"Souvenir?" Russell said, and tossed his NSA ID tag onto the kitchen table. Ben and Uncle Jim had made it together after some research at the library. The bar code at the bottom actually worked, but it was only good for a price check on orange juice. Making the ID had been much easier, actually, than faking the letterhead from the math journal.

Ben followed Russell to the door. "You're a pro," Russell said on his way out. "If you don't go into retirement after this, give me a call next time you need a shill."

The door closed behind him, and Ben turned to Uncle

Jim. From behind the kitchen table, his broad smile dropped as he realized what was on Ben's mind.

"In her room?" Ben said.

Uncle Jim nodded solemnly.

"How's she doing?"

Uncle Jim gave a small shake of his head. "Same."

⨏

Ben wished he had the check in his hands. He wanted to show her the actual thing.

She was lying in bed with more covers than the weather called for, but Ben had seen worse. He would have thought of it as a so-so day, back when he lived here. He sat on the bed and fixed the nightgown at her shoulder.

She put her hand over his. "My boy." Her eyes were lazy with sleep, but you could see the beautiful woman that she had once been.

Ben smiled for her. "Yeah, it's me. I'm back."

"Jim told me. You really did it, huh?"

"I really did it," Ben said. "I did it for you. For him."

Her mouth twisted with sentiment, and as Ben drew his hand away she held on to the lace of her nightgown. "He gave this to me, you know? He used to give me presents for no reason."

Ben had heard her stories a thousand times each, but he never tired of them. "Yeah."

"I'm gonna wear it till one of us wears out. Me first, probably." Her laugh was halfhearted.

"I know it's not enough," Ben said, "but we did it. We got 'em."

"I know, baby." She sat up in bed and asked for his hands. Ben gave them to her and listened. "I'm real proud of you. You're a good little man. Promise me something, though: Make this the end of it. We gotta live now. It's time to *live*."

"I promise, Mom." He was okay with that—he was ready to move on, too. "But can we look at houses for you?"

"Yeah, darling. No big mansions, though."

"No big mansions." Ben smiled with her, and this time her laugh had something behind it.

"Go and keep Jim out of trouble. Let me get dressed here, so I can take my son for an empanada."

Ben nodded. He didn't want to talk, because the tears were right in his throat.

✗

They got a bunch of empanadas from Mercado Rosanna and took them up to the widow's walk in a pink plastic bag. Ben and Uncle Jim ate at the railing, their legs swinging over the roof. Ben's mom spread a blanket and hugged her knees to her chest, a bittersweet smile on her face the whole time. She wasn't eating, but Ben didn't mind; he was just glad she'd come up.

Uncle Jim had brought his whiskey upstairs. He poured another glass for himself and asked Ben for details. There weren't many more to give—Uncle Jim had been there the whole time. Ben had been feeding him daily updates ever since he moved into the Pemberton with the money Uncle Jim had fronted for the plan.

"So proud of this kid," he said to Ben's mom.

She reached for his bottle of whiskey. "Pace yourself."

She gave Ben a wink, and he had one of those rare glimpses of the woman she must have been without the depression. It wasn't going to end today—maybe it would never end—but it filled him with joy.

"I'm proud of all those kids," Uncle Jim said, as if he'd never been interrupted.

"Here they come," Ben said, pointing to the edge of the parking lot below, where Erin and Zach had just appeared.

Uncle Jim stood up and crossed his arms above his head. "Oh, yeah! There they are!"

Erin saw them first. She flashed a piece of paper victoriously, then followed Zach in a sprint to the house and up to the widow's walk. Ben had found them both—Erin through his math research, Zach an old friend from grade school who had designs on being an actor. Their footsteps thundered on the stairs, and then they shot onto the roof. Uncle Jim lifted Erin off the ground and twirled her in the air.

They laughed. They grabbed up empanadas. They told stories.

Erin's piece of paper was a receipt from a Third Boston branch they'd stopped at on the way back to Boston. As planned, they'd wired the money immediately to an offshore account. "Went through while we were there," Zach said proudly. "It's in our account now."

"It's done," Uncle Jim said, holding the proof in his admiring hands.

And it was. They all beamed at one another, and it was a long time before they could sit down and utter anything but nonsensical sounds of joy.

At some point Erin cracked up about something, caught

up in her own laughter until she noticed them all looking on. "So we're at that *disgusting* fish place," she explained, "and Smiles gives Zach the check. It's fifty thousand dollars short, and Marlon Brando here doesn't even say a peep."

Uncle Jim cackled.

"What'd you want me to do?" Zach said. "Hold the whole thing up over fifty thousand dollars?"

"Of course not, but it was suspicious. You should have stayed in character. Never getting to Hollywood at this rate." She shook her head in mock dismay. "Which reminds me," she continued with the flush of excitement running through them all, "can someone explain to me how a guy who supposedly wears muscle shirts all the time gets a farmer's tan like that?" She pointed to the tan line well below his shoulder.

Zach looked at his arm like he was seeing it for the first time. "Yeah, well, luckily the guy's way too stupid to notice. How long did you have to ram that idea into his head at the blackjack table? Twenty minutes explaining to him about the government paying for prime numbers and he still barely got it. The guy's brain-dead."

Ben watched Erin. She crushed her foil wrapper and stared off. Ben knew how it felt. He'd spent more time with Smiles than anybody and didn't like hearing Zach talk about him like that, either. Part of the relief of getting back to real life was the relief of not fooling Smiles anymore. He'd never admitted to Uncle Jim how much he actually liked the guy.

He hadn't told Uncle Jim that he almost called the

whole thing off at the conference. It happened in the opening session, when Smiles's birth mother had appeared at the podium. They hadn't known that was coming at all—it was the worst possible complication. As soon as he saw her, Ben knew who she was. And then he saw that horrified look on Smiles's face, and it almost was too much. Was he a mark or a friend? The question loomed in Ben's mind while the theater rang with applause, and he knew that by the time it died down he had to make a decision. The presence of his birth mother was going to absorb Smiles entirely, mess with the fine details of their plan. So he made his choice, ad-libbing on the spot, feigning the discovery that he was supposed to make later that night. Hoping that it would distract Smiles enough from his mother to salvage things. It had worked.

Ben wondered if Erin had gotten close enough to Smiles for it to mess with her mind, too—or even closer.

He watched her pull herself back to the group. "Did I tell you guys he called me a skirt?" She narrowed her eyes at Zach. "A *skirt*? Where did that come from? A 1940s movie?"

Ben's mom chuckled in the background.

They all turned, happy to have her join in. But then she rose and kissed their heads in succession: Zach, Erin, Uncle Jim, and Ben. "I'm just getting a little chilly. I'll be downstairs."

Ben knew what that meant: She was going into her room for the night, probably not coming out again. He caught up to her halfway to the stairs and gave her a hug.

"Thank you," she said into his ear, and he knew that

something frozen in her had melted just a little. "Thank you, my baby."

"Time to live, right, Mom?"

"Time to live," she said, and went downstairs.

✕

One by one they left the widow's walk. First Zach went home, then Uncle Jim went downstairs, and then it was just Ben and Erin.

"So what are you going to do with your money?" Erin said.

Uncle Jim was getting a quarter of the money—Erin and Zach were getting paid out of that. Ben was getting the rest, but as far as he was concerned it was all his mom's. "Who knows," he said. "Are you going to, like, celebrate tonight?"

Erin sighed and lay back on the widow's walk. "I don't know. It was so draining, you know?" Ben did. "I might just go to bed. That'll be my big celebration."

Ben didn't know if he should ask, but Erin was the only one he could pose the question to. "You think you're going to miss him?"

Erin didn't answer. Maybe she thought he was stupid and loud and obnoxious at first, like Ben had. Maybe he won her over. Maybe at some point she stopped holding her nose and laughed at one of his jokes, if only on the inside. Maybe she thought it was unfair what happened to people in this world—even the ones who were supposed to deserve what they had coming. Maybe she considered him her best friend.

"You were great, Ben," was all Erin said. "You were really great."

"You, too," he said. She walked away and down the stairs.

And then Ben was alone on the roof.

He sat there for a long time, wondering what Smiles would think when he found out why they'd done it.

SMILES WAS ON his fifteenth call to Melanie's cell phone in the last two hours. She had to answer one of these times.

He held the phone to his ear as he raced up the stairwell at the Pemberton. His knees were stiff from the drive back from Squam Lake, most of which he'd done at over ninety miles an hour. He'd gotten three different calls on his way back, and each time he'd deflated at the sight of the 510 number on his caller ID. His mother. She was the last thing he could handle right now. Smiles rejected them and drove even faster. And now, finally, Melanie was picking up.

"Hello?"

"Mel!" He stopped in the stairwell, catching his breath against the cinder-block wall. Talking to Melanie was his only chance at getting any answers.

"Smiles, what's going on? You can't keep calling."

"I know I know I know. I'm sorry, don't hang up." He collected himself and tried to do his best impression of a person who was not currently going out of his mind. "I just had to talk to you."

"Okay, but I had to step out of English to take this. Are you okay?"

"Sure, right." Smiles was walking to his apartment now. Across the hall, the door to Ben's was open. Two members of the Pemberton maintenance crew were putting a fresh coat of paint on the apartment, which was otherwise completely empty.

"Oh, God."

"What?"

"You know that kid in my building? Ben?"

"Yeah—your friend, right?"

"I'm starting to think he just stole my trust fund money." Smiles entered his apartment, checked his fish (still alive), and dropped onto his sofa.

"He what? How?"

"It's, like, kind of complicated. But listen. I'm really sorry I wasn't calling you back this weekend. I listened to your voice mails, though, and right now I really need to know everything you know about that Andrei guy who killed himself."

"Okay, but why?"

"Because I think Ben is his son."

"His *son*? Whoa. I have no idea about that, but Tarasov was a Russian spy who stole research from your dad at Harvard. It's really sad."

Russian spy? Stolen research? "Who's Tarasov?"

"Andrei Tarasov. The guy you're asking about. Are you okay?"

"Oh, yeah, I just thought his last name was something else."

"Well, he changed it so he could sneak back into the States after he got deported."

"Naturally," Smiles said.

"I didn't learn that until yesterday. Turns out he caused your dad a lot of trouble—like, a whole lot. I actually spent my entire weekend thinking about that guy, 'cause I knew he had something to do with that letter from your mom."

"The letter from my mom is about *Andrei Tarasov*?" The letter would have the answers, then. But it was gone, destroyed . . .

"Well, I'm not really positive any—"

"Hold on, didn't you say there was a guy at Northeastern who knew about the letter?"

"I'm not sure what he knows, actually."

"Didn't you meet him or something?"

"I was going to. Today. But then my dad came to the lake and—"

Smiles was already out the door. "Do you know where his office is?"

MELANIE PRESSED HER back to the wall and slumped to the floor, landing hard on her butt.

His trust fund . . . stolen?

The bell rang and the classroom doors swung open. Melanie watched from kneesock level as her classmates washed to the exits in a faceless parade of Kingsley uniforms. Three minutes later only the stragglers remained, the rush of sound thinned down to individual voices.

Melanie remained against the wall, trying to let go of the strange news she'd just heard from Smiles.

Andrei Tarasov had a son?

"Melanie? Are you okay?" Her English teacher, Mr. Hardy, was calling down the hallway. "You left your books."

It took Melanie a moment to find her voice. "Yes, thank you." She rushed into the classroom and grabbed up her book bag so Mr. Hardy could lock up.

"Cross-country practice today?" he said as she breezed out the door.

"Off to it now."

But who was she kidding? Melanie couldn't let it go— she was heading straight to Northeastern.

IN NINE MINUTES, Smiles was supposed to meet the agents at the Prudential Center to get Ben back. But instead of being there, he was in a dusty corner of some academic building at Northeastern, talking to a small wizard. That's what the guy looked like, anyway, with his shrunken frame and mane of white hair. He actually looked pretty much the same as in the picture Melanie had left on the nightstand, which made it easy to spot him as Smiles ran down the hallway.

From his doorway, Smiles had spewed out a frantic explanation for his presence before Professor Worth cut him off and insisted he have a seat. The water cooler behind his desk burped as the professor drew water from it. He passed a small Styrofoam cup to Smiles, now sitting on a couch that had probably gone in and out of style a few times since the 1950s.

The professor stood by while Smiles downed the water.

"I can see him in you."

"Excuse me?"

"Your father."

"Oh, yeah."

"Just go slowly and tell me why you're here," Professor Worth said, refilling the water for Smiles and then taking a seat behind the desk.

"Okay, well, let me start with this." Smiles had brought the critical items with him. He pulled out the algorithm and the thumb drive from his pockets.

"Do you know anything about codes, sir?"

The professor laughed a phlegmy laugh. Pretty soon the guy was doubled over. His wrinkled arm raised in a thumbs-up gesture and he returned upright, red-faced but smiling. "Don't mind that. Standard operating procedure," he said. "Go on, please."

"Uh, codes?"

"Right right right. If you'll allow an old man to be immodest, I know an awful lot about codes."

Sounded like a yes. Smiles passed over the page from Ben's notebook. "Could you possibly tell me what that is?"

Professor Worth looked at it for about a second. "I most assuredly can. This, young man, is a bunch of gibberish."

"Gibberish? Somebody told me it was an algorithm to, uh, fast-factor the, uh . . ."

"The product of two primes?"

"Right."

"Oh, wouldn't that be marvelous!" Professor Worth was beaming. "But no. That particular mystery eludes us still. This is just a random string of math-looking symbols. As I say, gibberish."

"It was supposed to be on this drive, too," Smiles said, almost embarrassed to have him try it.

"Let us see," Professor Worth said, and placed the thumb drive in his computer. He clicked around for a while and swiveled back to Smiles. "Would you like to hazard a guess?"

"Gibberish?"

"Got it in one."

Smiles still couldn't wrap his mind around it. He had been right there when they tested the algorithm. He had seen it work . . .

You didn't see anything. You heard Ben read back a bunch of random numbers. Then you gave them to the agent, who was in on it, too.

It didn't matter that he was going to be late to the Prudential Center, because no one was going to be there. There was never any threat to Alyce Systems, because Ben hadn't discovered anything. All he'd done was find a sucker, and then stolen $7 million from him.

It hurt, but it also gave him clarity. Ben wasn't simply a thief; he was the son of Andrei Eltsin. Smiles had to find out the truth about that man if he was ever going to have any peace. "You knew my dad, sir?"

"Very well. We worked at Harvard together, on projects of some not insignificant import."

Another convoluted yes. "Something happened to me this weekend, sir. This might sound strange, but did you know Rose, too? Rose Carlisle?"

Professor Worth tipped back in his chair. "I did. And

I'll confess, I'm afraid of what your next question is going to be."

"Did she tell you anything about a man named—"

"Andrei?"

"Yeah."

"My dear boy." Professor Worth hacked into his fist, and Smiles feared the rambling soliloquy sure to follow. "Before you tread any further into these murky waters, I would ask you—"

"Professor, I have to thank you for talking to me, and the water, and everything. But I really need to know what my mom—Rose—told you about that guy."

"Yes, I understand. You're a determined young man. And you have a right to ask your questions, however troubling the answers may be." Professor Worth cleared his throat. "Rose knew of me from my work with your father at Harvard. Years ago, she came to me with a notebook."

"A notebook?" Smiles remembered the strange thing his dad had told him: that there would be a "package" along with the letter from his mom. *Not a regular gift*, he had said. *It's a notebook.* The letter might be gone, but maybe this notebook still existed somewhere. Maybe it had answers.

"Yes," Professor Worth said. "A notebook. She wanted me to look at it, and I did."

"Why? What was in it?"

Professor Worth shook his head. "I'm sorry, I can't. If you really want to know, you'll have to get that from the person who came here with Ms. Carlisle."

Smiles waited. Professor Worth swallowed.

"It was your mother, dear boy. Alice Taft, once Alice Smylie."

"My mother?"

Professor Worth eased back in his chair. "Yes. She's been trying to get you on the phone today, hasn't she?"

"How did you . . . ?"

"We've been in contact, you see. As you no doubt know, on Saturday I got a call from Marshall Hunt's daughter, a terribly nice-sounding young lady. And, well, I knew then that these old matters had resurrected themselves. So your mother and I have been talking, and frankly your visit here is not entirely unexpected. I'm rather of a mind that it would be far better for you to leave the matter be."

It's better left alone, Smiles could hear his mom saying.

"I can see, though, that you want to get your information," Professor Worth continued, "and your mother is willing to provide it."

"That'd be a change," Smiles said.

"Yes, I understand you had a rather unpleasant meeting at the conference?"

"That's one way to put it."

"You should know, son, that life has been extremely unfair to your mother. Much less fair than it has been to you. Believe me when I say she only wants the best for you."

Smiles didn't want to hear it. If she really wanted the best for him, she could have helped him out at Fox Creek. She could have stuck around until his third birthday.

"So does she have this notebook?" Smiles said.

"She's getting it right now, as it happens. And she told me that if you came poking around here, I should send you over."

"Over where?"

"To the bank, son. To the safe deposit box where it's been sitting for years."

MELANIE ALMOST CRASHED into Smiles. He was bursting from Professor Worth's office just as she was arriving, and he looked dangerously pale. Melanie felt an awkward smile on her face as they backed away from each other in the hallway.

"Hey. I thought I might as well come down," she said. "See what all this is about."

"Yeah, uh, thanks." Melanie had wondered if it would be weird between them, but it felt sort of good. It was like seeing her best friend from grade school. "Can you walk with me?" Smiles said. "I think I'm about to find out."

"Yeah," Melanie said, but she didn't even know if he was listening anymore. He was race-walking down the hallway and then out of the small building that held Professor Worth's office, a three-story outpost on Northeastern's campus in the South End. Melanie had a little laugh to herself when she saw his Infiniti parked illegally right in front of the entrance. Nobody got more parking tickets than Smiles.

"I've got to find my mother," Smiles said.

"Your . . . mother?" It took her back to that terrible conversation at the kabob place. The conversation that had started everything.

"Alice, yeah. She has the notebook I was supposed to get, and it's the reason all of this happened."

"Oh, okay." Melanie didn't want to touch the topic of his biological mother—it would be safer to douse herself in water and tap dance on the third rail of the T. "No offense, but you look sorta worn out. Want me to drive?" She used to drive them everywhere.

Smiles balled up the parking ticket and stuffed it in his pocket. "Thanks, but this is kind of my thing. Come with me, though, if you want."

✕

Melanie spotted her right away—she looked just like him. Or he looked just like her. They had the same features: the spread of their eyes, the wide mouth. At the same time, they didn't look like each other at all. His hair was floppy and wild, hers short and neat. The traits she liked about Smiles—the openness of his face, the calm of his eyes—were different on his mom. It wasn't quite a scowl that she wore, but it was in the neighborhood.

The security guard had been standing at the front entrance as they came in, waiting out the last minutes before he could lock up. They had slipped in just in time, swimming against a current of exiting bank customers. And then, down the length of the bank, right in front of the safe deposit area, they saw her standing in a tailored red jacket.

"Oh, wow," Melanie said, jarred by the resemblance.

"C'mon," Smiles said, and they walked down the grand room to his mother. The formality of the place felt appropriate somehow—like some kind of sacred ceremony was about to take place. Melanie stayed half a step back from Smiles. This *was* his thing, and she was going to have to fight her instinct to protect him every step of the way. His mom watched them coming, freakishly composed—her posture rigid, her clothes immaculate, her face stoic.

When they reached her, Melanie saw the tiniest fracture in her composure. Her face relaxed by a single degree, and her lips dropped from their fixed position on her face. It was the saddest smile Melanie had ever seen.

"Hello." The odd detachment of her voice wasn't a surprise. She didn't offer as much as a handshake. This woman made icebergs look warm.

"This is Melanie," Smiles said with a hollow voice.

"Not Melanie Hunt?" Melanie nodded, and she saw the fracture deepen another bit. "I knew you once," she said. "As a baby."

They were almost alone in the bank now. In a few minutes they would get kicked out. "I need to know something," Smiles began, and just then the door that said SAFE DEPOSITS opened up behind them. A man emerged—the name tag on his lapel said PERRY.

"Shall we, Alice?" the man said, before noticing Smiles and Melanie. "Oh my, Mr. Smylie. *Smiles*, that is. What a delight. You didn't have to get that signature so quickly."

"It's not that," Smiles said, then turned to his mom. "Just tell me. Do you have this notebook, whatever it is?"

Mr. Perry leaned farther out the door in his eagerness to serve. "Everything okay there, folks?"

"Give us a moment," Melanie said, hanging on the exchange in front of her. She had to see this notebook, too. Somehow, she knew, it would explain everything that had been going on all weekend.

"Are you sure you want to—" his mother started.

"I *need* to know." Smiles's voice was hot.

His mother drew her jacket tight against her trim body. She sniffed and said, "Yes, well, I have the notebook. I've kept it in a safe deposit box here for years. The letter I left for your eighteenth birthday, it told you that you're authorized to access it."

"I never got the letter," Smiles said harshly.

His mother's mouth twitched, and Melanie sensed that it was taking great effort now to maintain her rigorous self-control. "Well, let's go then," she said softly.

She nodded to Mr. Perry, and they followed him down a corridor to a series of caged areas. The size of walk-in closets, each was ringed with safe deposit boxes and had a block in the center like a kitchen island. "We're all very excited about the IPO tomorrow," Mr. Perry said breezily as they went, somehow oblivious to the unbearable waves of stress crashing between Smiles and his mother. One last time Melanie had to resist holding Smiles's hand, stepping ahead, doing whatever she could to shield him from the damage his mom inflicted on him.

Mr. Perry opened one of the cages and escorted them inside—Smiles and his mother first, then Melanie, then another bank guard who had appeared at the rear of the group. With a large ring of keys in his hand, Mr. Perry scanned a row of boxes at the back of the claustrophobic cage.

"Where are you now?" he mumbled to himself as he went along. "Ahh, there." Alice joined him at the box he'd singled out, and they both inserted keys into the wide, shallow safe deposit box. It was just like Melanie's dad had explained Alyce's encryption system to her when she was little—how you needed the two keys to unlock the code.

Mr. Perry left the box on the island, gave a short bow, and left wordlessly. The guard pulled a curtain across the opening of the cage to give them privacy. Melanie could see the backs of his shoes below the curtain, standing watch in the hallway.

"There it is," his mother said. She held a palm up toward the safe deposit box. Removed from the wall, it was less a box than a tray, open at the top. The thing lying inside looked like a parcel you might get in the mail. Smiles walked up to the box, keeping his hands carefully away from the package for the moment. His face was bloodless.

He looked to Melanie. She gave him a nod of encouragement, stepping forward to look on with him. Finally, Smiles grasped the package. As he pulled it out of the box, they could see that one end of it was open. Melanie inched right up to the island as Smiles reached in and pulled out another parcel-looking package.

This one had an address and postmark on it. It had been sent to Andrei Eltsin, at a Boston address. "Smiles, that . . ."

"Yeah?"

She remembered plugging it into her GPS, driving down the sad little street with the market at the end.

"That's where he lived."

"He mailed that package to himself," his mom said. "He did it to prove that the idea in there was his. The postmark establishes the date."

Smiles turned the package, and in the faded black ink of the postmark they could see that it had been mailed on a December day almost twenty years ago.

The gummy flap at the top of the package was loose. This was it—he was going to find out everything in a second. Melanie took a long breath to slow her beating heart.

Smiles peeled away the flap.

Inside was a thin spiral notebook, still new-looking. The red cover wasn't scratched at all. When Smiles flicked the pages, they appeared empty. But then he turned back to the front, and Melanie saw what was written on the top line of the first page:

A SYSTEM FOR ASYMMETRICAL ENCRYPTION

Melanie held fast to the table. She knew enough about Alyce to understand what it meant, and now she wished that she *had* held Smiles's hand, that she *had* taken charge, that she *had* protected him. She wished that she had pulled him out of the bank ten minutes ago, because she didn't want him seeing this.

No one said a word. Slowly, Smiles ran a finger across

the mathematical process etched onto the page in the hand of Andrei Tarasov. He knew, too.

It was his dad's breakthrough. His special encryption system. The entire foundation for Alyce Systems, and all the wealth that followed.

"Your father stole it," his mother said.

SMILES HAD GONE numb.

It was like hearing the doctors tell him about his dad's cancer. It was worse than that. It was like hearing his mom had died.

Across the island, Melanie spun the notebook to her, disbelieving. "Tarasov . . . My dad said he made everything up."

"He didn't," Smiles's mother said in that clinical way. "This is the proof. This is the basis for the technology Alyce Systems uses. It *is* the technology."

A shadow moved under the curtain, and the guard's voice said, "Folks, we can give you about five more minutes there, that's it."

"Yes, thank you," Melanie called behind her.

His mother took the notebook and the packaging and placed them all in Smiles's hands. "You know the truth now."

Smiles's brain fought it like an infection. "How did you even get this?"

"The night that man killed himself, he left this package

at our front door. I was alone with you at the house. I was the one who received it."

"And . . . what? You knew what this meant somehow?"

His mother smoothed her jacket, attempting patience. "Of course I knew what it meant. I'm a mathematician, a very good one. I was involved in your dad's company from the start. It's named after me. So yes, as soon as I opened it, I knew that it meant your father had stolen that man's work."

Her eyes challenged his, and Smiles felt a flame inside himself. "And so you left? That was your solution?"

Her head bowed, and Smiles enjoyed the feeling of breaking her down. Suddenly, he wanted to punish this woman for everything she'd ever done.

"I did a terrible thing in leaving you," she said. Her voice had lost its polish. She was all cracks and shards, broken pieces of herself. "I did an absolutely unforgivable thing, and it haunts me every single day. But when I found out what your father had done, it changed everything for me. I couldn't stay with him, couldn't live off a stolen fortune. But I wasn't strong enough to take you with me, not then. Your father is a resourceful man—he would have made it very difficult for us to leave together."

"You have no idea what he would have done."

"Yes I do. And I knew that if I was going to leave, I had to shut the door completely. It would have been too painful any other way. Staying away from you has been the hardest thing in my life." She raised her chin, resisting tears. "But it's made me very . . . tough. I think you'll find that your greatest sources of pain in life also show you your greatest strengths."

"Glad it worked out for you," Smiles said.

She closed her eyes against his sneer.

"Smylies?" It was Mr. Perry, outside the curtain. Melanie slipped outside and began whispering to him, buying them time.

Smiles still had stores of anger to burn. "But you didn't stay away, did you? You tried to get my mom involved—the one who was actually there for me."

Smiles took pleasure in the mud puddles of mascara on her face, the bloodshot stains on her eyes. She dabbed at them, collecting herself. "A year ago I heard about your father's cancer," she said. "I didn't know what to do, honestly—I'd always wanted you to get this information after you turned eighteen, when you were an adult and could handle it. But I felt it important that someone close to your father know before the end. In case there was a chance for amends. So I informed Rose. She didn't believe me, naturally. And that's when we went together to Professor Worth, to confirm for her that your father had stolen Mr. Eltsin's work."

Smiles refused to believe it. He fanned the fire inside himself—that's what he would hold on to, not his mother's accusations. "You don't know what he did. This doesn't mean anything." Smiles swept the notebook off the table. It fluttered and smacked against the wall.

His mother watched it fall. Something snapped, and when her eyes bored into him again, they were clear and white. "I know *exactly* what he did. He ruined all of us."

She was nearly yelling. Melanie had stepped back into the room. She looked on, her head retreating on her neck, a scared bystander. Smiles's mother took a stride toward him, closing the space between them. Her stiffened spine made her three inches taller. She angled over the table. "You want to know? This is what your father did. He took the trust of a beautiful young man and destroyed him. When Andrei Eltsin was doing work for your father, he was approached by the Russian intelligence service. They wanted him to inform on the advanced work being done here. They wanted him to spy. Andrei wanted nothing to do with it, but he made the mistake of going to your father for guidance.

"Unfortunately for him, he had also just gone to your father with his brilliant idea for making asymmetrical encryption viable over the Internet. He trusted your father. He looked up to him as a mentor. And do you know what your father did?" She leaned farther over the table, and Smiles felt himself retreat. *"Do you know what he did?"*

Smiles waited for it.

"He set him up. He told Andrei to meet with the Russian spies again, so they could get more information before going to the authorities. Then he called the State Department and told them he suspected Andrei of spying. They arrested him a few days later, at the meeting your father had told him to arrange. All so he could steal Andrei's idea and call it his own."

She backed down to her heels, her chest heaving under her blouse. Smiles felt as though he'd been cored out, as if some essential part of himself no longer existed.

"That's what your father did," she said as the calm returned to her voice. "He might as well have killed that man. He ruined his life, and mine, too. I wanted to be his wife. I wanted to run Alyce Systems with him." Her fingers clawed at the island. And she whispered, "I wanted, more than anything, to be your mother."

"I got the mom I wanted," Smiles said.

But when she turned and left the room, he felt abandoned again.

MELANIE WATCHED SMILES carefully as he started up the car. She wouldn't have blamed him for breaking down, or needing to be alone, or wanting to turn the car directly into oncoming traffic. In the short span of fifteen minutes, the burnished image of his father had been utterly demolished.

She didn't know how Smiles could face his dad now, but he was pointing the car toward the hospital. "You mind if we see him?" Smiles said. The first words he'd spoken since leaving the bank.

"No," Melanie said quietly.

It wasn't just his dad who had been revealed at the bank, either. Melanie now had her own demon.

"Your father wasn't the one who had that letter destroyed," she said. "My dad did it."

Melanie was sure of it. He'd done it for the same reason he'd lied to her and Jenna: He didn't want any of this coming out, because it would mean the end of his career as well. He must have known all along that Mr. Smylie had stolen the formula. Still, he'd chosen to go along with it. His entire career was a lie, just as much as Mr. Smylie's was. The truth hit her like a series of punches as they drove in silence to the hospital, parked in the garage, and walked across the skywalk to the cancer center.

Melanie had never been as proud as Smiles as she was at that moment. He kept himself firmly together while she dangled on the edge of sanity right next to him. Their lives had changed drastically in the last half hour, and she wondered how this would affect each of them down the line. But looking at him there, holding himself steady through the push of the crowd in the skywalk, she liked his chances of being okay.

He was never the cracked dish I always imagined him to be. She thought this as they pushed open the doors of the neuro-oncology center. At the reception desk, a striking woman with manicured dreadlocks offered tender eyes for Smiles. Her name tag said SHANTI.

Seeing their disheveled state, she leapt from behind the desk and locked her hands in front of her. "Your dad's okay, but he's in with someone. Let me see if I can clear them out of there. One minute."

They watched her disappear down the hallway, leaving them standing near a corner of chairs and golf magazines. Everything about the situation was horrible, but Melanie could at least enjoy the fact that her need to mother Smiles had left her entirely.

Shanti returned up the hallway and beckoned them back.

"Go ahead," Melanie said to Smiles. "I'll wait for you."

And then she saw the person coming up behind Shanti, the one she'd cleared out of Mr. Smylie's room. It was her dad. He labored over to her, looking sharp in a charcoal suit with subtle pinstripes. Starched white shirt. French cuffs. Gold tie. Ready for the IPO.

"How could you, Dad?" Melanie said.

HE LOOKED BETTER today. He looked much better, but somehow Smiles knew he was close to the end.

Smiles didn't go to his usual seat, the one by the picture of his mom. Instead he walked to his dad's side, pulled away the L-shaped tray with his dinner plate and *Economist* magazine, and took a seat at the edge of the bed. He felt no anger at all.

His dad breathed deeply. "You know, then?"

Smiles nodded. He wondered if his dad remembered their last conversation, when he'd asked if Smiles had seen the package. It didn't matter.

"You told me about the notebook on my birthday. You wanted me to know, didn't you?"

"It's the great burden of my life, that lie." He looked about the silent room, as if it might offer a way out of his past. "That poor man—"

"Dad, you don't need to." A group of nurses passed loudly in the hallway. From the next room, Smiles heard the deflating hiss of a machine. He shifted closer to his dad, laying a hand against his leg. "You've been a great father," he said.

His dad shook his head. "Andrei was a great father. He had a wife and child here, more important to him than anything. He snuck back into the country just to be with them." His eyes had gone away somewhere, going over the thoughts of Andrei Eltsin that must have plagued him his whole life. His father waved a weak hand toward the green screen. Tomorrow morning, the company would go public. Smiles was going to be here for it—he wasn't going to let them put his dad on the screen if he was weak. Smiles was going to protect him to the end.

"The frustration was too much for him," his dad said, unable to let Andrei Eltsin rest. "Alyce taking off, realizing the potential of his idea. He cracked, or perhaps the State Department found him again. That's when he killed himself."

Smiles nodded, and saw that his dad's lips were dry and cracked. He passed him a cup of juice from his tray and watched his dad suck at the straw, looking older than Smiles had ever seen him.

"Love of family. That's what I should have taken from him, not his ideas. Family is the most important, remember that." His dad let the straw go and Smiles returned it to the tray. "When you leave," his dad said, "will you call Mr. Hunt back here? It doesn't matter how late he comes."

"Sure, Dad," Smiles said. He got up and went to the iPod, scrolling through the classical music choices and settling on something from Mozart, his dad's favorite. By the time he looked up, his dad was asleep.

Smiles settled into the seat by the picture of his mom and listened to the whole album there. Every once in a while Shanti stopped at the door to make sure they were okay. When the music stopped playing his dad opened his eyes and found Smiles.

"Good night, Robert," he said.

SMILES HAD FORGOTTEN about Melanie. But there she was in the softest chair the waiting area had to offer, her feet resting on the table with the magazines, her cheek puffed out on one side. It was her I'm-doing-some-thinking-about-life look.

He was going to have to do a lot of that himself. He knew that what he learned about his dad hadn't really hit him yet. Still, the day had crashed over him violently. And maybe he was just dazed from the impact, but he felt a lightness as he walked over and nudged Melanie's foot. After so much had gone wrong in the absolute worst possible way, anything else he had to face seemed rather small by comparison.

Right now, he had to face Melanie. They'd never really talked after his birthday night, and they needed to clear the air.

Melanie stirred herself upright. "How are you?" she said, then shook her head at the question. "Scratch that. Ignore me."

"I'll manage. You?"

She nodded too enthusiastically to be the truth.

Smiles was starving, and he thought for a second about asking her to the kabob place. She might misinterpret that, though, and the truth was that his heart was in a strange place—stolen by a girl who'd taken $7 million with it.

"My dad wants your dad to come back and see him. Like, tonight. It doesn't matter how late, he said. Mind asking him for me?"

"Yeah, sure," Melanie said as she stood. "Is he going to be okay for the IPO tomorrow?"

Smiles shrugged. "So listen," he said, "probably not the greatest timing known to man, but could we talk about us for a second?"

"Yeah, uh, if that's what you want."

Shanti shuffled some papers at the desk, stuffing things in folders and wrapping up for the night. "Let's walk," Smiles said, and they waved good-bye to her on the way out.

They weren't alone again until they got to the skywalk. Night had fallen while he was in with his dad, and the hospital campus was a landscape of grays through the skywalk windows. "So after that night, you know, my birthday. Things got crazy, but I wanted to talk to you. Because you're really important to—"

"Hey, Smiles?" Melanie had stopped in the middle of the skywalk. "Would you mind if I said something first?"

"Uh, no—go ahead." He returned to her, watched her stare out at a crane glowing with yellow lights.

"I can't even imagine what you've been through, okay? I was dealing with some stuff this weekend, too, though."

Her eyes followed the sway of the crane. "And it's just . . . I've always defined myself in relation to other people. I'm your girlfriend, you know? Or my dad's daughter. Or somebody's student. Even in my own head. It's really stupid."

"You're not stupid, Mel. That's the last thing you are."

"Yeah, well, I guess it's time for me to be me. Whatever that is."

He saw, then, what she was trying to say.

"I get it," he said. "I never really deserved you, Mel."

She shook her head. "We just came to an end."

"You know," Smiles said, "you're much better at these breakups the second time around."

Her laugh soothed him.

"I think you're going to like being Melanie Hunt," he said.

"She's okay?"

"She's super cool," Smiles said, and they walked together to the Infiniti.

✕

Smiles got takeout from the kabob place, then let an action movie roll across his eyes just so he could stop thinking about everything for a minute. It didn't really work—he turned it off before the all-female special ops force even made it into the North Korean nuclear power plant. He had camped out on his sofa, where he used to crash three or four times a week. But his favorite spot no longer felt like home.

The ghost of Erin whispered in his ear. He went out to the all-night drugstore, then spent a good hour using the cleaning products all around the place, vacuuming and scrubbing and washing the glass of his aquariums clear. After the carpet cleaner set into the rug for half an hour, Lake Jägermeister came up without a hitch. By the time he'd put the second load of laundry in downstairs, the place was spotless and bright, looking three times larger without his junk strewn across the floor.

He stowed the cleaning products under the kitchen sink. "There," he said, not sure who he'd done it for, but proud all the same. He was going to have to leave this place soon, unless he found a job that paid the rent. And Erin wasn't walking through that door, either. Did he want her to? Did he even know her? Nothing in his life was real except a clean carpet and a sudden urge to get back to his dad.

He grabbed his duffel bag from his newly organized closet and threw some overnight stuff inside. Smiles didn't know how much more time he had left with his dad, and tomorrow was going to be a big day.

"The mathematics are usually considered as being the very antipodes of Poesy. Yet Mathesis and Poesy are of the closest kindred, for they are both works of the imagination."

—Thomas Hill

TUESDAY

"Revenge is profitable."

—Edward Gibbon,
The Decline and Fall of the Roman Empire

"THEY JUST LEFT," Shanti said.

It was after midnight now, but she was still at the hospital. Her purse still hung across her shoulder like it had hours ago, when she'd been getting ready to leave the first time. A team of businessmen had shown up on her way out, she said. They had come to see his dad.

"I didn't feel right leaving him," Shanti said. "Not tonight."

"Thank you." Smiles assumed that Mr. Hunt was one of the visitors, but didn't know why he would have brought a whole team with him. "Any idea what it was about?"

Shanti yawned and shook her head.

"Well, I guess I didn't feel right leaving, either. Okay if I spend the night in there?"

"Sure, honey. Blankets in that little closet." She fished her keys out of her purse, gave him a hug, and flashed a sad smile on her way out.

Smiles walked the darkened hallway to his dad's room, stopping for a moment at the open door. The beeping machines throughout the floor sounded like a twisted version of a summer night. Smiles cleaned off the whiteboard with his shirt, then wrote as perfectly as he could: *Robert Smylie*. He leaned against the doorjamb and looked on for a minute, his dad's small body lying peacefully under the sheets.

People do their best, his dad had said after he'd signed the document. *They do their best and they make terrible mistakes*. Smiles had thought he'd been talking about his mother, but he was talking about himself.

Smiles turned the Mozart album on low and found a paper-thin blanket in the small supply closet in his dad's room. He sunk into the chair in the corner, stretching his legs out on the wobbly ottoman and pulling the blanket up to his shoulders. The light from the hallway glinted off the metal clasps on the video production boxes. Above them, he could just make out the dark architecture of the lights and monitors assembled for the big show.

The thought of his dad performing tomorrow—touting his company to the world, the one built on a lie—made Smiles uneasy. But something told him, as his eyes fell shut for the night, that his father would never get the chance.

✕

They wheeled his body away at five o'clock in the morning, the nurses moving in a somber ballet about the room. Smiles woke just as an overnight nurse he didn't know was taking his dad's pulse, finding him gone. She gave him a moment at the bedside, and then the quiet rush of activity began—his dad being untethered from his hospital bed, calls being made, men in scrubs whisking the body downstairs until it was released to the funeral home, they said. At some point, Smiles signed a form that was thrust in front of him.

He wished Shanti had been there. He wished Erin had been there. He stayed in the room because no one asked him to leave, and because he could still feel his dad's presence. Morning hadn't broken yet. Smiles returned to the chair and pulled the blanket over himself. Looking around the room, it occurred to him that he would have to bring his dad's things home with him—the picture of his mom and the iPod with all his favorite music on it. It was then that he noticed that the music had been shut off, and it was then that he began to cry.

✗

Mr. Hunt found him shortly after six in the morning. Smiles was still cemented in the chair, wide awake but reluctant to move, when he saw Mr. Hunt pass quickly down the hallway, his head swiveling about. His shoes squeaked on the tile, and then a second later Mr. Hunt popped back into the door and said, "There you are."

He spoke it loudly, out of breath from his search, and then he seemed to remember himself and settled himself in the doorway. He walked gingerly over to Smiles and knelt before the chair. "Smiles, I'm so sorry. I just heard."

Smiles nodded. He didn't hold anything against Mr. Hunt. "Thank you."

"It's good that you were here," he said, an empty sentiment spoken to fill the air. Mr. Hunt stayed put at Smiles's side. He coughed and drew his hand over his mouth, and Smiles realized he was about to hear why Mr. Hunt had really come to the hospital.

"Smiles, umm, I know that you have only one thing on your mind right now, and if I had a choice I would leave you alone in your grief. But the fact is, we've been rather frantically looking for you since we heard about your father."

"We?"

"The people who work with me in Alyce's legal department. You see, something happened last night—something unexpected. I suppose, perhaps, your father knew his time was coming."

"He called you over here. Why?"

"Yes, that's right, he called us over here." Mr. Hunt stopped and cleared his throat. "And Smiles, he made you the beneficiary of his entire interest in Alyce Systems."

Smiles drew the blanket down from his chest. "He what? What does that mean?"

"Well, it . . ." Mr. Hunt stopped at a sound from the entrance to the room. Four people had appeared there—a man and a woman who looked like lawyers, and two older guys wearing shirts with the logo of the video production company. "A moment, please." Mr. Hunt shooed them with a hand, and they scurried into the hall.

"Smiles, you now own about twenty-five percent of Alyce Systems. But there's something more important. As you know, your dad liked to make decisions himself. So

Alyce mostly issued non-voting stock, which gives people a share of the company but no control over it. Your father managed to keep fifty-one percent of the voting stock for himself. The bottom line is, as of this moment, you control Alyce Systems yourself."

Smiles heard a laugh come from his mouth.

"Now, I hate to ask you this, but decisions have to be made about this morning. The market opens in only a few hours, and we're scheduled to open trading in Alyce at ten o'clock on the New York Stock Exchange. We have to say something to our employees and investors. That's why those people are here, to get ready for the broadcast." He pointed a thumb over his shoulder.

"I think the easiest thing, Smiles, is to go ahead as planned. You can simply designate someone from the company to speak to the employees. I'd be happy to do it myself."

Mr. Hunt waited. Smiles remembered how he had waited for Ben to give the go-ahead at Fox Creek. He had the distinct impression that Mr. Hunt wanted him to sign off on the suggestion just as much. A line of sweat trailed down the side of his face. Smiles fought a reflex to agree—to slide into the easiest groove life offered. He had a responsibility to someone—if only himself—to take this seriously. And now, with much more than his $7 million at stake, the last thing he'd be was an easy mark.

But why shouldn't he go along with it?

If he put it all on autopilot, he'd be the owner of Alyce Systems—a dream come to life. You didn't give up the thing you always wanted. You didn't give up the trust of your father—the trust that, when it finally came, felt like the greatest gift of all.

"Don't do anything yet," he said to Mr. Hunt. "I need to talk to somebody first."

LIKE EVERYTHING IN Back Bay, the Four Seasons on Boylston reeked of money. The sidewalk out front had been freshly hosed down, and the double doors at the front were framed with shining brass. A doorman opened them for Smiles. The woman at the reception desk beamed beside a massive bowl exploding with flowers.

His mother had said she'd be waiting in her room. It was a good thing he'd called so early—she had a morning flight, she said, and she'd be leaving for the airport soon. But yes, she would make time. She wanted to see him before going back to California. Smiles could hear, from her voice, that she didn't know yet.

He rode the elevator to the fourth floor, checking the time on his phone. It was nearing seven o'clock. In just two hours, someone would have to make that speech. Before that, Smiles would have to tell Mr. Hunt what he wanted to do about the IPO.

He found room 434 down a hallway lined with expensive wallpaper. Cream with blue stripes. Soft colors for an easy life.

Smiles could have an easy life if he wanted. He just had to turn around, give the all clear, and go to Fox Creek every weekend. A suite at Fenway. His eighteenth birthday every day, to make up for the one that had gone wrong.

He knocked on the door.

She opened it, and for a moment just took in the sight of him. She wore another smart suit, this one dark blue, her hair sleek from the shower. But there was little chill in her face this morning.

"Please," she said, and opened her arms. Smiles found himself wanting it, and her body felt small and feathery in his arms. She dabbed at the edges of her eyes when they parted, her mascara holding up. "I'm so sorry about yester-day. I shouldn't have . . . I had no right to . . ."

"Dad died last night," Smiles said, because there was no way to ease into it.

She nodded softly. "Yes, I see," she said. "Thank you for coming. Thank you for telling me." She pulled a chair out from the tiny desk in her suite. It was a French Victorian thing, fancy and proud on the outside, masking an essential fragility—more like his mother, he realized, than he ever would have thought just days ago. When she rubbed at her forehead, Smiles could see her age in the imperfections of her hand. "Would you like me to stay?" she said. "For the funeral?"

"It's not just about that," Smiles said. "It's about some-thing you said yesterday."

"Robert, I was terribly—"

"No, please, we don't actually have a lot of time. Yesterday you said you wanted to run Alyce Systems with my dad. That was your plan."

"Yes, it was."

"So what I'm wondering is: Would you want to run it yourself?"

"GOOD MORNING. I know that I'm not the person you expected to see here today."

It was so awkward, talking into the camera with the lights in his face, the huddle of lawyers at his sides, the green screen behind him. On the monitors at the edge of his vision, he appeared before an image of the Alyce logo, the great bronze keys locking into each other. Private key and public key.

Directly in front of him, in the flesh, five hundred Alyce Systems employees crowded the lobby of the headquarters. Smiles had insisted on doing the speech there rather than the hospital. His dad was gone now. These people deserved to hear from him in person. Mr. Hunt had spent ten minutes trying to dissuade him from moving the operation, but Smiles didn't care if a few lights were askew, or if they couldn't use the biggest camera. He thought his dad would approve, and it gave him the resolve to order everyone downtown.

Now they were here, and Smiles was sweating inside

a suit that one of Mr. Hunt's lawyers had procured for him on fifteen minutes' notice. He could feel the tag of the scratchy shirt digging into his forearm. Still in his tennis shoes, he stood on the X that had been duct-taped to the floor. Between him and the audience was just the thin glass podium.

Despite Mr. Hunt's protests, they'd done an amazing job setting up in under an hour. Smiles stood on a raised platform that let him see every last employee who had shown up. And if the heat of the lights in his face was any indication, those things were working just fine. He breathed and started reading from the teleprompter, where the speech one of Mr. Hunt's lackeys had written in record time scrolled slowly upward.

"I am Robert Smylie Jr., the son of Robert Smylie." The next line on the screen said something about how the people might know his dad as a friend, mentor, or inspiration— or probably all three. Smiles couldn't make his mouth regurgitate it. Time to wing it.

"My dad passed away last night. In his sleep, peacefully, and well cared for." Smiles felt the movement of lawyers behind him, worrying that he'd gone off script. "His death is a great loss to his loved ones and to Alyce Systems. To you, the people who actually do the work here." He could read the stunned reaction of the employees in the too-still body language of the crowd.

"I was surprised to find out just this morning that as a result of my father's death, majority control of the company has passed to me. But don't worry, I realize how scary that may sound." A riffle of laughter swept through the crowd. Smiles heard a clipped laugh burst from one of the lawyers behind him. At least somebody liked it. "And like I said, you do the work here, not me. I never had much to do with my dad's company, to be honest with you, and to be in control of it when others have worked so hard would feel like . . . stealing. So, as my one and only act as a shareholder, I'm doing the best thing I can to put the company in the right hands. They are the hands of a woman who was with this company from the start. It's named after her, actually. She is Alice Taft, and she'll now take over."

Smiles pulled away from the stares of the crowd, utterly drained.

His mom passed him on her way to the podium, giving him a peck on the cheek. "Perfect," she said.

MELANIE ACTUALLY TOUCHED the screen. She thought she had been proud of him yesterday, but this was something else. She wanted to reach through and give him the biggest hug she ever had.

She'd found the webcast on the Alyce Systems website and had skipped Early European History to watch it. She thought maybe she should take her laptop over to the cubicles at the edge of the media center, because she was going to start bawling in a second. A good cry, for once.

She typed out a text: *"Beaming with pride. Be good to yourself—you're super cool, too."*

The webcast continued—Alice was stepping to the podium now—but Melanie had seen Smiles's performance and that was all she cared about. She drew the headphones off her ears, ready to disconnect from the entire saga.

On the video feed, she couldn't help noticing her father in a line of suited executives behind the podium. He'd been up all night, Melanie knew. After she'd come back from the hospital last night, she'd relayed Mr. Smylie's request to see him. It was well past midnight when he returned, but Melanie was up to hear him. She was stirring honey into a mug of tea, still restless from the day, running the scene from the bank over and over in her mind. She didn't want to believe that Mr. Smylie was a thief. She didn't want to think her dad was involved. But she knew that both of those things were true.

Her dad entered the kitchen softly and stopped at the sight of her, like a cat burglar caught off guard. Melanie pulled her robe tight across her chest. She warmed herself with a sip of tea while her dad made his exhausted approach to the kitchen table.

He grabbed the back of a chair. "Do you mind?"

Melanie dipped her head permissively, not trusting herself to engage.

He sat and folded his thick fingers through each other, elbows spread wide on the table. The sigh that preceded his confession may have been the saddest sound that Melanie had ever heard. The story came out as Melanie suspected: He'd known what Mr. Smylie had done from the beginning. He should have stopped it—or at least left Alyce—but he didn't. He put off Rose when she found out the truth. And when he read the letter that would have given Smiles access to the safe deposit box, he destroyed it himself.

"I'm just as guilty, in a way, as Robert," he said at last. Melanie didn't disagree with him.

"Is there anything else you want to know?" her dad asked.

Melanie settled her empty tea mug on the table. "Just

about Rose," she said. She needed to hear it from him. "You didn't have any—"

"Oh no," he said, and finally she knew it was the truth. "I'm not that far gone, Mel."

She nodded and went up the stairs, and a few hours later the call had come about Mr. Smylie. The sound of the front door closing was the last she'd heard of him. Now, he looked tiny and uncomfortable in the corner of her monitor.

She clicked the webcast closed. There was still a half hour left in the period, but she was in no mood to fill it with homework. A thought was pushing itself forward in her mind, past her disappointment in her dad and even her pride in Smiles. After a few minutes she gave in to it, returning to the computer and pulling up the Vassar website. Just as she found the page she'd been looking for, the text response came back from Smiles: *Think I got a j-o-b already. Gonna be responsible like Melanie Hunt. Take care, you.*

She stared dumbly at it for minutes, then turned back to the website. She was responsible, yes, she'd always be responsible. But she needed to find the other parts of herself, too, and maybe this wasn't the place to do it.

DEFERMENT PROGRAM, the page said. Melanie clicked. Vassar could wait a year.

She spun a globe in her head and dreamed big.

In the search box, she typed: "Gap year Buenos Aires." She pressed return, and in her mind she was already off.

A GROUP OF nurses swept in, mopping the room down. A pretty black nurse folded clothes from the room's little closet. She did it carefully, slowly, like she didn't want it to end. She finally laid them quietly at the base of a cardboard box. She unplugged the mini-stereo and put that over them. The last thing to go was a picture of a bride—his mom, probably. The good one. Rose.

Pursing her lips and shaking her head, the nurse carried the box out of the room and to the front of the neuro-oncology center. Ben turned away and got a drink from the fountain, hoping to look like just another visitor. It had been easy to sneak back here, with all the comings and goings.

He stared at the bed inside the room. He'd planned to have his crowning moment right there at the foot of it. That's where Ben would have told Robert Smylie what he'd done to Smiles. Ben would say he did it for his father,

Andrei Eltsin—the man Robert Smylie had cheated out of life. Ben would say he did it for his mom—whose life he had ruined as well. The swindle was the best revenge they could get. Going to the police was never an option for them, since Ben's dad left his only evidence of the theft at the Smylies' front door. Along with his blood.

It would be revenge enough to hurt Robert Smylie. To stand at the foot of his bed and tell the great man that he'd taken his money. That he'd made a fool of his son. That his mom would now live in the comfort she deserved, a small measure of her rightful fortune returned.

But Robert Smylie had stolen that moment from him as well. There was nothing in that room except a tightly made bed and a television screen, cutting live to the Alyce Systems IPO. Smiles's biological mother, Alice Taft, was up there for some reason. Ben edged to the doorway to hear it.

"The first thing I want to tell you is that the public offering will not be going forward today," she said. "It's not appropriate in light of our founder's death, and the uncertainty in the market that could result. For those of you with stock, your shares might be undervalued if we were to go forward. What's most important is to step back and demonstrate that Alyce Systems continues to have strong leadership and a strong vision."

Ben hunted out Smiles in the phalanx of bodies behind her. The scroll at the bottom of the screen said: ALYCE SYSTEMS IPO HALTED. ALICE TAFT, COMPANY NAMESAKE, INSTALLED AS CEO. Somehow, his mom had taken control of the company. But Ben saw no trace of bitterness on Smiles's face. Just the same buoyant smile he'd worn every day, hour after hour, sanding Ben's hatred thin.

There was no revenge in this world. There was only going forward.

Ben went to the reception desk and asked the pretty nurse if he could leave a note for somebody.

FOR TEN MINUTES, Smiles watched his mom grab hold of the confused crowd and turn it in her direction.

That voice, he thought. The distant voice that he could never reach—he could hear, now, that it was the voice of a leader. Smiles didn't understand half of what she was saying, but the authority she projected cut through any doubt about his decision.

They clapped for her at the end.

"Masterful," Mr. Hunt said, shaking her hand as she led them off the podium. In the transformed mood of the lobby, employees gathered to greet her on her way out. The bodies pushed closer, and Smiles found himself turned to Mr. Hunt. Smiles nodded and made for the street—he knew the man's secret now, and it would never be the same between them.

Employees spilled from the revolving doors, then the lawyers, then the workers who'd set up the platform and all the rest of it. The lobby was emptying, the marble floor dull with shoe prints. Smiles felt sorry for the guy who had to buff it.

He stood outside the building for forty minutes, breathing the air and waiting for his mother. The huge logo shadowed him on the sidewalk. At last she came, exuding a tired energy. She cocked her head at the sight of him.

"You didn't wait for me all this time, did you?"

"I didn't mind," he said.

"Well, thank you. That was sweet." They had so much to say to each other, but nothing came out. In time, maybe. "So . . . when do you want to start?"

Her one condition of taking Smiles's stock and becoming CEO was that Smiles join the company, too. She had always thought Alyce Systems should have an educational program on the human side of security. Smiles would lead a team that would go to high schools, senior centers, and conferences to instruct people on being careful with passwords and avoiding Internet scams. He could make videos, too. She wanted him to make the program as big as he could. It would be *his own thing*, she said.

"How's tomorrow?" Smiles said, and she liked it. "You can find your way back to the hotel?"

"I hope so," she said. "It's my hometown, remember?"

They couldn't exactly be at ease with each other yet, but Smiles appreciated the effort.

"I think you're going to be good at this job," she said. She gave a small laugh then, shaking her head. "Can I tell you something? Before he nearly threw you out of the conference, the head of CRYPTCON thought you were the most charming student he'd met. He said, 'I was sure I was talking to the student whose research you presented.'"

"Just a little off on that one," Smiles said.

"Well, yes. Especially since that student was a girl," she said with a wink.

A girl?

ERIN LOOKED OUT on the street from the widow's walk, watching the day change to night and wondering where she'd be in a year. She had a place for the next month at least. Ben had given her keys and said the rent was paid through the thirtieth. He and his mom were going to stay in a nice hotel until they found a new home.

She could remember his first phone call, six months ago, as vividly as yesterday. He had skipped around things a lot, not saying too much at first, but somehow he kept her on the line. And then slowly his plan for the con had come out. He needed a pretty girl who knew a lot about math. He'd come across her name in his extensive research into every area of Mr. Smylie's life. A local girl who was doing research under his ex-wife? Candidates didn't get more perfect than that.

Erin thought it was perfect, too. She'd been half a year into an experiment to get her life on track and was already getting bored. Maybe she was a genius, but the life of a student fit her too tight. She liked counting cards, and she'd probably still be at it if she hadn't been blacklisted at every casino in Vegas by then. She liked playing with people. She liked gambling in every part of her life.

School was supposed to set her straight, but she'd jumped at Ben's plan.

And now she hated herself for what she'd done. Saying yes to Ben, it turned out, had been the ultimate act of self-sabotage.

She leaned back against the roof and felt the trapped warmth of the shingles under her back. She knew she would come up here every night and think about what it would be like if she had screwed the plan and stayed at that cabin with Smiles. If she'd told him the truth and crossed her fingers that he'd still want to be with her.

And then, looking down at the weed-strewn parking lot of Mercado Rosanna, she saw a black Infiniti going too fast down the cross street. He overshot the market, reversed in the street, and turned up toward the house.

Erin raced down the stairs and peered through the dirty glass of the front door. Her giddy smile faded as the minutes wore on. Maybe he hadn't come back for her at all. Maybe he'd come here to confront Ben. He could be dialing the police right now, waiting for them to arrive.

Erin stepped backward, scared.

✗

Smiles flapped the note in his hands, deciding.

Shanti had given it to him when he returned for one last good-bye. "Real little fella"—that was her description of Ben. The note said:

Sorry, kinda.
You never found me a girlfriend. There's one waiting for you here,
though, if you care anymore.

Ben

And at the bottom, an address—the same address from the postmark on Andrei Eltsin's package. Smiles was parked across from it now, unclear on what exactly he was doing there. The shabby house had a tree stump in its tiny front yard, a crack like a canyon in its front steps. Ben had probably grown up here, a million miles from Weston. Smiles looked at the small windows, the torn curtains, the sloppy porch, and he wondered if this was insanity.

Certainly, it wasn't smart on any level. No way could you call it the responsible choice. Definitely, there would be messy feelings to get through. He wavered, shifting the car from park to drive and back again.

Oh please, came his mom's voice. *This isn't brain surgery, pardon the phrase.*

Smiles was grinning to himself when the voice changed, and he heard his dad speak. *She's right. Trust your instincts—they're better than you think.*

Nodding, Smiles pulled the keys from the Infiniti and cracked the door.

He stood tall on the street. And then, with the house in sight before him, he broke into a run.

ACKNOWLEDGMENTS

The Cipher takes audacious liberties with the history of public-key cryptography, which is widely used in our daily lives and which was created by pioneers in the field, not fictional characters. Among those pioneers are Whitfield Diffie, Martin Hellman, and Ralph Merkle, who are credited with the development of public-key cryptography; Ron Rivest, Adi Shamir, and Leonard Adleman, the cofounders of RSA Security, who in 1977 developed the RSA encryption algorithm, one of the earliest and most popular methods used in secure data transmission; and Clifford Cocks, who developed a system similar to RSA's in 1973 while working at GCHQ, the British intelligence agency. Cocks was building on the insight of James Ellis, a cryptographer and employee of GCHQ, who earlier had conceived of "non-secret encryption," which we now know as public-key cryptography.

Due to its top-secret nature, the work of Ellis and Cocks was not revealed publicly until 1997. James Ellis died one month before the announcement.

It is my hope that *The Cipher* stimulates interest in the brilliance of these individuals and others in their field, rather than detracting from it. I also hope that it stimulates interest in the Riemann Hypothesis, the 1859 conjecture that remains unproven as of this writing. If you do solve it, the Clay Mathematics Institute has a $1,000,000 reward waiting. In the meantime, there are several fascinating accounts of the Riemann Hypothesis available for reading, including *The Music of the Primes: Searching to Solve the Greatest Mystery in Mathematics*, by Marcus du Sautoy; and *Prime Obsession: Bernhard Riemann and the Greatest Unsolved Problem in Mathematics*, by John Derbyshire.

I am thankful to those who shared my enthusiasm for this subject (or just listened patiently) as I wrote *The Cipher*. I am particularly grateful to the Fates that placed me in the hands of editor Kendra Levin, who guided me to numerous eureka moments as we solved the puzzle of this story together. You could call her the private key of this novel. Likewise, Sara Crowe, as she does, gave advice and support that exceeded the bounds of literary representation.

Many others at Viking have lent their talents to these pages (and the cover over them) in the publication process, including assistant editor Joanna Cardenas, copyeditors Kate Hurley and Abigail Powers, and designer Eileen Savage. All of them have my sincere thanks, as do readers Karen Barna, Tim Bentler-Jungr, Barb Goffman, Zachary Leffel, Gina Montefusco, Mindi Scott, and Laura Weatherly.

**TURN THE PAGE FOR AN EXCERPT FROM
JOHN C. FORD'S FIRST NOVEL—
AN EDGAR AND AGATHA AWARD NOMINEE!**

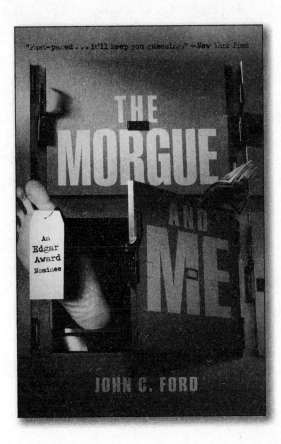

Prologue

When you're eighteen years old and you shoot somebody in a public place at two in the morning, of course you expect some attention. Especially when it's the person I shot, and especially when you're found right there on the scene with that person at your feet, gasping away in a pool of blood that seeps around your shoes. Still, I find it really embarrassing.

It's strange to be in the paper every single day. In the first story, under the giant headline, they ran a blown-up version of my high-school graduation photo. The cap looked ridiculous, not to mention my blotchy face or the magenta robe, four sizes too big. Over the next week, they used three different pictures of me in a parade of humiliating poses: fake smile, half-closed eyes, *in my pajamas*. I don't know where they dug them up, but they must have run out, because yesterday they called the house and asked for more. My mom called them "vultures" and hung up.

Reporters from the *Courier* have interviewed half the town about me. And it isn't just them—television vans from Grand Rapids and Detroit are sitting on the street outside, hoping to catch a glimpse of me. It's a waste of time for everybody; my parents have forbidden me to leave the house, and I'm in no mood to break that particular rule just now.

If you ever get famous (maybe I should say *notorious*) you'll notice something. People say things about you that are just plain lies. They pick up on something about you, and then they repeat it over and over until they think it explains all your actions. In my case, they say I'm a loner. In today's paper, this guy I barely know said, "Chris always kept 'way off to himself. He would sit alone in the cafeteria at lunch, reading books about astrology and stuff. It was pretty weird." First of all, it's *astronomy*. Second of all, having intellectual pursuits and eating by yourself doesn't make you some kind of terrorist, which is what the guy was saying.

When this happens to a group of people, it's called *stereotyping*. When it happens to an individual, it's called *in-depth reporting*.

My parents hired a psychiatrist for me. Our sessions take place on the back porch, over glasses of lemonade and my mom's oatmeal cookies. He says that I'm "disassociating" from my traumatic experience, which is why I talk about the shooting so lightly. My "levity problem," he calls it. I say my parents are paying that guy too much. Cops and soldiers use humor to get them through, and no psychiatrist beats them up about it. If I'm going to be a cop myself—actually, a spy—shouldn't I start adapting now?

Then again, maybe the shrink has a point. Maybe I'm a little screwed up right now.

My name is Christopher Newell. Classes start in a few weeks at Northwestern Michigan University. I'll be a freshman. Not to brag, but I was valedictorian of Petoskey High, and I won the Regents Scholarship—and no matter what anybody is saying, I intend to start college on time.

Some crazy things happened in Petoskey this summer, things that some people wouldn't believe. I guess that makes sense; I have a way of getting caught up in my own fantasies. But everything that happened to me was real—and I won't apologize for anything I did about it.

1

I t was the job at the morgue that started this whole thing.

It wasn't my top choice, mind you. I had planned to work in the NWMU astronomy department over the summer. My parents are both professors at the university, and I figured they could pull the appropriate strings. That was the idea back in May, anyway, before I got arrested during an unauthorized visit to the university's new $75 million planetarium.

It happened on a Saturday. Prom night, to be exact. I didn't go. I couldn't see myself dressing up in a tux and going to parties with people I didn't know very well and acting like a clod on the dance floor all night, just because you're supposed to. It's not that I'm anti-social, exactly. I'm just more the observing type, and stars are my favorite thing to observe, so I decided to check out the planetarium.

What else was I going to do—sit in my room thinking about Julia Spencer all night?

They hadn't quite finished construction on the planetarium, so they didn't have the alarm all geared up yet. I had just seen this Bruce Willis flick where he did a trick with his credit card to pry open the lock on a bad guy's apartment door. I couldn't believe it when it worked on the south entrance. The whole thing was a bust, though— they had me in plastic handcuffs within about five minutes.

The campus security officer said he didn't care how many moons of Jupiter were visible, it was still breaking and entering. He loaded me in the back of his car and carted me off to the campus police station, where I had a very unpleasant chat with the sheriff before my parents used their pull to get the charges dropped. Still, I wasn't going to be getting any job offers from the astronomy department.

My mom cried a little bit over the planetarium affair. She taught in the biology department and told me she could arrange an internship there. Her tone suggested that I should be very thankful and accept immediately. My dad said they always could use researchers in classics, too.

Around that time, though, the *Courier* ran a classified ad for a job at the morgue. It went like this:

MEDICAL EXAMINER seeks janitorial help.
Min. Qual. Flex. Sched. $8.50/hr. 15 hrs/week.

Naturally I hopped right on it.

"Naturally," I say, because my life's goal is to become a spy, or at least a spyish-type figure. Based on my preliminary research (namely, rentals from the "Cloak and Dagger" section of University Video),

I'm thinking seriously about the National Security Agency. Working at the morgue might teach me something about forensic pathology that could come in handy later, I figured. It's not like I had better alternatives; they don't train you in fingerprinting at the knickknack shops in town.

"Oh my Lord," is what my mom said when I told her that I was going to call about the job. She was making vegetarian lasagna at the time.

We were in the kitchen, where my dad was reading Chaucer. He lowered his book. "That's positively macabre," he said. That's how he talks. "Sometimes I think you would have enjoyed living in the Middle Ages."

My mom peered at the advertisement. "It's just fifteen hours a week."

"I don't need that much money," I said.

It was true, too. I had already won my full-ride scholarship to NWMU. It came with a housing allowance, which was like free money since I had decided to live at home. A part-time job was perfect—it'd leave me plenty of time to practice photography.

I put together a slapdash résumé that filled just under half a page, including a line for interests ("Astronomy, Comic Books of the 1940s, Edgar Allan Poe, Photography"), and faxed it over. To my surprise, they called me in for an interview the very next day.

The morgue isn't far from our house; nothing in Petoskey is. The sign on Route 14 says, WELCOME TO PETOSKEY: WHERE NATURE SMILES FOR SEVEN MILES, but every single word of that sign is a lie. For one thing,

Petoskey is six miles long at best. It sits on Lake Michigan—the West Arm Bay, to be precise—an hour's drive from the Upper Peninsula and, if you care to go farther, Canada. Tourists come up in the summer, when you could say that Nature winks at Petoskey. For the other nine months, it blows a harsh wind off the lake that freezes nose hairs and stunts tree growth. And snows in heaping portions.

The morgue sits in the basement of Petoskey General Hospital, a beige building that looks like the world's most unimaginative sand castle. My boss there, aka Dr. Nathan Mobley, aka the medical examiner for Emmet County, was a piece of work. He had pale, blemished skin—imagine a thin layer of cottage cheese and you won't be far off—and bulky shoulders that did a kind of roly-poly thing when he tottered around on his black cane. Basically, he was like an old, abandoned home creaking on its hinges.

I had my five-minute interview with Dr. Mobley in his office, where he sat behind a wooden desk about the size of the *Titanic*. Everything in the office seemed to be at least a hundred years old, including Dr. Mobley's faded gray suit and the sorry-looking briefcase at the side of his desk. He wheezed into his handkerchief and perused my résumé with narrowed eyes. The whites of them were yellowish, like his hair and his skin and his fingernails. We didn't have much of a Q-and-A session. He just asked me if I wanted the job ("yes, sir") and then grumbled about his office being a public trust and its importance to civilized society, or something along those lines.

After that he led me on a tour of the autopsy room. It had a tile floor with a black drain in the middle—for bodily fluids, I supposed—

and was trimmed with low-tech silver gadgetry. As Mobley explained it, my job was simple. I cleaned the dull green tiles and the grout between them. I cleaned the stainless-steel table bolted to the floor, the collection of different-sized bowls, the outsides of the body coolers. I cleaned the large, square windows that looked out onto the hallway and into Dr. Mobley's office. I cleaned the scale they used to weigh organs, and a bunch of other instruments, including the pair of pruning shears that had been made for hedges but apparently played some useful role in opening a cadaver.

When the tour ended, Dr. Mobley took me back to his office and explained the filing system. "The chores shouldn't take that long. Do them three times a week, I don't care when. If I need you for something particular, I'll call you in."

With that, he sat down again and fixated on a stack of documents lying on his desk. I sensed a conclusion to the interview.

"Look forward to working with you," I said.

I wasn't really looking forward to that; actually, I'd already decided to try to limit my contact with Dr. Mobley. It was quite easy to do, since he rarely came to work—at least, to his office in the basement. He also worked as a pediatrician on the second floor, but I tried not to think about Dr. Mobley tending to small children.

Another doctor—Dr. Sutter—kept a set of keys to the morgue. He was the one who let me in when I showed up. It may have been his only actual responsibility. Dr. Sutter had to be eighty years old, and as far as I could tell he spend most of his day doodling on a yellow pad.

"Ah, young Christopher!" he said with his customary good cheer when I showed up one Saturday in the middle of June. "Can't let you down there today, they're busy. Doc Mobley says come back tomorrow if you can. If not, just come around next week."

On the one hand, with Dr. Mobley down there, I was more than happy to leave. But the way that Dr. Sutter said he was "busy" got me thinking that there might be an autopsy going on, which I couldn't miss.

I nodded, told Dr. Sutter good-bye, and then headed straight down to the morgue.

Don't get me wrong. I'm no freak. Like I said, I had a vocational interest in seeing an autopsy. Plus, I was five weeks into the job and hadn't seen as much as a kidney stone—it was hard not to be a little jazzed.

The door leading to the morgue has frosted glass on top that says MEDICAL EXAMINER in black letters. Normally it's dark, but a yellow light was glowing against the window. It was cold in the basement, and the doorknob chilled my hand. Muffled sounds came from inside. A symphony of nerves started playing along my spine.

Act casual, I told myself. *You're just coming over to do your job. Whistle if you need to.* I waited for my breath to slow and turned the knob.

Dr. Mobley and a police officer stood in the autopsy room with their backs to me, looming over a body laid out on the stainless-steel table. A body bag lay on the floor, crumpled and looking like it might blow away any minute. I stood in the hallway, unnoticed, watching through the glass partition.

I couldn't see Mitch Blaylock very well. I didn't know his name then, of course. He was just the unlucky guy who phoned in dead that morning and whose body had ended up in the Office of the Medical Examiner of Emmet County.

The policeman, though—I recognized him right away. The broad back, the cropped red hair, the cocky way he had his hands on his hips. Sheriff Harmon. I hadn't seen him since the planetarium incident.

Dr. Mobley maneuvered a swinging lamp over the body; it threw a gruesome sheen on the man's waxy skin. I was rooted in place, absorbed by the sight and trying to calm my stomach, when Dr. Mobley looked my way. He clutched his handkerchief to his mouth and uttered something. The sheriff took the cue. He strode out into the hallway and closed the door behind him.

He had heavy cheeks with dark eyes pressed into them like chocolate chips lost in cookie dough. A smell of sweat, greasy food, and pure animal aggression radiated off the sheriff's uniform. He eyeballed me and grunted.

"Doc says you should go on home," he said.

Part of me wanted to run, but I was too curious to go away that easy.

"I left something in the office last week," I said. "I'll just grab it and go."

"Make it quick," he said, and I felt his eyes linger on me as I walked down the hall.

When I got to the office and looked back in through the window, the sheriff had returned to Dr. Mobley's side, their attention fixed on the body. The doctor pointed to something on the dead man's chest. The sheriff was blocking my view, but I had lost my enthusiasm for the project. What was I going to see, really? It wasn't like they had his chest cracked open or anything good like that.

Just get going before they kick you out.

I figured I'd just bang around the desk a little, pretend to do a search, and then scamper out. I lifted a few papers off the desk and then opened the top drawer with the pens and scissors and Dr. Mobley's nasal spray. The desk had large drawers on the sides, which I knew that Dr. Mobley never used.

I pulled one open, all ready to shut it again, when a glinting light caught my eye. It came from the clasp on Dr. Mobley's briefcase, which wobbled inside the drawer when I pulled it out. The briefcase shouldn't have been there—Dr. Mobley always kept it at the side of his desk, out in the open. It had been in that spot every time I came in, a little eyesore of cracked brown leather with Mobley's initials branded into the side: NHM.

It was a doctor's bag, the kind that pries open at the top. The clasp on the briefcase wasn't sealed, and the mouth of it was open wide enough for me to see an envelope lying at the bottom.

I checked the window. Dr. Mobley and Sheriff Harmon talked casually across the dead body. Quickly, I knelt down out of view.

The dull sounds of their conversation drifted in as I considered the envelope. Why would he hide his briefcase in the drawer? And what was that rectangular shape inside the envelope? The air in the office turned hot and close.

The sheriff is going to check on you in a minute. Get this over with.

The envelope crinkled against my fingers when I pulled it out. The flap, unsealed, pulled away easily. The mass inside was a few inches thick.

There were three stacks of bills bound in coarse brown paper bands.

They were hundreds.